BREATH & OTHER VENTURES

ALSO BY WILLIAM BRIDGES

Poetry

Common Places

Weedpatch or Jericho?

The Arafura Sea

The Perfect Country of Words

Eye

The Landscape Deeper In:
Selected Poems, 1974-2004

Other

Dear Viola: Reporting, Writing and Editing
for the Student Journalist

Under the Heaven Tree: An Indiana Childhood

Five-Mountain Morning: A Memoir

A Fine Smirr of Rain: Variations on a Theme

Places & Stories

A Weird Unfathomable Ordinary Everyday Life
(with Dianne Jenkins)

"Breath & Other Ventures," by William Bridges. ISBN 978-1-60264-719-0.

Published 2011 by Virtualbookworm.com Publishing Inc., P.O. Box 9949, College Station, TX 77842, US. ©2011, William Bridges. All rights reserved. No part of this publication may be reproduced, stored in a retrieval system, or transmitted in any form or by any means, electronic, mechanical, recording or otherwise, without the prior written permission of William Bridges.

Manufactured in the United States of America.

BREATH

& OTHER VENTURES

by WILLIAM BRIDGES

CONTENTS

CONTENTS

TALES

FOR MAC ROLLER

Good doctor, faithful reader

CREDITS AND ACKNOWLEDGMENTS

Deep thanks are extended to Colin Bridges for his illustration on Page 210, to Karl Bridges for various researches, and to Karen Bridges (always) for love and encouragement. Thanks also to Lindsay Hadley and Tim Lisko, who are not only fine cover designers but also friends. Their cover this time included, with her permission, Kate Egly Jones's photo, "The Path." I am indebted to Cody Crocker, computer tech par excellence, who solved a knotty problem during formatting of the text, and to Paul Newkirk, the best mechanic I know, who made a key measurement for me. Finally, I am more grateful than I can say to the doctors, nurses, and technicians who have helped me breathe better, and to those teachers who have guided me toward some understanding of Zen.

For permission to use various items, I thank: France Yu ("The Little Trees," Page 2); the estate of May Swenson ("Question," Page 8); Keith Kumasen Abbott ("Watching Sand Tell Time," Page 44, and the "Tea Bowl" brush art on Page 61); the Columbus (Indiana) *Republic* and photographer April Knox (photo of Barack Obama campaigning at Columbus, Page 130). I'm also indebted to various writers on the topic of breath, especially Tim Brookes, Larry Rosenberg, Carla Keirns, and J.B. West, all credited within the text.

The lines at the bottom of Page 41 are from "The Snow Man," *The Collected Poems of Wallace Stevens* by Wallace Stevens, copyright 1954 by Wallace Stevens and renewed 1982 by Holly Stevens. Used by permission of Alfred A. Knopf, a division of Random House, Inc.

Where no credit is given for poems or photographs they are mine, except for a few historical photos whose makers are unknown.

For the line about paradoxes that closes the "Breath" essays, I am indebted to a former student, Sarah Byerley.

BEGINNINGS

I took a break about noon from researching season-al affective disorder (for the Rain *book) to walk out on the front porch and soak up a little sunshine. I am not a SAD sufferer—have even been known to exclaim, "Hoo-ray! A rainy day!" The broken sky was pleasant, and lat-er, driving for lunch with Dick Martin at Mi Pueblo in Northwood Plaza, rays of "heavenly light" were stream-ing from a cloud. There were enough patches of blue to make a Dutchman's breeches. It was a good day.*

—Oct. 28, 2005

This journal item is notable only because it fixes, almost to the minute, the beginning of this book.

I had breathing on my mind that lunchtime. Two days earlier (at precisely 8:46:10 a.m., according to the report) I had taken a respiratory test leading to a diagnosis of chronic pulmonary ob-structive disease, or COPD. As I walked toward Mi Pueblo, I was thinking that I might write something—maybe even a book—about breathing and the human lung. As I waited for Dick, a title fell from the sky: *A Tree in the Body.*

But that book never happened. Others, I found, had already written it. Also, as my symptoms abated with treatment, I took less interest in the etiology of lung disorders. Instead, I became interested in exploring the intersection of medicine, meditation, and memory—an interest that led eventually to "Breath."

The rest of the book is about various explorations that have occupied me over time—poetry, public life, families, towns, and (in "Back Then") how changes in one's life happen in ways not always discernible at the time. There are also essays and

1

a few forays into short fiction; it pleased me, in the final story, to bring the 14th century Persian poet Hafiz-e Shirazi into a different galaxy in the far future.

The longer pieces (those in sections) are probably best read from the beginning. With the shorter essays and stories it doesn't matter. Because many of these were first published on my blog, *www.greenmarketpress.com*, there are some artifacts of time that I haven't bothered to smooth over.

If the experiences recorded here have taught me anything, it's the importance of the present moment and the certainty that it will change. My Taipei friend, France Yu, has expressed this transience movingly in a poem I've translated as "The Little Trees":

Time and space meet intricately,
held fast by a row of little trees.
Read their language carefully.

The computer won't help you,
the website's disconnected,
the time machine's
irreparably broken.
Those roads are closed.

Looking back, you'll see
nothing you recognize.
Even the little trees
have gone into another
time and space.

I. BREATH

Breath begins somewhere for each of us. For me, it was the Coleman Hospital on West Michigan Street in Indianapolis, where my mother had been taken from our home in Franklin for a caesarian delivery. Today the former hospital is a health center on the campus of Indiana University-Purdue University Indianapolis. A few feet away is the Indiana University Medical Center, where I go to have my current breathing checked, nearly half a billion breaths after the first one.

4

NUMEROLOGY

"BLOW BLOW BLOW blow blow blow blow blow blow blow blow blow blow blow blow blow."

With my teeth clamped tight on the digital blowmeter's plastic pipe, I blow for dear life. Patti, the respiratory therapist—who by now is almost as breathless as I am—is ecstatic. "Did you see stars?" she asks. And then, "These are wonderful readings, much better than last time. This is great reversibility!"

I am a successful asthma patient, back in less than three months from "severe" to "mild" pulmonary obstruction. No matter that the medicines I take cost roughly as much as my monthly mortgage payment or the annual sustenance of several families in the Sahel. I am healthy, I can breathe.

I also despise old gaffers who can talk of nothing but their health and their medications. So why am I writing?

There is something here at the intersection of body, spirit, and the world that nags at me, and it focuses on breathing, that simple autonomic act. It has never been entirely simple for me. My mother died in her fifties of a heart attack, probably induced by genetic emphysema. Her mother died after years of chronic asthma. At five or six, I wheezed with bronchitis and had to sleep in a sloping bed, its foot propped up on stools by my parents. "Postural drainage," they called it.

I grew up and out of such difficulties. But as a young husband, I was hit by asthmatic attacks, especially when visiting my wife's mother in her trailer home near farm fields. Mary and I got along fine—nothing psychosomatic here—but some dust or dander in her house robbed me of breath after about three days. Once, I got as far as a hospital waiting room before the attack passed.

5

But I grew out of this, too, and passed into my sixties and early seventies with no breathing problems that couldn't be fixed by popping an occasional Primatene tablet. In the meantime, my youngest brother had tested positive for alpha-1 antitrypsin deficiency, a genetic enzyme shortage that can cause the lungs to fill with goop. It sounded like Mom, and my brother clearly was worried by it, although he hadn't shown any symptoms.

How easy breath is when you have it, how terrifying when you don't. In a Sue Grafton mystery (stop reading here if you're not to the surprise yet), a victim endures a slow and horrifying death by suffocation in a buried car. The miners at Sago, West Virginia, suffered a similar death as carbon dioxide replaced oxygen in their lungs. (The sole survivor, as I write, has begun speaking a few words, the extent of brain damage still unclear.)

Zen masters through the centuries have thought a lot about breathing and built meditations around it. I have practiced some of these, letting my mind clear as I did slow breath counts. A Buddhist friend explains that breath partakes of "chi," the vital substance. During breathing meditation, activity and consciousness drop away "until nothing but breathing is going on," he says. A writer friend calls breathing "that place where the voluntary and the involuntary encounter each other."

Only humans can reflect on this. Batu, my cat, is curled up asleep on the desk, six inches from the pad where I'm writing. His side moves up and down as he breathes the world in and out, without knowledge.

Timing my breathing now, in repose, I find that the rate is about 12 in-and-out respirations a minute. Batu is making about 32. I love the numbers. If my rate had been constant since my first breath, on an April morning in 1935, I would now have taken exactly 446,848,920 breaths (including leap years—among them 2000, a rare leap centesimal year—but not occasional leap seconds). The number has, of course, changed since I wrote this sentence. It is also an absurd number, since it does not include breaths retarded by sleep, deep thought, or overeating, or accelerated by running up stairs, passion, or watching Reggie Miller shoot three-pointers.

Batu, by a similar calculation, has drawn and exhaled about 160 million breaths in his 10 years. Cats have lived into their twenties, so he could end up surprisingly close to my half-billion breaths. Can it be that both our lives are measured out in similar numbers?

Both numbers are of the same magnitude as the 300 million alveoli—tiny breath sacs—that we all carry in our lungs, on the misty frontier where the body exchanges carbon dioxide for oxygen. A book, *Human Anatomy and Physiology for Dummies*, compares the tiny clusters of alveoli to raspberries, but it would take a long time to gather enough for a pie. Try to think of 300 million of anything inside your chest. Try to imagine each alveolus filling and emptying with every breath.

Scientists and writers have to use analogies. A student of genetics has sent me articles describing DNA repair in terms that sound like little backhoes and dump trucks at work. But in truth, at this microscopic level, life begins to sound less like earthmoving and more like painting.

What is it, really, this tree in the body?

Patti is not concerned about such things. I'm one of her first patients of the day, I'm taking my medicines, and she's downright chirpy about my progress. She loves her craft, and I am a success story. She's not at all surprised that I've had a good winter, with no colds, bronchitis, or wheeziness. I mention that my Burpee seed order has arrived in the mail. "You'll have more energy to dig in the ground!" she exclaims. "More energy to write!"

I take a deep breath and begin.

'Smart Little Feller, Ain't You?'

Body my house
my horse my hound
what will I do
when you are fallen . . . .

—May Swenson, "Question"

PEOPLE SURVIVE, and even live lives of meaning, despite the most dreadful afflictions. Victims of "Ondine's Curse," a rare disorder of the autonomic nervous system, must remember to take each breath. There are about 300 of these sufferers in the world, according to a registry kept in Paris, and as a rule they do not sleep well or live long. Those of us who don't have to think much about the body and its health should feel profoundly grateful.

Which I do. As an airplane passenger, I go for much of the flight without thinking about just where I am, but it takes only a tremor of turbulence to remind me. I was referred originally to Patti Huesman, the cheerful respiratory therapist, after a puzzling round of chest colds in the late summer and fall of 2005. Her report on my breathing numbers, at 8:46:10 a.m. on Oct. 26, is a tremor. The poet Stanley Kunitz, writing in his 100th year, joked about "the rumors of my immortality," and while I like his panache, I suspect that in my case the rumors are unfounded. The largest part of my life is over, and I leave Patti's place more thoughtful than when I arrived.

One can respond to mortality in a variety of ways, from indifference to rage to joy "in the hope of a glorious Resurrection," as stones in old graveyards still say. My stepmother, Marie, died several years ago at the age of 94. She was the daughter of a

8

wildcat oil driller, and was born in New Mexico before it became a state. She had a rich life that included running a hair salon, teaching prison inmates to read, and—in the 1920s—learning to pilot an airplane. In her last days, my stepbrother David asked if she was afraid to die, and she replied, "No." But when he asked how she had reached this state of peace, she said only, "I dunno."

At her memorial service, a gallery of pictures from her life ended with a fairly grim one taken shortly before her death. I heard someone wishing the picture had been left out, but I could understand why it needed to be there. At the service, David said, "Mom had a great trust in life. Her response to something unfamiliar or threatening was to go out and engage it."

I would like to do the same, but am not always good at it. Patti has diagnosed asthma and something called COPD, or "chronic obstructive pulmonary disease," which seems to be a term popularized by Medicare billing. It can include asthma, chronic bronchitis, and emphysema, but whether it is something in itself or only an umbrella term is unclear. That I "have" it, though, has certain results, such as my insurance company's refusal to extend my coverage, though by every test the company's visiting nurse employs I am the world's healthiest old fogy.

So how to go out and engage with this? I can write about it, as I am doing. I can get a second opinion, maybe one that won't sentence me to a life of oxygen tanks or ingenious and expensive inhalers. I can exercise more and take better care of myself.

But since I'm a writer, I don't want simply any old second opinion—I want one from *the* expert, who will answer all my questions and maybe even be sympathetic to a writer's perpetual curiosity. On Jan. 25, 2006, I take my retired family doctor, Mac Roller, out for coffee, and a few days later he calls with a referral to Dr. Michael Busk, who is a pulmonologist at the Indiana University Medical Center in Indianapolis, as well as medical and research director of the nearby National Institute of Fitness and

Sport. Mac used to teach at the center and cautions, "Just remember that these are very busy doctors. Their time is valuable."

A web search adds to Busk's credentials. The *Indianapolis Star* quotes him in January, 2005, a week after Johnny Carson's death from emphysema: "If he would have come to see me 20 years ago, we would have interceded, gotten him to stop smoking, gotten him on some medicines." But Carson didn't, so here's Johnny, on the slab, sooner than he needed to be.

Busk sees patients only on Tuesday afternoons, but I'm able to make an appointment, through his delightfully named secretary, Susie Circle, for March 21. But then Busk has to cancel all his spring and summer appointments, and it is Aug. 22 before I'm finally at the IU Medical Center. I have arrived early, to see a Chihuly sculpture in one of the buildings and to visit the Coleman Hospital, on the nearby Indiana University-Purdue University campus, where I drew my first breath 71 years before. (The first breath is always an inspiration, the last will be an exhalation.) Coleman is now a college health-services center; I tell a slightly puzzled receptionist that I was born there, and that the hospital did good work—I've held up remarkably well. Outside, I chat with Drew Wade, a med center employee, who also was born in the building. "Always good to meet someone else born in Coleman," he says. (Later, Busk will look for me in the hospital's birth records, but I'm too far back to be computerized.)

In Busk's waiting room, an energetic nurse named Arletta Young takes me in tow for the preliminaries. "C'mon, angel," she says, leading me to the scales. And then, "What have you written for me?"

"I've written a lot of things. What did you have in mind?"

She eyes me a little narrowly. "You just *looked* like a writer to me," she replies. (It turns out that she wants me to compile a medical history.)

Eventually Arletta turns me over to Busk's office nurse, Paula Puntenney, and then the doctor himself arrives, pretty much on time. He is surprisingly youthful, almost boyish, though he must be in his 40s or early 50s. He forgoes shaking hands until he has washed his, "and I'll wash them again before the next patient," he says.

He's a good listener, who despite Mac's warning seems to have all the time in the world. We talk about asthma and COPD, about my family's history of lung disorders, about the second-hand smoke to which I'm exposed at home. He thinks Patti's diagnosis and treatment are on the mark, although he's slightly surprised at my quick rebound from "some very bad figures" on her first tests. Maybe it's because I exercise and am in good shape, he says.

I've sent him all Patti's tests, which he has in a folder along with my little essay on numerology, which he has read. Despite the improvement in my breathing, he advises carrying an inhaler of albuterol, a fast-acting bronchodilator, at all times: "It's the life saver." Call Susie Circle, he adds, and get a letter that will allow me to take the inhaler on the plane when Karen and I go to Europe in the fall.

Finally, I get a chance to ask some writer's questions. Where's the best place to start researching the subject of breathing? What book should I commit to memory? Foolish questions, in a way, and instead of answering directly, he offers to copy some articles for me, and refers me for an information session with Jan Hutchins at the Lung Center in the sport fitness institute. (When I ask Jan later about her role in the Lung Center, she looks briefly flustered and replies, "Well, really, I'm Dr. Busk's nurse. It's Paula in the office, me over here.")

We've been at this nearly an hour, and I think we're done, but no. Now it's up on the table, shirt off, a stethoscope exam, nose and ears, more note-taking. Very thorough. I've asked for a full battery of tests, including one for alpha-1 anti-trypsin deficiency, and Busk prescribes all these plus a CT scan, after carefully explaining costs and that a scan sometimes discloses "nodules," which are usually non-cancerous but may require follow-up scans just to make sure.

Then we *are* done, and another appointment is set. "We'll know everything about your lungs then," Busk says.

A few minutes later, while I'm waiting for a nurse to schedule the tests, Busk comes in to copy the articles he's promised. He runs them off himself, after a little trouble with the copier, which amuses the office staff. This is reassuring. When the staff is comfortable teasing the doctor, it's a good sign.

Earlier, while waiting for Busk, Nurse Arletta and I have hung out together for a few minutes. She has told me her life story, from her birth in Erlangen, Kentucky, to her prospective retirement in another four or five years. Her speech is vivid and colloquial, its casual grammar not disguising a quick mind. I tell her the two-minute version of *my* life story, and she replies, "Smart little feller, ain't you?"

Indeed I am—and where has it gotten me?

DUST

For he knoweth our frame; he remembereth that we are dust.

—Psalms 103:14

DUST IS A SERIOUS PROBLEM in a flour mill. The reason is simple. Each speck of flour dust is mostly surface, exposed to the air. If someone strikes a match in a dust cloud, that speck and millions of others oxidize instantly, and you can plan on calling the fire department.

There is an analogy here with your lungs, which also are mostly surface. Those 300 million air sacs, or alveoli, that you carry around in your chest are as tiny as dust motes, but their interior surface area would carpet a room 30 feet square. If your lungs were finely milled flour, they would explode at a spark.

An alveolus has a diameter of about 200 microns, or 127th of an inch. This was first measured, with remarkable accuracy, by the Rev. Stephen Hales in 1731. Such minuteness is hard to think about, so I took a straight pin to Paul Newkirk, my auto mechanic, and asked him to use a micrometer to measure the diameter of its head. "No problem," Paul said, pulling out his little gauge shaped like a question mark. "We measure all kinds of things in here—but this *is* a first."

The pinhead measured 685 ten-thousands of an inch—or a little under a sixteenth, to use a more familiar term. Its diameter would hold nearly nine alveoli. There is no answer to the theological conundrum of how many angels can dance on the head of a pin, but if angels were alveoli it would be about 75. Two alveoli could line up across the period at the end of this sentence.

What tiny structures, and how complex! As so often happens, language offers insights into function. "Alveolus" comes from the Latin *alveus*, a hollow vessel, a tub, a channel. "Alveolar" also applies to the sockets of the teeth and to other organs pitted with small cavities. "Alveolariform" means shaped like the cells of a honeycomb, and indeed the alveoli of the lungs look, in a photomicrograph, like such a comb—they are polyhedral, many-sided, rather than spherical. (In 1893, a young German scientist, Hans Kohn, described tiny channels between alveoli, and these "pores of Kohn" are also visible in the photomicrograph.) Finally, there is a rare English meaning of "alveus" as the bed of a river or a trough of the sea. "This mass of Water fell back again . . . into the Alveus of the Ocean," John Woodward wrote in his *Natural History* (1695), fusing the very large and very small in one image. Pulmonologists do the same thing today when they talk about the "tidal volume" of air inhaled by the lungs in a normal breath, or "inspiration."

Inspire means to breathe in, but more often it connotes the creative impulse, "a breathing or infusion into the mind or soul," according to the *OED*, which adds that writers of scripture are held to have been breathed upon by the divine. "Breathe on me, breath of God," says the hymn. Such a view of breath can itself inspire a deep respect and calmness. A friend with whom I discussed breathing says his family has noticed that he often pauses for several seconds between one breath and the next. There are no doubt biochemical reasons for this, but he believes it also indicates a confidence in life—that his next breath will come.

Medical writers like to compare the alveoli to clusters of grapes or raspberries. They also look a bit like barnacles on a ship's keel, but all this gives a much enlarged view. In a typical lung, about 2,000 alveoli are gathered into a "primary lobule" that itself is not much bigger than a granule of tapioca. Rather than ask Paul to measure tapioca, I calculated that if my pinhead were a sphere, between three and four of them would make up about the volume of a primary lobule. The alveoli within the lobule are not precisely the same size, and this would appear at first to be a problem. Because of natural laws governing pressure and surface tension, air ought to desert the smaller alveoli and flow into the larger ones. It doesn't, and the reason is a chemical "surfactant" that lowers the surface tension of the smaller alveolus as its radius shrinks, thus keeping everything in balance.

All this minute immensity has one main function—to provide a surface large enough to handle the pint of air each of us takes in at every breath, exchanging its fresh oxygen for the blood's carbon-dioxide exhaust. A healthy breather at rest makes that exchange 12 to 15 times a minute, every minute, for a lifetime. At this level, the alveolar and capillary tissues are so thin—one micron, a millionth of a meter—that the gases exchange directly across them. All the body's blood comes through once a minute, and some have suggested that this "respiratory zone" of the lung looks more like a sheet of blood than a network of vessels.

At this point, one's reaction may be that of an old Buddhist monk who, when finally persuaded that the Earth was spherical, inquired, "Are you any happier knowing this?"

The answer is no, and it points up the frivolousness of statistics. In seeking the size of an alveolus, I found reputable sources that blithely doubled the number in the body, to as many as 700 million. The writers apparently thought 300 or so million was the figure for one lung. After the first 100 million, who's counting?

My pulmonologist, Dr. Michael Busk, eventually confirmed for me the two-lung total of about 300 million, but wouldn't indulge my mania for statistics by suggesting an average size for alveoli. "You're thinking like an engineer," he said. "We're physicians, and everybody's different. Let's just say they're *tiny*."

Writers (and I do not except myself) also strain for comparisons—"an interior surface the size of a racquetball court" or "half a tennis court." One assertion does stand up, though: the lung's interior surface is by far the largest area the body presents to the

15

atmosphere—more than 30 times that of the skin. In an increasingly dirty world, the gravest insults to the body are to the lungs.

Most of us never see a lung, although pictures are easily found on the Internet. Even a healthy adult lung looks a bit battered; a smoker's lung looks dark and leathery, like something found in a sarcophagus. A slice of a healthy lung resembles a pink sponge with innumerable holes and bubbles. It's more romantic to think of the lung's airways as an inverted tree, with the alveoli as the topmost leaves absorbing oxygen instead of sunlight. As it is, they lie at the end of a long ramification, beginning with the trachea or windpipe and descending through some 23 branching levels to reach the lung's "working face." The descent of air into the body is called the oxygen cascade, because its pressure falls from 160 millimeters of mercury at the mouth to between 4 and 20 in the ultimate tissues. A website for anesthetists suggests a bit whimsically that this last pressure may represent the oxygen that "our ancient unicellular ancestors first found they could effectively use."

The same site refers to the lung as "a low-pressure air pump"—an amazingly efficient one compared to the clunky and accident-prone circulatory system. The pump is triggered by rising carbon dioxide and acidity in the blood; receptor cells send alarms to a respiratory center in the brain's medulla oblongata. (My Uncle Bill once received, for Christmas, an exceedingly long, narrow box bearing a tag with various content possibilities, among them "medulla oblongata." "Well, I know it's not *that*!" Bill said, and his gift turned out to be a smoked eel.)

Upon getting an alarm, the brain signals the diaphragm and rib-cage muscles to contract, expanding the lung and lowering its air pressure, so fresh air can pour in. A key part of breathing is not, as one might think, a labored sucking in of air, but rather an emptying that allows the new breath to enter. The diaphragm is much stronger than the rib-cage muscles, so "belly-breathing" is less strenuous and is recommended by breath therapists and those who practice breathing meditation. A Zen instructor advises greeting the new year "buttocks back, belly forward."

There are other parts to the mechanism of breath. The lungs are sheathed in a set of membranes, and between these is the pleural cavity with a bit of fluid that allows the lungs to slide easily during breathing. An elephant has connective tissue rather than fluid in this space, creating a larger vacuum so the elephant can suck in air and water through its trunk—and also snorkel across rivers. (The uniqueness of these lungs was discovered in 1681 by an Irish scientist who dissected an elephant killed in a fire.)

Besides their role in breathing, the lungs can serve as a reservoir of blood, a fact important to oceanic free-divers. As recently as the last century, it was thought that no one lacking special equipment could dive deeper than about 50 meters without the lungs being crushed. However, because blood can "pressurize" the lungs, that limit has now been extended to more than 150 meters. Still, there is a limit beyond which the accumulation of blood would overwhelm the heart. Free-diving is like "free-soloing" for mountain climbers—gravity wins in the end.

But this is enough, perhaps too much, about the mechanics of breathing and the lungs. Those who want more might consult an elegant little book by J.B. West titled *Respiratory Physiology: The Essentials*. It makes clear that the respiratory system, like much of the body, is really the province of biochemists. Things happen to us because one molecule binds or doesn't bind with another. As a young UPI reporter in Germany, I wrote about Stefan Bandera, a Ukrainian nationalist, who was sprayed in the face with cyanide by a KGB assassin. West's book told me that cyanide blocks the use of oxygen in cell tissue. If Bandera had not inhaled . . . .

The Rev. Stephen Hales, who was Perpetual Curate of Teddington and perhaps had time on his hands, did many experiments in respiration and blood pressure, including taking the arterial pressure of his horse. He seems to have been motivated by wonder at God's creation, but even those who discount theology can meditate with deep respect on the breath. You are breathing now, and can pay attention to that, while sending your thinking mind on a short vacation. Done long enough, this can be deeply satisfying. Just breathe, slowly, into the networks of bright dust. You will eventually hear in your own breath the sigh of innumerable leaves, and the endless soughing of the sea.

Dispatch from the Asthma Wars

I AM GRATEFUL to Tim Brookes for writing the book I once thought I might write, but didn't.

In 1991, Brookes—a teacher and an essayist for National Public Radio—suffered a terrifying asthma attack that could have killed him. Over the next two years, he wrote *Catching My Breath: An Asthmatic Explores His Illness*, which is a well-written and informative account of his experiences with disease and doctors.

Brookes is a trench correspondent in the battle for breath. He did everything that I, as a journalism teacher, would have advised a reporter to do. He read copiously, did dozens of interviews, and put down his own astute observations. And he went and looked at a lung.

He also wrote entertainingly about his sometimes grim subject, and there are moments of wry delight, especially for another scribbler. "I wanted to write an accurate, interesting, comprehensible explanation of the process of chronic inflammation," he declares, "so vivid and accurate that it would win not only a Nobel Prize for Science but a Nobel Prize for Literature as well, and get optioned as a screenplay. In the end I failed."

But it was his determination to see a functioning lung that made me love him—and also helped me realize why my own explorations had led in a less clinical direction. Brookes's description of his two and a half hours in an O.R., watching lung surgery on an elderly priest, is enthralling. I learned from it and corrected at least one of my misconceptions. I had imagined a lung as a fairly solid chunk of meat, shot through with millions of airways but still standing up fairly well on its own. Brookes made it clear that

a deflated lung is about as solid as a rag of punctured balloon—
"no more than a cup of tissue" lying limply in one corner of a surprisingly large chest cavity.

Brookes writes that he had feared he might faint or vomit, but
instead "was reeling in sheer wonder" at the delicate arrange-
ments of the body he was observing. I think my reaction would
have been the same, and perhaps would have included Brookes's
eventual boredom—he left for a tennis date before the operation
ended, and never tells whether the priest recovered.

So what was it that made me content with looking at lungs on
a website, one that included, playfully, a portrait of Dr. Patricia
Lung?

Without disparaging Brookes's work in the least, the difference is one of age and outlook—and perhaps between reporter
and editor. Every young reporter, someone has noted, wants to
write about a fly describing arabesques on the ceiling. Every editor has already seen too many arabesques.

That said, I'm still grateful to Brookes for covering so much
ground, and for exploring (it seems) every possible asthma treatment from dairy avoidance to tea made from roach intestines. He
describes the mechanics of the autoimmune system about as well
as anyone could, and avoids what I've come to think of (after
some reading about DNA) as "the little dump truck" fallacy in
describing the body's microscopic parts. At least his images are
fresh; an antibody rides a bacterium, he writes, "like a spider
clinging to a barrage balloon."

Brookes also gets passionate, even angry, about things that
medical scholars take more equably, including the continuing ina-
bility of researchers to pin down exactly what asthma *is*. "Are the
symptoms under control?" one doctor asked Brookes. "That's the
goal, you know."

Brooks wants something more—a better understanding of
what's happening to his body, a little more actual (not just rhetorical) empowerment of patients, some true two-way communica-

tion, even bonding, with his doctor. Lack of these, he suggests, is among reasons why only about 25 percent of patients actually follow "doctor's orders." (He has a real hate relationship with one specialist, whom he describes as callous, condescending, and rich. "He made five times my annual salary, yet the sign in his front office still demanded payment in full at each visit," Brookes writes. "Fuck him.")

My own relations with doctors have been happier. Yet I still wonder why it's hard for me call my excellent and friendly pulmonologist by his first name. The one doctor I could do this with, "Mac," looked out for me much of my life, with compassion, humor, and wisdom. He was also the best diagnostician I'd ever known. Had he told me to treat my asthma by setting fire to my hair, I would have bought matches on the way home.

It's not until nearly the end of his book that Brookes marches off into some (to me) dubious country. He warns the reader with titles like "Celestial Ankle" and "Strange Seas of Thought." I don't fault him for consulting a psychic about his asthma. Had I thought of it, that would have been part of my advice to a reporter.

But his skepticism turns to warm butter a little too readily. By his account, the psychic said only the most banal and predictable things, but those worked on him so powerfully that "for almost a week I wandered around in a daze, wondering about a new-found universe that overthrew all my old notions of time and space, life and death." Ummm, yes. He regained his balance fairly quickly, though, and some of his amazement at the psychic may have been firing for literary effect.

He writes with more conviction and great personal candor about the disputed role of the emotions in respiratory distress. If asthma can be caused by hidden emotional conflicts, he notes, then his own case is classic: "By not only having the attack but then *choosing to write a book about asthma,* hadn't I given myself a glorious, enjoyable, and thoroughly worthwhile focus that enabled me to avoid thinking about my unresolved conflicts for sixteen months?"

My own experiences also suggest some mind-body connections. Earlier, I described asthma attacks at my mother-in-law's house, but discounted anything "Freudian." Dust is still the likely culprit, but I'm not so sure that being away from my own home, routines, and psychic weather didn't have something to do with it. Stress is not always what we think it is.

Brookes also has a keen eye for our deplorable health-insurance system and the rapacity of Big Pharma. (Why did my old inhaler cost $17 while my new eco-friendly one costs $87? Not all the difference will go to save the ozone layer. But luckily, Medicare Part D is bailing me out, at taxpayer expense.)

Brookes ends his short book (readable in a couple of hours) with an epiphany, not about asthma but about human behavior. As *Catching My Breath* was about to go to press, he realized that his 1991 asthma crisis might have been caused by the tartrazine dye in the Rolaids he had taken that evening. He rushed to a hospital for a tartrazine "challenge" test, which proved nothing.

"Even after all this time," he wrote, "I was still looking for the single causes, simple cures."

I'm no smarter or wiser than Brookes, just a little older. When I decided, long before reading his book, not to go the clinical route—not to go all out to look at a lung—it was in part because I have less time and energy for in-depth reporting. But also, the physiology of breathing, the etiology of disease, engage me less than they did even a year ago.

To me, the most interesting things in Brookes's book are a few intimations that illness may not be quite as it's advertised in our health-happy culture—not so much a terrorist breaking into our lives with a box cutter as something ordinary and expectable, that we live and die with. I'd like to be better at doing both. In a book about Zen, a student asks the master if his legs will ever ache less from the sittings. "No," the sage replies, "but you won't notice it as much."

Brookes was in his fifties when I wrote this and directs a writing program at a Vermont college. I may run into him sometime, since my son lives just across town. Meanwhile, Google tells me that he is a guitarist who has written a book about how those instruments are fashioned by mountain craftsmen. All in all, this sounds like more fun than asthma.

ROUTINES

FOR A TIME, in the fall and early winter of 2006, I was driving a 38-mile round trip three days a week to the pulmonary lab of St. Francis Hospital in Beech Grove, Indiana. I had been referred there by my doctor for "pulmonary rehabilitation," and it was a comforting routine—so much so that I was disappointed one day when Bev, the lab's director, called to say that my late-afternoon session was being cancelled because too many of the staff were sick.

For most of my time, there were no other patients in the late lab. About 2 p.m., on Mondays, Wednesdays, and Fridays, I put on my gym shoes and threw a Taipei shopping bag into the car with an apple, bottled water, a cell phone, and taped music— Patsy Cline, Newfoundland folk songs, Cole Porter. Then I headed north to the Indianapolis suburb where the lab was located. Arriving at the hospital (old, slightly shabby), I parked in the lot for pulmonary/cardiac patients and walked to the basement lab, through a drab cement patio with a few cigarette butts under the tables. These were not from patients or the pulmonary staff, the lab workers emphasized.

Rehab was a scheduled 10 weeks, with two opening class sessions, followed on each ensuing day by 90 minutes of exercise. This took place in a narrow room with a desk at one end, a warm-up area at the other, and exercise equipment in between. I shared the class sessions with Ray, a retired plumber trying to kick a 50-year cigarette habit, and Ralph, who looked and talked like an old farmer but was really a retired office-supply salesman. Between them, they took an astonishing array of breathing medicines. After the first week, they went off to other sessions; except for one brief glimpse of Ralph, I never saw them again. I did my warm-ups and cool-downs, my treadmill and exercise-bike time, alone until almost the end, attended by a shifting cadre of therapists who took careful heart-rate and blood-pressure readings and listened to my chest. It was as routine as an Army morning formation.

I didn't know for sure why I was there. It seemed at first as if I might not get in. Ann, the "intake" therapist, had trouble deciding, even with my help, what my goals should be (a requirement for Medicare reimbursement). When I did a six-minute walk up and down the lab corridor, she shook her head. "We don't usually see figures this good," she said. But I had been referred by a respected physician, and she eventually wrote down "undiagnosed asthma" and admitted me.

Near the end of my time in the lab, I asked Patti—the cheery therapist at my family doctor's—to explain just what rehab was supposed to do. She said it was educational and that the exercise would build me up. But it's also socialization, she added. "Some patients never see anything but their own four walls. Going to rehab gets them out and improves their lives." When I passed this comment on to Ann at the lab, she said, "And here you are, all by yourself!"

The lab workers had their own routines. Mary, a gifted and empathetic teacher who referred to the lab as "the service," gave lectures on lung function, exercise, diet, and "the main event"— how to have sexual intercourse, even if tethered to an oxygen tank. Karen, the pharmacist, talked about medicines and gave us her phone number in case we had questions. Ann and the other therapists had their routines of checking vital signs and charting patients' progress toward their goals. Much paperwork was filled out.

And behind all this, unnoticed except by those paying attention, were the routines of the lab itself—the filling of shifts, decisions on which patients were ready to leave the program, and occasionally office politics. "We're all going to be out of jobs!"

Mary exclaimed one day, about some unspecified internal crisis. There were also seasonal routines, and jokes. At Halloween, a hospital employee came through with his son in costume, passing out candy. Thanksgiving came and went. "What did the hen say to the scrambled eggs?" Mary asked us. "You crazy, mixed-up kids."

I progressed and began moving toward a home-exercise regimen, the main purpose of rehab, the therapists explained. I started walking through my neighborhood, and also did some short uphill runs that boosted my heart rate to an athletic 140. I had been a runner once—it was exhilarating to try it again at 71, and I loved the feeling of flying over the ground. But Mary was unhappy. "It's too hard on your knees," she said, and reluctantly I had to agree. It was about this time that Bev called to cancel the session because of staff illness. "That's okay," I told her. "I'll keep exercising at home." "But *don't run*," she ordered. How did she know I'd been running? At the next session I told Mary and Dana, another therapist, that I'd figured something out: "You people talk to each other. I'll bet you even have staff meetings to discuss the patients." "Right," Dana said. "It's called communication!"

Although patients were encouraged to talk about their own routines, it was more unusual for lab personnel to do so. Being a writer I asked questions—from how they spelled their names to what was going on in their lives outside the lab. And they were not unwilling to talk. Janet, I discovered, lived in the same town I did and served on a civic beautification committee with a good friend. She was well into a second marriage. The first husband, she said, "worked too hard and never read anything." Mary had wide interests in nutrition and in slightly new-age health care— and in walking, if not running. "You know, the bottom of your foot *is* called the sole," she said, with a laugh at her own dubious etymology. Ann found out I liked Patsy Cline, and brought in some tickets she couldn't use for a performance by a Cline impersonator. Dana, the mother of three sons, told me she volunteered "at the Boys School." Mishearing, I said, "You work with delinquents?" "No!" she said, cracking up. "I meant at *my* boys' school. But maybe you're not so far wrong."

Friendly people, professionals, doing their routines with patients.

What are your readings now?" with a gesture toward wall charts showing levels of dyspnea (breathlessness), exertion, and pain, the last calibrated from "none" to "the worst pain possible. "

No, don't start the six-pound weights today. We'd have to kick you out of the program.

I'm hearing rales in your chest. Better take your albuterol [a fast bronchodilator] before we start.

Routines.

I had routines of my own that had nothing to do with the lab. Knowing exactly where I would be at 3 p.m. three days a week, I organized the rest of my life around these times. I drove back from St. Louis for a Monday session. Working one week in Orlando, I went to the hotel spa at the appointed hour.

Back home, I worked out my route to the lab. The way to it was partly familiar, partly strange. I had known the road north to Greenwood since college days, when it lay among now-vanished farms—a friend and I once took an hour to travel it in a car with a cracked block and no water in the radiator. From Greenwood a bypass led to Emerson Avenue, which I knew as far as St. Francis Hospital South; my wife, Karen, was having minor surgery there just as I was starting rehab. But from that hospital to St. Francis North in Beech Grove, my knowledge was spotty.

So I made maps. From Greenwood to County Line Road was an area of old and new business—South Park and Emerson

Pointe. St. Francis South was at Stop 11 Road, where the Interurban had halted until it went out of business for good in 1940. There were mysteries, like the rusted water tower with a single word, PIPE, painted on its reservoir. From there, Emerson curved up and over Interstate 65, descending into a confusing intersection with Southport Road, and then into a woodsy stretch as far as Edgewood Avenue. (Who lived in the neat white farmhouse at the corner of Edgewood?) Todd Road led off to the Smock Golf Course, which I had never visited but where, I knew, there was a martin house that Karen and I had donated to a bird-loving golfer friend. So much history, so many routines.

As I approached Beech Grove, the going got steadily more urban (although with such touches as a Japanese cherry tree, its fruit glistening in the autumn rain). In Beech Grove itself, Emerson Avenue was being reconstructed. When I began driving to the lab in October, I followed temporary lanes and corridors of cones—when I finished in December the new highway was done and the workers had gone on to other jobs. Living in Taipei, I once walked the same street to work for a year, attuned to its rhythms of traffic and change. Now I was doing it again.

Near the end of rehab, Karen and I drove north one day, looking for a Christmas tree. We turned off Interstate 65 at Southport and a minute later were in the Southport Road/Emerson interchange that I was seeing every other day from a different direction. "Oh, I know this place!" I exclaimed, pointing out landmarks to Karen like a native guide exhibiting his expertise to a tourist.

Over the weeks in the exercise lab, I never reached the first pain threshold, or got beyond the lowest level or two of exertion and dyspnea. But I did advance several levels in treadmill walking, biking, and weight-lifting, and established a daily home-exercise schedule.

On a Wednesday, eight weeks into rehab, Ann approached me as I trudged on the treadmill. "I have some news for you that you may not like," she said. "You're kicking me out?" I asked.

"You saw this coming, didn't you?" she replied. "But yes, you've met your goals. The patient-review committee got together yesterday and decided we can't keep you any longer. We prefer to call it graduation."

The next day I came in for a final evaluation, doing the six-minute hallway walk again—300 feet further this time. My systolic blood pressure zoomed from 130 to 180, but the diastolic "resting" pressure stayed at 80, right where it was supposed to be. I came back one more day for an exercise session with Mary, during which a fire alarm went off. We stayed in the lab (steam had escaped from a compressor), but Mary checked it out on the phone with her boss. "There are firemen in the hall with hats and everything," she said.

The firemen left, and Mary and I—alone at last—finished the exercises. As I did my cool-down routine, I heard her rummaging in a filing cabinet behind me for a graduation certificate. And then I heard the scratchy sound of "Pomp and Circumstance" on a tape recorder.

"You've been a good patient," Mary said. "We'll miss you." And with that we both went off to our own lives and other routines.

OXYGEN

I ONCE WROTE about two college students who got progressively more lovey-dovey in my journalism class, as part of a sociology experiment to see how far I'd let them go before calling a halt to front-row romance.

That was in the 1980s, and the students—Tim and Patricia—showed up again 20 years later, married to each other, with a teenage daughter, and still involved in theater of the absurd. This time they materialized as something called Mental Entropy Productions, which was filming a script by Pat titled "Before the Devil Knows You're Dead." Would I play an elderly curmudgeon who yells at children? Three lines, no money, but I get to die spectacularly. Who could resist?

There was an added fillip for me, one I didn't tell Pat and Tim about. "Mr. Hardy" would appear in bathrobe and slippers, pushing a walker and dragging an oxygen tank. Given my preoccupation with breathing, this looked like a chance to explore vicariously a situation I had thought about but was trying not to experience for a while.

Oxygen tanks call several images to mind for me. Near the end of her life, my mother struggled with emphysema. For religious reasons, she wouldn't see a doctor, but my father—an industrial-arts teacher—went to a welding shop and bought a large metal tank of oxygen, which stood next to Mom's bed where she could take whiffs at night to ease her breathing. Today this would be illegal. Respiratory therapists have explained to me that oxygen is a medicine and should be obtained only by prescription, from a doctor not a welder.

Other images were similarly upsetting—old people in church trundling oxygen tanks, and younger ones in pulmonary rehab, on the treadmill but still tethered to their tanks with hoses and nose clips. There is a helpful and sympathetic pamphlet on how to have satisfactory sex while still hooked to the tank. Not reassuring images, although I had come to understand that these sufferers were actually a lot happier and more comfortable because of their apparatus.

The projected film had a fairly simple premise, based on an old Irish blessing: "May you be in Heaven half an hour before the Devil knows you're dead." Pat had written a sparkling script, in which the Devil—"Scratch"—shows up at a wake for Marty, an engaging reprobate whose friends still love him and manage to rescue his soul in a slow-motion car chase during the funeral procession.

I was to appear in a flashback to Marty's youth, in which he and the friends torment Mr. Hardy by playing catch with his garden gnome. After he chases them away, yelling and swinging his walker, they return and set fire to a paper sack—"dog poop flambé"—on his front porch. Mr. Hardy stamps out the flames, but his bathrobe catches fire, his oxygen tank ignites, and he blows up.

This would all happen on my (real) front porch, and the flames and explosion would be dubbed in later, digitally. "They'd better be," my wife said. "If these people show up with matches and tinder, they're going to meet Mrs. Hardy. It won't be pretty."

The filming, scheduled for a quiet Sunday afternoon with minimal street traffic, got delayed several times by weather and a cast member's sprained ankle. But on a November day of mingled sun and clouds, the movie makers finally arrived. I had been practicing snarling, and had added a line to the script: "Damn teenagers!" Would that be okay, I asked Tim? "Sure," he replied, "just don't drop the F-bomb."

The "child" actors, including Tim and Pat's daughter, Megan, arrived. Did I mention this was a low-budget movie? Waiting for them, I lurked behind a lace curtain in my living room, scowling and muttering, getting into the part. (Helpful friends had suggested that, since Mr. Hardy was clearly typecast, I didn't need to rehearse.)

The kids took off immediately to a nearby Village Pantry for sugar snacks, while Tim and Pat hooked me to a shiny oxygen tank on wheels. I got a few minutes' practice negotiating the front door with the tank and a walker left over from my mother-in-law's last years. The kids returned, high on sucrose, and began singing and dancing on the sidewalk. "Quiet on my set!" Pat ordered, and filming began.

It went with remarkable smoothness, despite retakes and waiting for cars to pass. No neighbor called the cops. I remembered my lines. I got to say "Damn teen-agers!" not once but twice, and Pat liked the addition so much she wrote it into the script. I stamped, perhaps a little too vigorously, on a non-flaming paper sack that contained something into which I did not inquire too closely. The clip on the oxygen hose irritated my nostrils. Struggling through a double door with walker and tank may have produced just the touch of macabre comedy that Pat wanted, but it left me uncomfortably aware of playing for laughs something that's deeply serious to many. Still, if Borat can get away with it, why not me?

In about three hours we were done. Actors, producers, technicians, the oxygen tank—all rolled off in a couple of cars to shoot street scenes downtown. I put the walker and my acting career back in the closet.

But stay tuned. Mr. Hardy may be coming (though perhaps not very soon) to a theater near you.

A BREATH OF ZEN

"I'M GOING TO BE DOING some Zen breathing meditation," I told Karen, "so if you see me sitting and staring into space, don't be alarmed."

"Okay, but how will I tell it from all the other times," she replied.

Her comment, besides deftly puncturing the balloon of pomposity, also pointed up something about Zen, meditation, and maybe breathing itself. They shouldn't be taken too seriously. Or rather, they are serious and not serious at the same time. This is deeply paradoxical, and if your tolerance for paradox is low, you probably should not be reading this right now.

My casual interest in Zen went back to a year spent in Taiwan in the early 1990s. In a bare room in the east coast city of Hualien, I wrote a poem that now seems like a foreshadowing of the Zen absorption with "emptiness":

There is not much here,
a cupboard, a cot,
something to write on.
People are friendly
but distant. Sometimes
I go a whole day
without one thought.

But my interest in Zen and meditation went no further until several years later, when Sam Hamill, owner of the Copper Canyon literary press, visited my college to speak and meet with students. Sam is a high-octane publisher, poet, and translator, whom

Karen and I still refer to as "the Buddhist ex-Marine." He was a delightful and perceptive visitor. We took him to see the Tibetan Center (directed by the Dalai Lama's brother) in Bloomington, Indiana, and dropped in at a bookstore where Sam recommended a little book called *Zen Mind, Beginner's Mind*, by Shunryu Suzuki, the founder of Soto Zen in the United States.

The book got a grip on me, not least because it was highly paradoxical. Suzuki, in these informal essays, seemed to be saying things that contradicted each other. Disciplined sitting meditation, or *zazen*, is the heart of Zen practice, he kept saying. But also, "I think that if you try to do *zazen* once a week, that will keep you busy enough." And, "Do not be too interested in Zen." There were some cryptic statements, like these about duality: "Our body and mind are not two and not one . . . . Our body and mind are both two *and* one."

For several years, I carried Suzuki's book around like an amulet. It was comforting, for some reason, to read and re-read. And paradox was familiar territory. I thought of Tertullian's comment on the miraculous: "It is impossible, it must be true." But finally I saw that it was a deep mistake to keep reading and thinking about something that had no meaning except in the doing of it.

So I began sitting *zazen* with some regularity, often in the early morning at my dining room table. I remember a day of winter darkness with a candle doubling its flame in the window— duality made visible! I sat in a chair, because my legs will not fold to the usual cross-legged position on a pillow. I began counting my breaths as a meditative technique. Other writers than Suzuki had warned of the difficulty of this practice. Some beginners, one teacher wrote, can scarcely keep their minds quiet enough to get to the count of two. But this was not my problem. As an experienced multi-tasker, I could go into the hundreds without losing count, keeping track of the breaths in one corner of my mind while thinking about the rest of my life in another. I was even a little proud of my ability at this, although I knew it was destroying the point of the practice. Eventually I quit doing such a futile exercise.

I also put Suzuki's book away, even lost it for a while somewhere in the house. And this is almost the last I will say about it, since copies can be found in any well-stocked bookstore.

I began to think about Zen and meditation again when breathing became a more serious concern for me. What was such meditation really, and what did the breath have to do with it? Why not focus on the circulation of the blood? Why not stand on a chair for 30 minutes every morning, as a friend was doing? The answer seemed to be that the breath was handy—as an object for focusing the mind, it would do. Various writers supplied suggestions for practice. Do it each day without fail. Don't try counting beyond 10—at that point go back to one, or if you lose count start over. Half an hour is about right—use a timer with a bell. Try to have a regular spot for *zazen* (one suggested appropriate pictures, and incense). Get a teacher. Try not to let your practice cause division in your family; if possible involve your spouse and even your children in social activity at the *zendo*, or practice hall.

Many of these suggestions I didn't adopt. I did, as noted earlier, warn Karen, who has a sense of humor and after nearly 50 years of marriage is not surprised by much that I do. I'm often up by 4 or 5 a.m., so early morning still seemed a good time for the practice. I put a straight-backed chair with a bed pillow in one corner of my upstairs study and arranged the corner with some books on Chinese themes and a little painted folding screen atop a bookshelf. No incense. I found—startlingly—that a candle placed in front of the screen cast a shadow on the wall behind it reminiscent of a lake bordered by mountains. But I quit using the candle; the image was too vivid and distracting, and the candle a possible fire hazard, should the meditator nod off.

This is as much as I want to say about mechanics. I don't put my "practice" forward as one to be followed by anyone else, or exemplary of proper Zen—which may be an oxymoron. It's also difficult to write about something that aims at direct experience of a state of being, rather than an intellectual understanding of it. And which warns against even "aiming" at this experience, since to have a goal subverts the practice. Trying to attain goal-lessness is itself a goal. We have entered the Hall of Receding Mirrors here. Just sit.

I noticed some things after several months. The practice didn't become boring, as I thought it would (and as it probably will—students are warned to expect this and deal with it). After a life of fast-paced, on-deadline activity, it's been strangely satisfying to do something that has no result, or at least none that can be described. I have finally been permitted to stop doing, and to be.

Zen practice makes me aware, a little uncomfortably, of how frenzied my mind usually is, and how many directions, all fascinating, it shoots off into, given the chance. There are mornings when I have trouble counting breaths to 10 (although I usually can make it past two). "Stopping your thinking," a tenet of Zen and of other meditative techniques, is not really inimical to the intellect. Rather, it affords the thinking mind a rest, from which it can return, like an overtired muscle given a day to recuperate.

"What do you think about in meditation?" is a question that misses the mark. The answer, such as it is, is "Nothing. I'm aware of the breath, that's all." But it's not that simple. The experience resembles that of the child who loses a tooth and is told not to put his tongue in the spot, so that the new tooth will grow in gold. Or the philosopher's challenge of going a year without thinking of the word "hippopotamus." The busy, thinking mind throws up many obstacles. Sometimes it thinks about how successful (or not) the meditation is. Sometimes it mouths the names of the numbers, even though teachers urge just becoming "one with the breath." Sometimes, the thread simply is lost and the mind goes off to think about breakfast or the afternoon's appointment. There's nothing to do then but laugh and start the count over.

At first the slightest distraction was enough to derail me. In my corner, a price tag pasted on a book made me lose count. Another book, *The Glory and Fall of the Ming Dynasty,* reminded me of the friend, now dead, who had given it to me, and I remembered that I'd always intended to read it. I tore off the price tag, and the Ming Dynasty eventually sank back into its shelf. At times I pictured "monkey mind" climbing down from its tree and going to sleep at my feet. Of course that was a delusion, too, in several ways. The picture gave my busy mind something to dwell on besides the breath—and anyway, as Zen teachers point out, "monkey mind" is neither bad in itself nor something separate from "big" or universal mind. No duality, please.

My experiences have probably been the small change of meditation for any beginner. Eventually I quit worrying much about them, and let awareness of the breath fill as much space as possible. I was able now and then to focus on breathing for a minute or two without actually counting or having words arise in my mind. It was not a dreamy state at all—rather sharper than ordinary perception, with the intake and release of breath a little more of a direct experience than before. But there was no revelation here, nor anything out of the ordinary. It was just breathing. And there was no sense that anything much had been achieved.

Which, as far as I can tell, is the way it should be.

I did notice a peculiar thing—I lost the sense, at first, of how much time had passed. Having decided against a timer and bell, I would turn my wristwatch to the wall, and "sit" until I'd done about as much as I wanted that morning. For several weeks, I guessed that I'd been sitting about 20 minutes and found it was nearer 40. Whatever internal clock regulates such things has now reset itself, and my guess is often within a minute or two. I usually quit after 30 to 50 minutes, although one morning I sat for an hour so that this would no longer be a goal. And now and then I stop short to remind myself that the time doesn't matter.

So are there any results at all from this goal-less activity? Even those who caution most against expecting gain, still seem to think *something* happens, whether it is that elusive state called enlightenment or some more homely outcome. They also agree that one should not limit the practice to the *zazen* hour, but in some way take it out into the everyday world.

I believe, without a lot of evidence, that my mind is more focused than it used to be—slightly more able to attend to the activity of the moment without flying off into irrelevancies. I'm more aware of the extent to which joy and misery arise in my head, rather than directly from outside events. A possibly apocryphal comment makes sense to me now: "I am an old man and have had many troubles, most of which never happened." But many people learn this without counting the breath.

When Karen and I went to Europe several years ago, I took along a book on breathing meditation, not specifically centered on Zen. It became operational in Munich, where Karen aggravated a leg ailment and we found ourselves trapped, as it were, in a fourth-floor walkup hotel room. At another time, I would have been worried, annoyed, and a little frantic. What if it gets worse? Will we get out of here and home safely? How will we eat? What about all the things I want to see and do in Munich? It was becoming more of a problem for me than for Karen, but reading for once came to the rescue. We were in Munich, after all, that wonderful city, which has excellent medical care. We spoke German. We could move to a lower room. I could go buy bread and cheese. Breathe in, breathe out.

For a couple of mornings we sat in the outdoor garden of Munich's farm market, the Victualienmarkt, drinking coffee, reading the papers, and watching people. It was brilliant late fall weather with golden light filtering through the trees. The Pope had just left town, and the Oktoberfest was about to start. "Pope's gone, time to party," Karen said one morning. She was back, and we had a lovely time, even though we passed on the Oktoberfest.

When I began writing this, I wanted to quote the seemingly contradictory statements by Shunryu Suzuki that appear near the beginning. No problem—I knew this book by heart. I would just flip through and find the passages again. But I couldn't find them! Impatience began. I was ready to write the paragraph, where were those damn quotations? And then I started to laugh. Of course, Suzuki was hiding them from me. I sat down and began re-reading the book from the beginning, enjoying it again, until I came naturally to the words.

I am not very good at this and maybe never will be. Buddhism and Zen are a vast religious and cultural complex; it would be pretentious and foolish of me to comment further on them, except to say that many of their tenets parallel those of other faiths including my own Christian one. And I like the Buddhists—they have never started a war.

Even in the limited practice of breath meditation, my cat Batu is more accomplished than I am. For about a week, he came to my corner in the study and "sat" with me each morning, either atop the shelves to the left or the futon on the right—eyes closed, totally at peace. Then he stopped coming. I think he had found Nirvana.

BREATHING THROUGH SATURDAY

MORNING ANNOUNCES ITSELF in gold through the bedroom window. It sets the louvers of the wooden shutters alight, glances from depths of the mirror, drops the corners of the room back into darkness. I am awake.

Today, I've decided, I'll watch every breath I take, which is outrageous and impossible for anyone not a monomaniac or a yogi. But I've been thinking about it for a while, and experimenting—"being with the breath," one meditator calls it. And today looks like a good day for a further step. Several things are going on in the house, but at least I don't have to worry about the book I'm editing, since one author is seriously depressed and the other has gone to the beach. I am free.

There may be, probably are, those who can observe every breath, but what meditators usually mean is just frequent awareness of this process, which extends without a break from the slap in the delivery room to the sigh of death. In theory, you might observe the heartbeat or the circulation of the lymph, but these are harder to watch.

And the breath has no history, no past or future. It's pure present. Aside from an asthma attack or the first gasp after nearly drowning, no one remembers a particular breath or plots how to breathe in the future. The breath is the enemy of nostalgia and dreams.

This unique "presentness" has an unexpected effect. When you focus on the breath, the world around you is also present more vividly. Being aware of the breath makes you a better driver, a more alert and prepared walker on a dark street. You can be fully conscious of the breath only in this moment, right now, while you're reading this, in fact.

Easy to say, but what does it mean to practice it?

Today is an ordinary Saturday in April. I do 30 minutes of *zazen* meditation in the upstairs study and go down to breakfast, intending to spend the day watching the breath—not every breath, probably, but enough to see how doing this might change things. At 7:40 a.m. sunlight is coming in low over the field behind the house, illuminating the old truck that Randy the roofer parked in the driveway last night. Birds weave the air over the back yard, and Garfield, a yellow cat from two doors down, comes stalking toward the house and then mysteriously vanishes. Teachers arrive at the school beyond the field, car doors opening like wings. A vista between trees leads to a distant road on which other cars are passing.

> *Those far-off cars, those distant susurrations.*
> *all of those purposes, those destinations.*

I wrote that once, in a poem illustrating rhetorical figures, and the cars are still going by.

Tristan, the six-year-old at Garfield's house, comes soodling out on the rear deck, to inspect a tree house his father is building for him and to practice leaping back and forth between the deck and a box on the ground. Then he goes back in the house. Hannah, the dog, squats under the tree house, looking bored.

At 8:30, walking by the bookcase, breathing, I notice a pamphlet bought years ago at a yard sale for $1.98, but never read: *Wallace Stevens: The Poetry of Earth*, a Library of Congress lecture delivered in 1979 by A. Walton Litz. Reading it now—it's only 12 pages—I come to these lines from "The Snow Man":

> *. . . the listener, who listens in the snow,*
> *And, nothing himself, beholds*
> *Nothing that is not there and the nothing that is.*

BREATH & OTHER VENTURES

Wallace Stevens as a Zen Buddhist? This is what my friend Susanna would call a wonderful synchronicity, but it takes me away from the present, to a barracks in Fort Benning, Georgia, in 1958. I'm sitting on my bunk, reading "The Emperor of Ice Cream" by Stevens, my first real poet, in a book given me by Natalie Darcy, a New York City schoolteacher. She also has introduced me to Sean O'Faolain's *A Summer in Italy*, inviting me "to see Venice with the eyes of an Irishman as well as your own." And a few years later, I do. (I think Natalie is no longer alive. For several years we kept sending the annual card, but it was neither returned nor answered.)

I come back to the breath, to the present, in which my son Karl calls from Vermont, to say that he's finished his new book and has been off spending his prospective royalties at a used-book store. On one table, he says, was *Gathering of Animals*, the centennial history of the Bronx Zoo by his Great-Uncle Bill. "I think Bill arranged for it to be there today," he says, and on this morning of synchronicities I don't disagree.

Don't worry if you lose track of the breath, the meditators say. It's always there, you can come back to it.

I come back, while putting water on to boil for my morning job of decanting some two-year-old pear wine from gallon jugs into sterilized bottles. By this time a rain of bricks is coming off the roof and thumping on the driveway, as Randy and his crew dismantle two old chimneys. As the bricks fall, their shadows also fly over the drive. There isn't a hardhat (or an OSHA inspector) in sight. I go out, at a safe distance, and ask the roofers to save the bricks for me, which they do, piling them neatly by the garage. "I cleaned those gutters for you while I was up there," says a workman in a Superman T-shirt.

Since the workmen have their ladder against the bathroom window, I go off to piss in the upstairs john, and resume following the breath. You breathe every moment of your life, from the the most ethereal to the earthiest.

42

Back in the kitchen, Karen and I begin siphoning off the wine. She guides the upper end of a plastic tube, splinted with a chopstick, into the gallon jug, keeping it free of the sludge on the bottom. I suck (a breath?) at the lower end to start the siphon, which could bring on a buzz if, like a wine taster, I didn't spit frequently. This is a sour wine, not very good. "Paint thinner," Karen says. But the blue bottles are beautiful on the kitchen counter, a Matisse still life with bananas and a bowl of grapefruit.

By 11 most of the wine is bottled. I stop to write to another son, Colin, in New York City, and then walk to the post office. It's a good day to walk, breathe, and look at the world—at lawns sprinkled with violets and dandelions, at the sign for a new Sky Bank (blue-sky financing?), at the still leafless white bones of sycamores. In the post office, a mother copes with two kids while addressing a package. One nearly knocks a box of forms off the counter. "See, that's exactly what I meant!" Mom exclaims, triumphantly.

Coming back along Walnut Street, counting breaths, I look down its long prospect of spring leaves, and remember writing about a man walking into that diminishing vista:

He shrank
until he was the same size

as television people,
then disappeared in a green tunnel. Eye,
how shall I be well

and artfully deceived today?

At home, Randy and his crew are packing up, after sealing the chimney holes with new decking and shingles. Karen and I eat cheese sandwiches and bottle the last of the wine. I take coffee and my breath to the front-porch swing—yellow swing, yellow tulips next to the porch, more dandelions. And noise. My neighbor Greg is mowing the lawn, and five-year-old Audra is throwing a tantrum (and a broom, for some reason) in the front yard. Now and then Greg kills the mower with a dying-duck gargle. A wind chime bangs, birds screech. Only a blissninny (Finn Wilcox's delightful word) would expect following the breath to be always idyllic. That's the point—you have to breathe with what's there, in the moment.

I go back upstairs and sit *zazen* again, this time with two cats who do it better than I do, except that with them it looks suspiciously like sleep. By now, I need sleep, too—awareness of the breath, or of anything else, takes energy. I nap for an hour, badly, with dreams in which my mother and I are fighting because she wants me to go somewhere and I'm resisting. But, as with noise or distraction, the idea is not to avoid any of this—look at it instead, get intimate with it, breathe with it.

When I get up, Audra is riding her battery-powered toy car full speed down the driveway, with her grandmother in pursuit. I drink coffee beside the driveway window, breathe, and notice the objects around me. Uncle Stephen's painting of a church, which languished for years in a cheap frame and dirty mat, but now shines in a new setting. A poem by Keith Kumasen Abbott, set in type and sent to me by Jerry Reddan at Tangram Press in Berkeley:

> *watching sand tell time*
> *waiting for water to turn*
> *into tea*

I am one of Jerry's faithful customers and have a box full of his exquisite printing, which my executor can decide what to do with.

Later, I take a walk through town and meet Cliff Cain, a former college chaplain, who is mowing his lawn this fine April afternoon. We discuss heaven and hell for a while, and I ask why present-day Buddhists sometimes talk about these, even though the Buddha never did. Cliff fills me in on Theravada and Mahayana Buddhism, as the mower cools. Early practitioners were silent on an afterlife, he says, but later ones discovered a heaven of 33 levels. "You mean the theologians got hold of it," I say. "Yes," says Cliff, no mean theologian himself. And with a laugh, "The same thing happened to Christianity."

I go on walking and breathing, past my great-grandmother's house, where the family gathered on the porch for a Christmas photo in 1914. The last person alive from that picture, my father, died in 1996. I walk on, past two men carrying a plant in a tub to the front porch for the summer, past bulbs unfurling their leaves on the lawn of a prominent attorney, dead now a few weeks, in a car accident while terminally ill with cancer. A gravel driveway, numinous in pale sunshine last week, is only a driveway today. I walk through a puddle and the wet footprints follow me a little way, then fade out.

Coming home, I mow the lawn, not concentrating on the breath every moment, but doing the work with attention, because the yard is still littered with small limbs shed by the ash tree over the winter. Audra comes running across the yard to hug me, as her grandmother yells from the back step, "You get right back over here!"

"Audra's not having a very good day, is she?" I yell back.

"No, she's not been a good kid today."

There is more to this Saturday, and to the breath. Karen and I go out for supper, meet up with friends, come home. The house is dusky now, in western light. I go upstairs to write this essay, and before long it's midnight. This particular day—an ordinary one in April—has ended. I haven't succeeded in my goal, if it was ever that, of continuous attention to the breath. But I've been more aware of it than usual, and this has anchored the day. I have not been absent from my life this spring Saturday.

Going to bed, I think of the *malkos*, a traditional melody of India composed for midnight prayer and "the soul's abandon in the sublimity of night." I am ready to sleep now, without dreams. The breath can go on without me until, God willing, we meet again tomorrow.

WALKING THE BREATH

Then, after a while, I was in the road going to the house and looked up and there it was, on the little rising piece of land, waiting for me. Through the mist that lay between us it seemed that the house was built of the most fragile web of breath and I had blown it—and that with my breath I could blow it all away.

—From *The House of Breath*
by William Goyen

I STARTED WALKING. That had been the reason, it now seemed, for all the trips to the pulmonary lab and the hours on the treadmill and exercycle. I was supposed to carry all this practice home and keep doing it and keep breathing.

This was exercise at first, and then it became a discipline. I knew that every afternoon—whatever the season or weather—I would be walking and paying attention to my breath.

And since this town was my old home and I had been in house after house of it for 70 years, this seemed right, to walk its streets and breathe it back into life around me. Fifty years before, as a young newspaper reporter replaying *Winesburg, Ohio*, in my head, I had walked every part of it, day and night. Now I would do that again. I would see the little stub streets (Palmer, Second Street) that butted into the railroad. I would explore the far reaches of the North End ("Kentucky"), and stroll along the Champs Ulysses, named by a returning World War I doughboy who couldn't spell. I would walk the boggy subdivision meadows, where so many geese wintered that my wife and I had coined a word for them: "megagaggle."

47

And I would breathe the way I had been shown, a deep breath into the belly and then an expansion of the rib cage. I would walk for an hour every day, fast, taking in air through my nostrils and warming it for my lungs. I would breathe out long, through pursed lips. Coming home, I would walk fast up the little hill on Banta Street by the old catalpa tree, working my legs and my heart.

There would be fallbacks for really bad weather—an indoor track at my old college or (a last resort) Walmart, which looks different when one is walking, not shopping. It has its own street pattern, its own houses of merchandise, its own community of clerks, loafing and gabbing on the corners.

It was a good plan, but it didn't work out quite so simply. This was because the town suddenly came back to me and began to talk. And also because of a question by a writer in a book, who asked himself, "How do I want to live my life?" Not, "What do I want to do with my life?" the more usual question. A difference.

First, the town: Franklin, seat of Johnson County, 20 miles south of Indianapolis, founded by entrepreneur George King in 1823. An old town, full of trees and history. Full of family memories, too, because my great-great-grandfather came to the county only six years after King. It's a town where restaurants decorate their walls with pioneer photographs. Drawing on one of these, I once wrote a poem called "Letters from the Town":

> *Here are five huts along*
> *a dirt street where a horse*
> *stands at a paling, and the fields*
> *are just visible in this photograph*
> *the color of dust.*

This was South Jackson Street in the 1880s, although the horse may be an invention, like the Arab leading a camel on the cigarette pack. "What color is his fez?" my father delighted in asking, and when we guessed red hooted at us. "There's no Arab, he's off behind the pyramid drinking arrak."

I have my father's storytelling blood in me, and his humor, and his knowledge of the town. But too much time has passed, and it is not his town anymore, nor mine. He and his brother sat one night over a bottle of scotch, recording their memories of 60 years before. They tallied more than 100 stories of the town and its people, and I have their notes, but only the first half are legible. And my own memories twist and dissolve like a drunkard's scrawl or an old letter blurred by tears.

So I walk and breathe among the ruins of my past, starting on King Street and going east past all the family homes remembered from childhood. My great-grandmother's house is nearly derelict now, with no sign of life and with soiled sheets hung at the staring windows. Aunt Alta Henderson's house is clean and painted— almost, I think, I could walk in and see her treasured heirlooms again, and look through her genealogical scrapbooks. Further on, the house where I woke to the clatter of the sun has been remodeled and its cozy "galley" kitchen removed. The North House on Duane Street, to which my grandparents moved about 1900, is gently decaying. So many people, so much breath now stilled.

A whole street of houses, in one of which I lived as a student, has been picked up and moved to another part of town. I walk past it now on a different street, and past the window where I once looked out on another landscape. In those days, I walked the length of Madison Street every day, going to and from the college and my job at the *Evening Star*. A few years ago Madison was closed at the railroad, a trade-off with Conrail for a new grade crossing in an industrial park. After griping about this for years, I tramped across the tracks one day, "opening" the street again to foot if not vehicular traffic.

Some familiar landmarks have burned. In fact, the whole town is burning down, a slow conflagration that has been going on since George King's two-room cabin disappeared, probably sometime in the 1830s. A town earlier than my memories is entirely gone. A "bird's-eye view" painted in 1876 shows settlement ending at Banta Street, with green hills beyond, where I now live, in an aging subdivision. I walk across this boundary, trying to see this earlier, greener town, the old contours of gently rolling ground dropping down to the confluence of Hurricane and Young's creeks. And to other creeks, long since turned into storm drains, never to be "daylighted."

This could go on. Franklin has done a better job than most of "preserving our heritage," as the phrase goes. An excellent county museum occupies what was once the Masonic Temple. A preservation society restores old homes and has rescued the Artcraft Theater, for decades the town's social center. (My father cleaned brick from the house demolished for construction of the theater in 1922. People still living remember being in the Artcraft on a Saturday afternoon in 1930 when the movie was halted to announce that the body of Amidor Wyrick, a leading businessman, had been recovered after a boating accident on Sugar Creek.)

The city's streets are mostly asphalt now, but a few stretches have the original brick. This is due to the hell raised some years ago by an organization called SOBS, for Save Our Brick Streets. There are also some brick sidewalks, much damaged and heaved up by tree roots. In fact, many of the town's sidewalks are in terrible shape, making it hard to walk, especially in bad weather. But I am a careful walker.

And walking in the rain one night, I come to one of the hidden rivers, a little stream once called Roaring Run, which now pours from a pipe beneath Jefferson Street, the town's main thoroughfare. On the other side of the street, I trace the paved-over swale through which the creek once ran. This was also the path of the Big Four railroad, which went clanging past my great-grandmother's back yard. The Big Four, too, has gone under house lots, but its roadbed reappears alongside the stream below

Jefferson Street, following its trickle down to Young's Creek and a ruined trestle with "1928" pressed into a concrete pier.

Near the stream, a sign marks the site of George King's primeval cabin. We are a people who tear down buildings and then put up handsome and expensive signs ($1,500 each, from the Indiana Historical Bureau) commemorating them. One day, I walk between the sites of the old North and South schools, buildings that have vanished within my memory. Built in 1870 and 1887, these were high-ceilinged, Victorian structures with pine floors worn down by generations of children and redolent of cleaning compound. (At five or six, my father was taken to the North School by his brother, shoved in the door, and told, "Get a back seat.") When I last saw the South School, it had become a boys' club, with a box cut into the ceiling of the third-floor gym. This was so basketballs could be arched into the goal—it limited rather sharply the spots from which players could shoot.

In 1928, during a commemorative fit, the city declared that the North School would be forever known as the Philander W. Payne School, for "the physician and Christian gentleman" who had been on the school board when it was built. The South School was renamed at the same time for Kittie Palmer, "the splendid woman who was principal of the high school" housed there. The Payne School was torn down in 1969, and Kittie Palmer's school in 1981. The first site is now a park and playground, the second an arboretum. But sometimes the historical site is still intact. A plaque marks the house in which Paul Vories McNutt was born: 34th governor of Indiana and the first ambassador to the Philippine Republic—and, briefly, a presidential hopeful. (Another hopeful, Roger Branigin, the 42nd governor, has a boulevard named for him, but his birthplace is now a vacant lot—with a sign.) A while back the town was concerned about a state plan to route a superhighway through the neighboring countryside. At a meeting of the county historical society, a board member said, "Maybe we should put up a sign commemorating farmland."

Some people and happenings have no monuments. Seventy years or more ago, my great-grandmother remarked one day to my mother that a prominent citizen and contemporary (she named him), had been conceived "in a buggy coming home from the Sprunica Fair." I could probably confirm this, at least circumstantially, with a few minutes in the wedding and birth records at the county museum. But research has to end somewhere.

Is it bootless nostalgia to remember all this? What pain is associated with these reflections? Nostalgia has long since lost its 19th century diagnosis as a serious malady, a type of melancholia. But a writer has observed that "the phenomenon did not disappear with its demedicalization."

I walk and count my breaths. What I feel is not a desire to return to some idealized home, but rather a sense of time's irreparable passage. "Change and decay in all around I see," wrote the hymnist, and he was looking mostly at himself.

And here I come back to the question, "What do I want to do with my life?" For many of us, the time for answering that is over. The doing is finished, for better or worse. But "How do I live my life" is still an open question, one I think about as I walk and breathe, a dozen times a minute, 18,000 times a day. The question isn't what to accomplish or how to fill the days—those are easy. It's how to live in the present moment, more deliberately and with intention. It's how not to do, but be.

Today is cold and clear, and I'm walking my breath again, past old family houses as far as Hurricane Creek, where at six I launched rubber-band boats in the purling current. A crew of high-school runners trots by, naked to the waist in 35-degree weather. An old man (and yet not much older than I am) hobbles past, watching the runners. In the park beside the creek, teenagers play pick-up football, and I shout to them, "Will you be ready to go in if the Colts call you on Sunday?" "You bet!" one yells back. "Aw, they're gonna lose," says another. (But they don't, and go on to win the Superbowl.)

BREATH & OTHER VENTURES

This is their town, not the one of memory. The people who lived in that one are done with their doing; reminiscence will not bring them back, or change one thing that happened there. I have to leave them behind. Walking on, I turn off Breckinridge and onto Banta, quickening my pace and breath to bring my heartbeat up to workout level by the time I reach the galled and twisted catalpa at the crest. I wrote about that tree once and how ivy hid the rot in its heart, like a hand raised to hide a scar. And about how

> *. . . even the new tree*
> *in its circle*
> *of bricks and earth,*
> *its fine lace glistening*
> *with rain, was turning away,*
> *but with such generous*
> *and tender transience*
> *I could let it go.*

PARADOXES

A warm day leaves only
dirty peninsulas
that rot bottom up.

Detail revives. A leaf
skitters on brown grass,
sticks sail in gutters,

floodwater hangs and flashes
over the Conrail tracks.

No more white wideness,
just the beautiful
specificity of the world.

—Snowmelt

THESE SHORT SKETCHES on breath have been full of para-doxes, one of them being my preoccupation over several years with both medical treatment for breathing disorders and with Zen. While Zen does not, as far as I know, discourage medical treatment for its adherents, it seems to have little interest in the clinical aspects. While celebrating life, it counsels facing the certainty of death and getting beyond undue concern about it.

Dianne Jenkins, my co-author on another book, has carved a rubber stamp with a quotation from Stephen Bachelor that shows up often in her letters: "Since death alone is certain and the time of death is uncertain, what should I do?"

Neither of us has a definitive answer to that question.

As a writer, I began by exploring the clinical aspects of lungs and breathing, but discovered quickly that I didn't want to write a book about a disease—which had been done anyway. What my medical experience did was open a door to more acute observation of the world—an effort Zen study has reinforced. A third skein of this composition has involved the history of place and family, old preoccupations seen through a new lens.

This final essay begins with a story.

Karen, my wife, tests positive for tuberculosis. She's never had the disease but has the antibodies, probably because of Johnny Vieke. Johnny and his wife, Laura, were friends of her parents, Fritz and Mary, in the American Legion post at Vincennes, Indiana. When she was born—a late-in-life baby—Johnny was delighted and held her every chance he got. Then he was diagnosed with TB and went away to Hillcrest Tuberculosis Sanitarium, on the outskirts of town, where he died. Fritz and Mary visited him, but Karen wasn't allowed inside. She remembers Fritz holding her up, on the hospital lawn, so Johnny could wave to her from behind the window of his sickroom.

This image moves me, as does any picture of Karen as a child. It's also easy to look at the figure in the window and think of isolation and loneliness. While writing the first draft of this essay several years ago, I was seeing reports on the news about Andrew Speaker, a young lawyer who traveled while infected with tuberculosis. One photo showed him, like Johnny, wraithlike behind the curtains of his Denver hospital room.

But this melancholy impression is less than the truth. Hillcrest Sanitarium (now condominiums) was an important support for sufferers and their families. Johnny watching and Karen waving are a poignant but not a sad image, and this is not an essay about dissolution and death. Breathing is life itself, a moment-by-moment miracle of process and order. Still, one celebrates while being aware of its opposite, and while holding at bay the fear of not being able to breathe at all. I am breathing well these days, but back of that well-being is the fear of not being able to breathe at all.

At three or four years of age, I woke mornings terrified by a recurring dream of suffocation—of something pressing down all night on my chest, so that each breath was a struggle. I was sickly, with an overprotective mother, and would have fit neatly into the mid-20th century Freudian view of childhood asthma as "a suppressed cry." It was during this time that Marie, later my stepmother, urged my mother to "let go" of me and quite possibly saved my life.

Later, as I have written earlier in these essays, I wheezed with bronchitis and slept with the foot of my bed elevated. Meanwhile, my grandmother was dying of asthma in Arizona and her daughter, my mother, was developing the emphysema and (probably) the *cor pulmonalis* or enlarged heart that would kill her at 58.

But I outgrew my childhood ailments and went on, even lettering in cross-country at college (no great feat, since there were seven runners and seven letters given). Then in my early 30s I began having asthmatic attacks now and then. These subsided until my mid-40s when we moved to our present home. There the attacks recurred, and it's these I remember vividly.

It is 3 a.m. I am standing, braced against the kitchen sink. I can hardly breathe. It is the most intense effort to draw even one breath, and after that another and another. I have no past or future—nothing beyond fighting in this moment for this breath. Every muscle is tense. I've tried breathing the steam from a teakettle, hoping it will somehow warm and loosen the cold lump of my chest. I cannot think. I am utterly exhausted. Calm sleep is not even a distant memory. How long can I go on like this without dying? There is nothing in the world except this hopeless struggle for the next breath.

This describes a fairly routine asthmatic attack, not even a truly severe one. Some have it much worse. About 5,000 Americans die each year of asthma, writes Carla Keirns in *Short of Breath: A Social and Intellectual History of Asthma in the United States*. She quotes a second-century physician, Aretaeus the Cappadocian, who describes asthmatics in a way I can relate to:

> *They breathe standing, as if desiring to draw in all the air which they can possibly inhale; and, in their want of air, they also open the mouth, as if thus to enjoy the more of it; pale in the countenance, except the cheeks, which are ruddy; sweat about the forehead and clavicles; expectoration small, thin, cold, resembling the efflorescence of foam . . . .*

Keirns writes "about the transformation of asthma across time and space" and also "the transformation of the medical gaze" from the patient's symptoms to the pathology of disease—a progress to which asthma has been a troubling obstacle at times. In her engrossing, unpublished work (a 2004 doctoral dissertation), I see how my own experience has paralleled the story of lung disorders in the 20th century.

When I was born in 1935, tuberculosis was a major killer in America, as it still is in much of the world. My father discovered, in a routine x-ray, that he had tubercular lesions. Apparently he had had the disease in youth, but his body had walled it off. Only a few years earlier, sufferers were still called "lungers." If not actively diseased, they had "weak lungs" and spent their lives pursuing relief—at expensive spas if they could afford them, or with the help of patented nostrums like the Vapo-Cresolene lamp, which maximized sales by printing a different diagnosis on each side of the box. Accidents might doom one for life. John Bridges, a son of my great-great-grandfather, was 14 in the mid-1800s when he ruined his lungs beating out a field fire started by sparks from a passing train.

Keirns traces asthma from its first literary mention (in the *Iliad*) through the start of the 21st century. To the Greeks, ασθμα was simply breathlessness, and it remained that until about 1810, when Parisian hospitals began treating poor patients in return for permission to dissect their corpses. The autopsy findings under-mined ancient theories about the body's four "humors" and led eventually to modern "evidence-based" medicine. Other lung ailments once were seen as precursors of tuberculosis. When the TB bacillus was isolated in 1882, asthma began emerging in its own right. But no asthma germ was ever found, and patients often seemed entirely normal between seizures. At autopsy, Keirns writes, "asthma became the disease you had if you died of suffo-cating shortness of breath and had nothing wrong with your heart or lungs."

She adds: "Asthma remains, in many ways, a holdover from an earlier medical world, a condition whose reality depends on the testimony of its sufferers." And she quotes a medical historian, Charles Rosenberg: "In some ways, disease does not exist until we have agreed that it does, by perceiving, naming, and respond-ing to it."

What then *was* asthma? Clinically, it was a spasm or parox-ysm in the smooth muscles of the bronchial tree, attended by overproduction of mucus. The airways closed up. But what trig-gered this? The field was open to every speculation. In the 19th century, climate was suspect, and great spas arose in salubrious spots like Saratoga and the White Mountains of Vermont. Colora-do became "the Switzerland of America." (Andrew Speaker's Denver hospital began as a home for the children of asthmatics and consumptives seeking relief in the mountain air.)

Along with its relation to climate, asthma was often considered a neurotic or "nervous" disease, treatable with stimulants and de-pressants. Inhalations of chemicals and smoke were popular—Calvin Coolidge treated his asthma by breathing chlorine fumes. The term "allergy" was coined in 1906, and shots were developed for sensitivity to pollen and other substances. By the time of my birth, asthma was being redefined by psychoanalysis into a disease associated with childhood trauma. "Parentectomy"— removing children from their smothering parents for months at a time—was sometimes prescribed. The stage was set, Keirns writes, for a struggle in mid-century "between allergists, pulmonologists, and psychiatrists for jurisdiction over asthma." The medical treatment path would lead through steroid and cortisone injections, antihistamines, "β-agonist" inhalers, and eventually inhaled steroids.

In middle age, unaware of all this, I had found an over-the-counter remedy. Primatene (containing ephedrine) relieved my asthma symptoms even though it left me woozy for a few hours. I got through the '80s and '90s popping Primatene tablets, until I found I no longer needed them. By the time symptoms returned, in the fall of 2005, medicine had moved on. Primatene was now terrible stuff "that shouldn't be sold over the counter," a respiratory therapist said. Instead, she prescribed daily doses of Advair and Spiriva, the newest inhaled bronchodilators.

My asthma is now "under control," she tells me. But when it is under control, what do I actually have? Keirns writes, in a fairly startling sentence, that "even though a range of tests, from spirometry to immune desensitization, may support a diagnosis of asthma, in the absence of a complaint of shortness of breath, cough, wheezing, or limitations on exercise caused by breathing, a patient does not have asthma."

I am assured, though, that I do have COPD, or chronic obstructive pulmonary disease, an illness not labeled until 1968 when it was added to the *International Classification of Diseases* as an umbrella term for a congeries of respiratory ills, including bronchitis, emphysema, and sometimes asthma. Today I hear people say casually, "I have COPD," and insurers pay for its treatment.

"Classification matters," Keirns observes.

My doctor, a pulmonologist, also calls what I have "fixed-airway disease" and says it exceeds the degree of pulmonary dysfunction normal for someone in his seventies. My airways have been "remodeled"—apparently by an inept interior decorator—and they will never be as good as they were. The doctor is pleased I don't smoke, wishes Karen didn't, suggests I could be just as happy with a gas log in my fireplace as with a wood fire (which I've not been willing to give up yet).

But still . . . . in what does this paradoxical disease consist? Is it simply that lung function deviates significantly from statistical norms? An article tells me that a COPD patient who is careful may have 10 more years before becoming seriously ill. How does this differ, I wonder, from ordinary aging, illness, and death? Sometimes I imagine my doctor looking at me quizzically—even speculatively—and thinking that a good autopsy might answer some questions with more certitude.

Keirns ends her treatise with a review of asthma "narratives," including the interesting if unproven idea that our lives may be too "clean," leaving our immune systems to turn on themselves and cause "mischief like the vestigial appendix." There is certainly an asthma epidemic, she notes, especially among children, some of whom can't fly on a plane if another passenger is eating peanuts. But she leaves for debate the extent to which this epidemic reflects reporting changes or "domain expansion"—the tendency of doctors and patients to find diseases when easy, safe treatments are available for them.

Meanwhile, I take my "meds," as they're called in the current medicalization of life in America. I have no noticeable breathing difficulties, am mostly unbothered by allergies, can walk briskly for several miles without becoming winded. I get medicine cheaply under Medicare Part D—about the only initiative of the Bush II administration with which I agree. I haven't had a cold in months, although my researches into breathing may simply have made me more careful about going out in the rain.

But I know this good health is transitory. I will fall ill again. I will die—in 20 years, next month, a day or two from now. A writer on meditation, Larry Rosenberg, observes that death is not something waiting for us at the end of a long journey. It's beside us now, in each moment. It is as near as being unable to take the next breath, and it will happen on an otherwise ordinary day.

How do I feel about that, after several years of a medical regimen and Zen practice? I may be "a smart little feller" as Arletta said, but it's gotten me no closer to unambiguous answers. What it has done is make me worry less about the answers and perhaps use my time here better. "Pay attention," says W.S. Merwin, our new poet laureate.

Shunryu Suzuki, during his last illness, told his wife, "I don't want to die." Some younger followers faulted him for that, but I don't—it was a statement of fact. Who would want to leave the beautiful specificity of the world?

Suzuki also said, "We die and we don't die," a paradox as profound as Tertullian's on faith: "It is impossible. It must be true." One can take it as that or hold out for something more definite. The choice is a free one. "Paradoxes," one of my students once wrote, "are the brightly blazing banners of the liberty of the soul."

TEA BOWL

BRUSH PAINTING
BY KEITH KUMASEN ABBOTT

II. Back Then

The house at 502 Mockingbird Drive in photo of May 20, 1970, soon after our move there. At left, Karen with Colin, next to the porch with swing and rosebush, April 1976.

BACK THEN
(AN UNINTENDED MEMOIR)

NOT LONG AGO, Karen searched for one of our old houses on Google Earth—502 Mockingbird Drive in Jeffersonville, Indiana, where we lived from 1970 to 1977.

She got a surprise. The house was there, but Viking Drive was gone. This was the short cross-street we had traveled daily going to work, to Ewing Lane School, and to the neighborhood grocery known only as "Convenient." It was the street down which Karen and her friend Carol once carried a cardboard Conestoga wagon to a Cub Scout Night at the school, almost sending a motorist into a telephone pole. How could anyone live on Mockingbird Drive without the Viking Drive outlet?

A few days later we were in the area, across the Ohio River from Louisville, and decided to see what had happened to our old neighborhood. Viking Drive had indeed been closed, by an expansion of the Viking Village apartments, although it was still possible to reach 502 from either end of Mockingbird.

I last visited the neighborhood perhaps 20 years ago, when I was feeling anxious about the swift passage of life. The visit was therapeutic—the neighborhood hadn't changed much, and I found my memories of it being "unpacked," as if a dried flower had reconstituted itself in water. I relaxed. Life had not, in fact, disappeared without a trace.

But the experience this time was initially different. More than the street plan had changed. Our home at 502 had been new and shiny in a treeless subdivision. Now the trees had 40 years' growth on them. Some of those bright little houses were showing wear and neglect. The open spaces behind our house were now

65

built up, and there was a house next to 502 that I didn't remember being there (although Karen says it was built shortly before we moved—and since she is 27 percent smarter than me, according to a study of successful marriages, I'm sure she's right about this).

Most disturbing of all—I had difficulty reconciling our house with my memories of it. It seemed smaller, perhaps because of the bigger trees, and the porch now seemed hardly deep enough for the swing we had hung on it. There were cosmetic differences—shutters a different color, a hedge gone, and a junky mailbox on a post in the front yard. But what struck me was my uncertainty whether this was really the house where we had lived during an intense period in our lives. I asked Karen to turn the car around and drive past again. The house was indisputably the right one, but I no longer felt a connection with it, or with our lives there.

This is making too much of a routine occurrence. We were not depressed, and as we drove we recalled stories of that time—the Conestoga wagon, the woman down the street "who had kids by the litter," and our across-the-street neighbor and friend Maurice (our first African-American neighbor in the long-ago '70s). Then we went on to a happy lunch with our son Mike and his wife, Amanda, at a riverside restaurant.

But there was a shadow of some sort over the day. Had we really lived in that tiny house, with three kids until the arrival of a fourth dictated a move to larger quarters? Except for a generous basement (not very usable because of seepage), the house was a shoebox—three small bedrooms, a living room, and a kitchen that doubled as a dining room. We put a lot of work into the modest back yard, laying a brick "patio," planting a hedge, and fitting in a small flower and vegetable garden.

I've long been intrigued, if not obsessed, by nostalgia, which until Civil War times was recognized as a medical disorder. As a child, lying awake in my grandfather's house, I had been prey to a sort of "prospective nostalgia"—thinking about how time was passing, how I might someday revisit and buy this house, and live there.

But I had no desire to live again in 502 Mockingbird. The house struck me as cramped and dead, someone else's house in the wrong neighborhood.

It took about a day to think this through.

Change does not come as a surprise to me, nor am I overly concerned by the inevitability of death, which lies behind the fear of change. "If you didn't die," Shunryu Suzuki says, "you would *really* have a problem."

What I eventually realized was that I still had clear and vivid memories of "back then," which depended little if at all on the house where they were made. In that "now" of 30 to 40 years ago, we had lived our lives fully, with some courage as well as the usual human quota of joy and sorrow, anxiety and peace. I could still visualize those days clearly, with their memories of grubbing in the garden, writing my first poems at the living room desk, waking up in bed with Karen, a kid, and a cat. The set of bookshelves I built for that house is a few feet away as I write, and it is only momentarily disorienting to think that its width was dictated by the distance from the living-room closet to the hall—33 inches. It was a *very* small house.

We live in a different "now" now. One can revisit the past but not live there. We outgrew that house and that life. It is, in Auden's words, "a place we remember as unchanging, because there we changed."

BACK THEN: DECEMBER 13, 1975

When I wrote in the preceding pages about returning to Mockingbird Drive, I thought I'd exorcised whatever shadow had been over the visit. But it didn't turn out that way. I was suffering from a deeper sense of loss—those days on Mockingbird, gone, irretrievably, with all their joy and pain.

No matter how much one intends to live in the "now," the past pulls one back and never can be experienced vividly enough. I am the child who hoarded pine needles and bits of ribbon because he hated so much to see Christmas go. I wanted to go back to Mockingbird Drive as it actually was, and couldn't!

But then, almost accidentally, I looked in my oldest notebooks and found diary entries forgotten for years, including several so detailed that they brought those days alive again, as much as anything could. They told not only what we were doing, but about a sea change in our lives that we barely realized was happening at the time.

As I read and wrote, I realized I was creating a sort of memoir of a particular time and place—the house on Mockingbird and a slightly later one on Beckett Street in Clarksville, Indiana. This evolved eventually into the entries that follow.

I began writing poetry in the Mockingbird house in 1974—shocked into song by a holiday in Venice—and also began keeping a poetry journal. For the first few months, it was simply a repository for other poets' work I liked, or for general comments about the practice of poetry that I was beginning. Eventually there were a few diary entries. I was an editor on the night shift at *The Courier-Journal* in Louisville, so had days free to mess around with such things.

Then on Dec. 18, 1975, there is an extended entry, which brought that time into sudden and sharp relief. Karen (Kit) was in the kitchen with her Cub Scouts, and I was in the bedroom writing—not very far away in that small house. I wrote:

"Sitting by the bedroom window, while Kit's Cubs make cookies—voices drifting down by the window. Sweeper running. Imagining—if I were an invalid confined to this room and window for the rest of my life, what would I observe, write about?

"There is a physical world outside the window, dead grass, last of the peppers lying in it like bloodstones. The bale of straw in the raspberry patch with grass growing out of it. Benny's trees (the invalid would begin to learn the shape and every limb of each tree—one has limbs extended and curved like arms in supplication). The patch of plowed field between the far houses is medieval, a woodcut, a man pushing a plow should be going across it. Flash of a car going through the space. The fantastic fragility of trees—what visitor from another star system would believe them?

"Someone is working on Hobson's roof—two people, I think, because the hammer blows are contrapuntal—now just tapping, now bang bang bang decisive. Let your mind go. Bob Hedge appears suddenly out of Benny's house—unexpected event. Boy keeps on playing basketball in back of Fisher's—Bainbridge 70, Monroe 68. [An allusion to imaginary games I played as a child.] Suddenly aware of the relation of our back yards to those of houses on the circle.

"The exact curve of raspberry briars [a drawing here].

"Five wires across sky—a stave—no bird notes on it today. Pigeons would be whole notes. Spatzies 1/16ths. Quarter notes are the solid workhorses, so dependable. Then there are hemidemisemiquavers . . . .

"Enough of this, a la Creeley's *Day Book*. But if one sat here 8 hours a day, every day, how well he would know, get deep into, this particular landscape. Eisenstadt photographed the same tree, day after day, for years. To exhaust, to learn everything about one scene. Impossible. And this minute cataloguing of physical appearances means nothing in itself—mere practice of observation, on this warm sunny December morning. The poem is those cars flashing between the two houses, across that medieval field—people arriving in and leaving this particular windowscape.

"The boy is no longer playing basketball. Nobody is pounding at Hobson's—but a saw is starting up. Particular sound—how to describe it? 'Whine' is too bland for that sharpness. Good to be idle, simply to look and listen. A sudden weakening of the light—cloud over the sun—cold. Also an event—a vast number of events out this window. Roar of a jet fighter—silver. White car flashing north. High-pitched bird cry. Bell in the other room. Voices. 'Cookie man,' says somebody. More bird noises. Constant movement of hedge, briars, grass, trees in wind—the world in motion. Another jet coming, going. I don't see it. Piece of fluff drifts by screen. Particular shadows—slow-moving events. Crash of pan in kitchen. Now there are <u>5</u> boys playing basketball. Paper blows across the plowed field, disappears past the house. Airliner coming in toward Standiford—2-engine prop job. A paper blows across back yards of two far houses.

"Standing up (expanding the frame) discloses a tan and white dog beyond Hobson's back yard, nosing at something on the ground. More crashing from kitchen. Green pickup goes north. So ends this 10-minute catalog of events."

I said something to Karen while transcribing the piece above about how small the house had been, and she bristled slightly. "It was a <u>nice</u> house," she said. Indeed it was—we were too busy living in it back then to be concerned with size.

BACK THEN: BECOMING A POET (1)

[Journal, early summer, 1975] . . . . and out of the side of your eye, driving by, you see a girl balancing on a railroad track—a figure in T-shirt, blue jeans, tennis shoes, her back to you. Loose brown hair, I think.

It gets to your heart—something does—maybe the simplicity of the child's absorption in the balancing—something we have all done, but probably don't do much anymore. She is just being a child, walking a rail—you'd be wrong to leap to easy comparisons with ballerina, aerialist, bird—though there is something high-legged and in the hands bent back from the wrists that suggests a bird.

And there's the balance itself—you lose it if you think about it. You have to forget that you're up there, relax, and stroll as though you were going down the widest promenade—right up to the moment you fall.

GIRL ON THE RAILROAD

She isn't
a fifth-grader now
or anyone's daughter—
just girl walking the track,
balanced
above weeds and cinders,
high-legged in denims,
tennis shoes skewed
to the crown of the rail,
arms thrown out, hands
planing air,
keeping a balance
that's lost if thought about.

BACK THEN: BECOMING A POET (2)

[Journal, 7/3/1975] For the last few days, reading Robert Duncan's *Bending the Bow*—a background against which my various difficulties with poetry are illuminated.

I'm drawn to this poetry, sensing its great good, craft, and human-ness—yet put off again and again by its difficulty, by my laziness, by Duncan's huge scholarship, and even by his stance as poet. Where would one begin to understand—or to sense—this poetry? By studying and understanding depths of mythology for starters, perhaps. That seems necessary—but more necessary, perhaps, is calm, careful listening and attention.

[Journal, July 1975] I have found that some things work, become poems, and that others don't—that there is a sort of line that can be traced there, a line that one feels. A phrase or a word *feels* right or doesn't—and sometimes an entire poem labored over and carefully crafted can be all wrong—and fortunately can be recognized as wrong.

Poems are true or fake—or have true bits embedded in the fakery. Erica Jong, for me, is a fake poet—she shocks without being true. "Eat this poem" indeed. Eat shit.

[Journal, 1/27/1976] Grass on the hill moves continuously, is never still an instant. Slim-wristed hands of grass, of wheat-colored grass. Darker on the stalks where light and shadow play more intensely, a swarming as of gnats, a vibration, an oscillation.

The grass does not wave in the wind, it does shimmer—like looking at it through heat waves. It is rooted, but still is continually moving. The oscillation of molecules.

Why do I remember for 35 years the look of one field of grass (or maybe of grain) on Sugar Creek above camp where the stream turned and there was a sort of headland.

Shimmering of molecules—molecular shimmering—any one movement impossible to keep in the eye, but the whole going forward. Something else, like the way light sequins on the river, "photons falling now in the sun's bright rain."

A FIELD OF WINTER GRASS

The slim-wristed grass
asks tremulously
to be gone,
but is held fast—
a crowd of prisoners
hoping for notice,
lifting wheat-colored arms
at the barbed wire.

[Journal, 2/11/1976] Letter from Wade Hall today, returning "Boustrophedon" but accepting "Footprints in Snow" and

"Uproar on Mullins Lane" for next two issues of *Kentucky Poetry Review* (formerly *Approaches*). The first poems to be accepted anyplace.

BACK THEN: WINTER IN THE ZOO

[Journal, 12/3/1975] To the [Louisville] zoo today to take another look at the Siberian tiger. Almost deserted, and I get the female tiger to play a little by stalking her, hiding behind bushes, etc. Very aware of anyone doing anything out of the routine. Their eyes probably are bigger than human eyes, but in the expanse of those big-cat faces they do look "man-sized." Wolves were out running—how to describe that soft—deathly soft—bounding. And it is "deathly," not "deadly." A real linking of the feelings of beauty and death. The last horror of seeing those beautiful soft-bounding forms coming toward you across the snow.

The lynxes—Mephisto.

Having trouble writing now. Conscious of great limitation and of true feelings being blocked, so that I stumble around in language. "Tiger" suffers from this, as does "Teek." The latter does have a line that's right—"Winter morning sun/pounds on Teek's door." The pounding is there in the line.

Also inhibited by wondering if Beloit is going to print anything—now that they've had poems for a month. Like losing virginity—at this point I want to get something in print and get it over with.

Will all this look like a waste of time someday? I don't think so—if no poetry at all came out of it, I'd still not regret the observing, the opening up—the effort that [Donald] Davie calls tracking feelings "with scrupulous and sinuous fidelity." The effort actually to live, here, now.

People in Kroger's—old black in a snappy hat; happy, 50ish woman at checkout. Many worn-down faces. None of us asked to be here.

[The poem "Tiger" turned out to be "Wolves," reprinted below in its eventual form. No great poem—I would hesitate now to haul in the personal vignette. But it is what it is.]

WOLVES

Nothing is more beautiful/menacing
than the deathly soft
bounding of wolves,
absolute zero of malice,
they just
want to kill us.
We will not cajole them
when the fire goes
and they bound toward us
over the snow
like our favorite shepherds,
but daintier,
beautiful death.
Soft, beautiful and cold
as the snow above Meiringen
when I climbed too far
and night came on.
Then mountains were stone cold
as burnt-out planets
and as lonely,
dead ranges
out of which moon wolves
might have prowled.
All suns are anomalous,
glowing nodes in a matrix of ice.
Build up the fire.

BACK THEN: A DAY ON MOCKINGBIRD DRIVE

[Journal, 2/22/1976] A nice day. Boys dropping by the bedroom, one at a time. (Do they think I'm a lazy bum?) David talking about fishing, vacation, getting something to eat. "Calm," Stephen and Bill [his great-uncles] call him, catching a quality about him immediately. Mike coming through with plastic monsters—a lovely and lively imagination. Karl not coming—well, he was in earlier with a tub of cherries from the freezer. Pie later, maybe. I like him (and yet have a harder time getting that across to him).

Karen is here for a while, too. _Very_ pregnant now. Wonder what this 4th will be like? A boy we think certainly (tho what a fine surprise if a girl!) So we think about boys' names—Colin Petersen was first. Now we play around with John (Jack) Stephen Bridges or Colin Matthew Bridges, or Stephen Matthew Bridges.

I haven't felt much urge to write about him, and envy a little poets who wax lyrical about their offspring-to-be—"there you ride in your penny balloon," etc. Yet young John Stephen is still a cipher to me—a little like a coin blank waiting to be stamped—although he's well-stamped already, of course. A Bridges, for God's sake! Time really to drop the joke and let people be who they will . . . . So, John Stephen, come and be who you will (or Mary Kate).

And Colin Matthew arrived a few weeks later . . . .

BACK THEN: HEARING RICHARD WILBUR

[Journal, 2/27/1976] Went out to the University of Louisville last night on supper break to hear Richard Wilbur. He read "Events" (telling us with great enjoyment about Manfred Dog's letter in the _American Poetry Review_, threatening to kill anyone who criticized his poetry).

He also read a piece—I didn't get the name—about himself as a young hobo in Kansas, trying to put the make on a girl while her father went by "with cold, conniving eye." He said Jacques Barzun had attacked him for his use of "connive," which Barzun apparently defined as "conspiring." "I always bear down hard on it," Wilbur said, because it actually means to turn a blind eye to evil. Someone else who thinks Barzun doesn't know English!

Wilbur reads well—program had a lot of light verse. He read "To His Skeleton" which he must like—a *New Yorker* piece. I wonder—"Events" is a superb poem and unlike anything else he read. He told us it was one of his favorites, but that no one else had taken to it and so he had laid it away. If he stopped thinking about what was popular and just let his sense of things come out . . . . ? Unfair, probably—yet I'm not satisfied with a "To His Skeleton" or "A Late Aubade." And still it's admirable that he doesn't try to be "a fun-loving monk who's pretending to be Savonarola."

Wilbur is a rather heavyset man, 54, full head of bushy hair, mostly gray or tan suit, glasses, a full, rather boyish face with flat planes—something Slavic about it and something Tatar about the eyes. The first time we applauded, he hushed us a little with his hands & seemed embarrassed.

He read some Villon translations, a poem about April, one on domes and Emily Dickinson (Thoreau is pronounced "thorough," he says), and a poem about a visit with Sylvia Plath and her mother.

Wilbur remains one of my favorite American poets, and the mild criticism above sounds carping today. Poets.org tells me that he is 89 and lives in Cummington, Mass. Jacques Barzun is living in France, at the age of 102. I don't know how I managed to get to the U of L, hear Wilbur's reading, and get back, all on my supper hour from the Courier-Journal *copydesk. It was a very forgiving newspaper.*

BACK THEN: A REMARKABLE NEWSPAPER

Under the Bingham family of Louisville, *The Courier-Journal* was a most remarkable newspaper. The owners had a deep commitment to spending money on the news, and on taking progressive leadership in their conservative southern community. (Soon after my arrival there, I took some malfunctioning appliance to a mechanic and mentioned where I was working. "Oh, Red Star!" he exclaimed.)

Barry Bingham Sr. was a devoted Anglophile, a leader in Louisville's English-Speaking Union. So when the celebrated novelist C.P. Snow visited the city, it was not surprising that Barry invited him to address the newspaper staff. The journal of April 7, 1976, records his appearance:

"Reading C.P. Snow's *Strangers and Brothers* just now. Heard Snow speak at the *C-J* this week. Quick-minded, funny—he spoke to us for about 10 minutes, then answered questions for an hour. The burden of his own remarks was the growth of world population, the necessity to control it. The Western world as an island. Very strong response to a question from Carolyn Colwell [a reporter] on the lifeboat theory—the idea that we should save Nigeria by letting India go: 'Immoral!'"

Interesting to read this post-Copenhagen, where the developed world seemed basically unconcerned about pleas from island nations that are likely to be submerged during global warming.

On the *C-J* staff, we didn't know we were living in the last days of the Bingham "empire." A year or so after I left to enter college teaching, the paper was sold to Gannett. Today it is . . . . a Gannett paper.

BACK THEN: WORDS, 1; ME, 0

[**Journal, 6/2/1976**] A bad month. Deep trouble trying to review R.D. Laing's *The Facts of Life*. Done, finally, even though I'm unhappy at the result. Words, 1; me, 0.

Jon Anderson's books and Thomas James came this week. There just can't be any real doubt that James was seriously unbalanced—no one with that mind (and probably an addict, too) could have lived long in the world (much less Joliet, Ill.). But what a poet!

So where am I after this month? Strange dream this morning—I'm at Tolson's, trying to talk about politics. Words won't come, can't talk, what comes out are only cant phrases—can't talk.

[Journal, 7/27/1976] Reading Robin Skelton's *The Poet's Calling*—very Jungian, and daunting in his utter lack of compromise. What hope is there for any of us whose daemons are rather small and uncertain, and who have not "stored our memory banks" with all of Yeats, Graves, etc., and *The Golden Bough?*

Well, he does give us a little hope at the end, and some very good things by Kathleen Raine and Jeni Couzyn. And I'm delighted to catch him in a Latin howler—"magnus opus."

Right now I am at this point. I am realizing my deep ignorance of much of the craft involved in poetry, have come to see that what ability I have at it is very modest, but am learning not to be entirely disheartened by this. I am becoming less interested in publishing, because I am afraid of letting bad work loose—it is good, though, to have some kind of an outlet in the *Kentucky Poetry Review*. I have to be careful to send Wade Hall only good things like "Land's End," not more "Footprints in Snow," which was well meant but not very good.

I also have made the decision that I, at least, can't put poetry ahead of everything else. I wouldn't shirk an obligation—that is not as noble as it sounds; if I did shirk job, family, etc., that wouldn't make me a poet. It would be much more likely to destroy me by throwing me into guilt and depression where any writing would be impossible.

So I go along—unable to perform the task, not permitted to quit—the Talmudist's dilemma—and once in a while something goes right.

BACK THEN: SKYDIVER

[Journal, 9/13/1976, from Mockingbird Drive] Got up at midnight after sleeping all evening. Children sleeping and Karen asleep on the couch. Read for a while in O'Faolain—"A Sweet Colleen"—and later Camus' essay on "creating dangerously."

In front of me on the white linen tablecloth, on the kitchen table, are two created things—pottery bowls we bought yesterday from Suzanne Sidebottom at the fair on River Street. Beautiful pottery—as pottery like that always is, with its imperfections, the artist's hand on it.

I can't get yesterday's skydivers off my mind (they were at the fair). I was watching one jump with binoculars, and saw him a split second before his chute opened, a falling human shape against the smoke behind—or like the human shape being blown into the distance in "Hindenburg."

Free fall is a misnomer—it's absolutely determined, right to the 120 mph of terminal velocity. Then the chutist pulls the cord and goes tootling off through the sky, like someone in an aerial armchair or the driver of some fantastic old-time automobile with a colored canopy. That's what's "free," because exquisitely controlled, not the plunging "free fall."

SKYDIVER

He leaps into our world with a yell
we can't hear and falls smoking
ten thousand feet.
We can just see him then
through binoculars,
tiny swastika man
blown sky-high but dropping
back on us corpse-quick.
This is called free fall
and lasts forever.

But now his chute is out,
a squarish surrey top,
and he is
motoring through the sky
in his funny car.
We are all laughing.
Which of us could have worried?

BACK THEN: DOWN BLUE IN DRY WEATHER

[Journal, 9/30/1976] A lot of things interfering with writing just now, but it's a good time. Back to 10-hour days under a new *C-J* editor.

Karl, David, and I went canoeing on the Blue River last weekend—a real survival exercise. The Blue is beautiful on a hazy fall day, with a constant fall of leaves into the water—some water-logged and sinking, others spinning, sailing like dhows with bright orange sails. Some image here of an autumnal harbor, full of ships in a dying light—or in the light of fires from the shore or burning ships—a vast darkening harborscape. Water like blood in a fiery evening.

The canoeing is exciting—coming down onto rapids (the water was very low), looking for the dark V of water between riffles, heading in, and shooting through. Or slipping just barely past rocks in minimal water—something about the just making it with nothing to spare, a risk taken.

The sexual image of entering the body of this land on this thin conduit of water, easing one's way.

Little things—knotted fringes of roots along the bank, the debris on the surface, cleared off after the night's rain.

[Journal, 10/27/1976] So much change in the last month. Excitement of a new job [as day city editor]—all that challenge. The switch from night to day work. Poetry has gone by the board—slowly coming back to it now. Or back to an attitude of observing, feeling—not just motion. These past two weeks have been just motion. Now coming to myself. And this is just rambling and trying to fix again, letting words spill. Writing just to write something . . . .

Strange thing—in these two weeks of great activity my fear of death has been very sharp. Why is this? Does intense involvement in daily life make one more uneasy, unsettled, less at peace? Does it have to be one or the other? Can one keep peace and balance while involving himself fully in daily life and work? Can I be both a hard-working, imaginative, competitive newspaperman—and a poet? Is that gap too wide? Filiatreau can't seem to bridge it, or doesn't want to, and is lacerated.

I would have said once that the gap couldn't be bridged. Now I think maybe it can, if I think truly.

[Journal, 11/18/76] In a long period of not writing. Being diverted by a new job, etc., has made me realize what intense care and concentration poetry takes, in distancing and in minute-by-minute observation, and also in being open to feelings. Am tired in the evenings now, very little fresh, free time. So I'm looking for some new avenue, and meanwhile keeping afloat here.

[Journal, 12/2/76] Poems came back from Beloit today, though with an encouraging note. May resubmit "Venice."

What is the trouble now? "Something we were withholding made us weak" . . . . Begin where you are, Levertov says. Wait creatively. In the beginning were the emotions, only later brought to words. All this writing—a way to keep afloat.

I am going down into it. I want , I want . . . . Very dry, not much hint, break it, get through it—getting through—live, alive, by any crook, live as much as you can.

THE NATURAL WORLD
(Written on the porch at 502 Mockingbird Drive)

The arrowed light of evening,
stones growing in caves,

81

plantain's aerial cities,
rose-steeples in leaves,

crows gravely walking,
all things that are
without our talking,
or even our being there.

BACK THEN: LIVING BEHIND THE FACTORY

By early 1977, we had moved from Mockingbird Drive and into a huge, unkempt barn of a house at 401 E. Beckett St. in Clarksville, still just across the Ohio River from Louisville. We moved in one of the great snows of the century, and it was spring before we saw our sidewalks. Poetry was not coming easily, although a friend and practicing poet at work, John Filiatreau, was giving me welcome encouragement. The journal continues:

"Nothing doing these days. Perhaps, as Karen says, if you wanted to write, you would write. As [Uncle] Stephen says, 'Boy, you need stirring up!' (Actually, I think that's a quote from his father, Harry.) Saw a line in the *NYT Book Review* that I wanted to send to Stephen—new biography of Corvo, and the reviewer said *Desire and Pursuit of the Whole* was about the author's troubles with publishers—like saying (what?) that the *Book of Job* is about Job's troubles with his complexion? (I'm not sure what *Desire* is about, but it's not publishers.)

"I'm continuing in a time of intensely practical activity—working on the house, dealing with things on the city desk. Shouldn't be inimical to poetry, but is. Inimical to feelings, & to emotions. They get shoved aside.

"What have I felt or what has gotten to me lately? Inge with her talk about Germany and her gift of a can of coffee—we almost felt like war refugees ourselves. Filiatreau saying he felt 'strangely comforted' that I'd criticized the police column—how seldom does anyone express a feeling of any kind of gratitude directly.

"I still kick around 'Living Behind the Factory.' We do, in fact [behind the old Palmolive factory in Clarksville]. And we try, with more or less success, to stay alive behind the clanking machinery around us. The cars grinding all night and all day, too. Karen being so wound up in day's affairs that she has trouble quieting—so do I.

"An inventory of the front bedroom of 401 E. Beckett St. in Clarksville, Ind., about 10 p.m., 7/24/1977.

"The sliding doors nearly closed to let Colin sleep, and hiding the hanging planters and Stephen's medallion of the basketball player.

"A box of love letters on the mantle—box made by me, in the North End Boys Club at Vincennes, as gift to K. the Xmas week before our marriage. At moment it is part of furniture.

"One half-breed [our name for an armoire made of mixed woods] with doors open—another memento of a (generally) happy marriage.

"Rackful of ties, all old, most dirty, and all hated by me.

"Four empty beer cans at various points—only 1 from tonight. Pointing to some relaxation in housekeeping which we shall blame on the hot weather. Ugly chandelier with only one bulb, for thrift. Assorted clothing in various attitudes around room. A bed, early-marriage period. Me on it.

"Telephone, bottle of pills, blue marble ashtray, sack of shoes, banana peel, bedside table, child's alphabet block with the letter P, & other items too numerous to mention, and they will not be mentioned."

LIVING BEHIND THE FACTORY

This bastard side of town's an orphanage
for houses, some scrubbed and hopeful, some
too streetwise now to expect parentage.

No trace here of suburbia's noblesse.
The corner light is high, and cold as thrift.
To live here requires poverty or stubbornness.

Some people move rather than pay their bills.
Some stay and root like ailanthus trees,
which no one ever plants and nothing kills.

[The *Beloit Poetry Journal* accepted "Sunday Morning in the Gesuati," my first acceptance in a national poetry magazine.]

BACK THEN: WHEN WE OWNED A POST OFFICE

We moved to a new house at Clarksville, Indiana, in the winter of 1977, and found that we had unwittingly purchased a historic landmark—the onetime Falls of the Ohio post office was in our back yard. We had thought it was just an interesting shed. Eventually, we agreed to a request from the Town of Clarksville to disassemble it and put the pieces in storage. As far as I know it's still there.

[**Journal, 4/24/77**] A day of alternating rain and sunshine. One shower drove us onto the back porch, from which we watched the rain fall over the old post office—a beautiful building in its ruin. I'll be sorry to see it go. Buildings like that seem to reach a point where nothing more can happen to them, or at least the outer shell can't get any more dilapidated. There's a house like that at Campbellsburg—some old people still live in it.

Wind the other night blew down hundreds of maple seeds in the back yard—parachutists on a landing ground.

The yard has turned out to be full of flowers, an old-fashioned farmyard like Aunt Laura's. All we need is a wisteria vine. Pale blue iris are out today against the scabby gray of the p.o., in the chilly April rain. Beauty that just is, unplanned, even made up of things we think are unlovely.

Not long after this, we cleared the contents from the old post office, and a town crew came to take it away. One of the workers proudly showed us a board with a slot in it—that's all it looked like to us, but he assured us it was the very slot into which all the town's letters had once been deposited.

BACK THEN: HELP FROM A POET

John Filiatreau, columnist for *The Courier-Journal* in Louisville, wrote fine poems of his own, and took the time to read and comment on mine, even inviting me to his house so we could discuss them at length. More than 30 years on, I remain grateful for his kindness to a beginner. The journal of June 2, 1977, records some of his comments:

"Filiatreau and I had our get-together. He spent most of the evening critiquing my poems—very little time on his own. That puzzles me a little. Good criticism, surprising at times. (He picked 'Old Ellerman' and 'The Mill' as the best.) Part of that is his apparent great concern for metrics—no organic poet. Don't think he really believes there is such a thing. Has studied [William Carlos] Williams and is baffled by him.

"Perhaps his most interesting comment on my stuff is that it seems to aim at the monumental—not in size, but in the sense of something immovable—W.S. Graham's thing 'that will stand and will not move.'

"Good cautions—against 2nd-person poetry, commas, sentimentality, 'what's' for 'what has,' poems that say (however well) what is already known (his comment about 'On the Road at Nightfall'). Curious objection to 'selvage,' 'skerry,' and 'skirl' so close together in 'Land's End' ('as though you'd looked them up in the dictionary'), poems without enough payoff.

"Really strange objection to the last line of 'Cineres Manini' because of its length. To me it's that length and flow that release things.

"Best results—a poem ['Living Behind the Factory'] coming out of his suggestion that I do best with a formal metric, and poems he lent me by Alasdair Maclean, a Scottish peasant-poet."

SPRING POEM
(For John Filiatreau's daughters)

Crumbly spring
is big square chalk
that always breaks in the box.
It doesn't matter.
Take a piece and make
pastel smudges of redbud.

BACK THEN: 'THIS HOUSE'
(For Karen)

Sometimes we thought changing houses
would make a difference.

Driving miles into the country,
we came to one
next to a sort of rural tavern.
Evening forgave the faces of farmers,
there were almost hay wains in the yard.
What warm lives we would have lived there!

Elsewhere, young architects
were building their dream homes,
the rich renovated mansions,
couples planned extensions
of their personalities.

We came home then
to this house, which seemed

odd for a moment, like someone
approaching in a shop window,
stooped and fraying
but strangely faithful to us.

I wanted to tell you I loved you
more than houses,
that in this house somehow
we have to be changed.

BACK THEN: LEAVING BECKETT STREET

We lived for about two years on Beckett Street, fighting a ceaseless battle with a huge house that would have required far more resources than we had to repair and put into good shape. We couldn't even afford a new roof, and as soon as we repapered a downstairs room there would be new water stains down the wall. Years later I dreamed of trying to restore an immense house, which crumbled behind me as I moved from room to room. It wasn't a mystery where the dream came from.

And yet it was a happy time. Our four boys were healthy and growing. Newspaper work was going well, and I was writing more poetry—and was now officially published in a well-known "little magazine." Karen remembers luxuriating in all the space we had, even though some of it lacked wallpaper.

There were alarums and excursions. The journal mentioned that Colin, at a year and a half, had ridden his four-wheeled horse down the stairs from the second floor, but I had little memory of this. "Tell me again what happened," I asked Karen.

"I was in the kitchen, two boys were in the living room, and one in the dining room," she said. "I think you were at work. We met at the bottom of the stairs in record time." Was he knocked out, I asked? "No, but he was squalling his head off."

She wasn't sure if she called me immediately or if a neighbor took her and Colin to the Clark County Hospital. She remembers that the emergency room was stacked up—a bad accident, a shooting. "We were about fourth in line." The attendants had to strap Colin to a board so head x-rays could be taken, but aside from cuts and bruises, it was basically "put a Band-Aid on him and send him home." "At that age they just bounce," the emergency-room medic said.

Karen added, "I still don't know how he got his riding horse up 17 steps without making a sound, the little snot."

Karen also made another foray into journalism, the first in a dozen years, covering a horse show for *The Courier-Journal*. (Dave Adams, the *C-J* sports editor, had called her while she was under the house, fixing plumbing.) And in a ferocious winter, I called from work, telling her to grab a camera, dress warmly, and head for a nearby parking lot where a newspaper helicopter would pick her up to take aerial photos of the snowbound city. But the paper's own photographer managed to fight his way in to work before she could carry out this mission.

And yet changes were coming. Many months earlier, I had noted in a journal, "I'm enjoying my new work, but still feel it's essentially empty—the capable performance of a task not necessary in itself, but providing food and clothes for my family. Working always around the edges of something sensed as central but not seen."

I applied to be city editor of *The Courier-Journal*, but lost out to a man who was unable to do much with the opportunity. I think I didn't really want the job. I could have stayed there comfortably, but when the chance came to teach journalism, at the small college from which I had graduated, I took it. Then there was the uproar of moving again, supporting two houses for a time, moving the kids to a new school system. The job was in my old home town, not theirs. Karen recalls it as a time when she was in "survival mode"—with three teen-agers and a 3-year-old—and she eventually got some counseling to help her through the upheaval.

As I have noted before, she is 27 percent smarter than me.

BACK THEN: 'AS PERMANENT NOW AS CARTHAGE'

This series of small essays began with a return to a small house at 502 Mockingbird Drive in Jeffersonville, Indiana. It's appropriate to go back there one more time.

When we moved into that tract house, we stepped directly out of our back door into a muddy yard. So before long we decided to build a brick terrace, about six feet wide and running the length of the house. We had found bricks somewhere (the journal notes that some were incised with names like "Louisville No. 1 Wedge"). One summer I laid them out in a herringbone pattern on what turned out to be an inadequate sand base.

The terrace served its purpose well, but over the years weather broke many of the bricks, and grass covered parts of the surface. I wrote a poem about it, called at first just "The Old Terrace" but now bearing a different name:

ON THE DIFFICULTY OF CHANGING ANYTHING

This herringbone terrace gets shabbier
each year. I remember laying it out,
neat as a new suit, a careful weave
of old bricks on sand, but they didn't wear well.
Each winter crushes more of them in its hand.
Spring pries the fingers open and sifts
down dust and crumbs of red rock.

Gradually the terrace becomes what it it,
a barren of small weeds, miniature shrubs
in bombed squares. Ants pursue
private purposes among the ruins.
Vines creep over the inscriptions.
Sometimes for days no one passes.

A new patio would be better,
but we delay and leave the old terrace there,

like a suit we don't wear and won't throw away.
a habit we can't shake. The grass
grows up in angled rows, remembering
where the bricks were,
as permanent now as Carthage.

BACK THEN: CODA AND CONCLUSION

The mind, it has often been observed, works in strange ways.

For several weeks before visiting Mockingbird Drive, I had been thinking about vocation, or "call." This might seem at first to be a strange thing to occupy the mind of someone 75 years old. But it isn't. I've joked all my life about wondering what I would do when I grew up, and with luck one never grows up and never stops posing the question. It is the hidden theme of the essays in "Back Then."

If I listen to my soul or "true self," as described by any number of writers and mystics, what will it tell me I should be doing at this moment on my journey? The soul, one such writer, Parker Palmer, observes, "is not responsive to subpoenas or cross-examination. At best it will stand in the dock only long enough to plead the Fifth Amendment. At worst it will jump bail and never be heard from again."

As I thought about this, I knew—knew—that I had written something once about "true vocation." The idea went far back, but I couldn't find it in any published poem of mine, or in a scan of notebooks. And I couldn't get beyond those two words.

Then, not far from the description of looking out the window at 502 Mockingbird Drive, I found it:

Today, for the first time in weeks,
I stopped, looked out across fields deep in snow
to slab-sided houses, smoking chimneys, yards,
cars winding off among the snow-duned streets,
and stopped to think of what is true vocation.

This is a slight poem, untitled, with no number in any list of my work. But it still speaks to me after nearly 40 years. It tells me that my true vocation, apart from any job of the moment and the necessity to put bread on the table, has always been, and is, to look and then to tell, in the best and most compassionate words I can, what it is that I see. The circle is completed, the gap closed. This is, finally, what I want to do when I grow up.

The house at 401 E. Beckett St. in Clarksville, Indiana. This photo was taken in 2010, but the house's exterior is mostly unchanged since we lived there in the late 1970s.

Pioneer

I don't know much about Grandfather George.
He came up from Kentucky
with a tar bucket swinging on the axle,
married several neighbors in succession,
had fifteen kids, raised mules, and ran a sawmill.
He owned a thousand acres once, all gone.
His photo, unretouched, in Forsyth's History,
shows him staring, frightened almost, at something.

Why tell you this? Was it unreasonable
to wonder whether I could save such stuff
a little longer? He lived, after all.
It seems as if somebody should remember.
I don't know why. All that you know of me
is not what mattered then—
not what I loved, or how I never could
say what I wanted to you, and cannot now.

—To a Descendant

MANY YEARS AGO, I had ideas of writing a family history, based on a pioneer ancestor, my great-great-grandfather, George Bridges.

I did a lot of research, rooting in old records of the Mt. Zion Baptist Church at Trafalgar and the *Forsyth History*. At the Johnson County Courthouse, clerks brought down dusty boxes of century-old records from the attic. But after several chapters, the project lagged. I don't expect to resume it, although there are profoundly American histories to be written by those willing to delve deeply into late 19th and 20th century records.

DAGUERREOTYPE

The plump baby born on the Fourth of May, 1800, would go through life in double harness with the new century, and would see nearly three-quarters of it.

Isham, his father, belonged to the Kentucky frontier and never sank deep roots. "Went to Texas" was the family's epitaph on George's youngest brother, John. Only George would invest all his life and energy in one piece of earth, seeing the years turn from frontier to dawning industrial age, from log huts in the forest to Victorian mansions in the cornfields.

George was the first child of Isham and Elizabeth Forsyth, married in Louisville a year earlier. He was the heir on his father's side of minor landed gentry in Virginia, and on his mother's of Scotch-Irish ancestry, with a tale of a whirlwind romance and a flight from Ireland to America.

When he came to Kentucky in the 1790s, Isham had no land of his own, so he went to work for his brother Benjamin. He brought along his two slaves and three horses. George grew up on the horses, or following them down a furrow; he would be intimately involved with horses all his life, riding them, trading them, breeding them, and seeing them through foaling and illness. And when old, his last bequests to his sons would be horses and saddles.

Life for a boy in Kentucky was mostly work, although there was plenty of hunting and fishing, too. George went to school little if at all, and never learned to write—at first because there were few schools and little time, and later because he got on very well without writing. Progressive in farming and business, he had an old settler's stubbornness in this.

But if he had no books, he grew up hearing stories—the ones his red-haired grandmother, Margaret McGibbon Forsyth, told of Ireland, and those of his Uncle Benjamin about the Revolution.

And there were blood-curdling tales of Indian raids and how an early settler on Benjamin's place—Abraham Linkhorn—had been killed by an arrow as he raised the last rail of his fence into place.

When George was 21 and a strapping young farmer on Floyd's Fork, east of Louisville, he married his 15-year-old cousin, Matilda Forsyth. His mother and her father were sister and brother. The age and close kinship were not unusual then; a year or so later, George's brother William married Matilda's small, pretty sister Margaret, who was 14 and ran away from school for the wedding. (Returning, she passed her mother standing in their cabin door. Neither spoke, defiance on one side and disapproval on the other binding their tongues.)

A first child, Elizabeth, was born to George and Matilda in 1825, when George was already getting the urge to go north. Each week, it seemed, some neighbor—often a relative—loaded his wagon and left for the rich, uncrowded land in the new state of Indiana.

On Oct. 27, 1827, "George Bridges of Jefferson County, Kentucky" paid $250 to Henry Musselman for 80 acres of hilltop land in the northeast corner of Hensley Township, Johnson County, in the center of the state. Each man signed the agreement with an X.

George and Matilda prospered, for George had bought the best land in a place where the quality of the glacial soil varied widely. He worked incessantly, pushing his big body to its limits, taking on enough for two or three lazier men. He rolled logs as much as 30 days a year, rising before daylight to "right up" his smouldering pile, then going off to fell trees and roll logs with his neighbors before coming home at 10 or 11 at night to tend his own pile again.

A second girl, Matilda, arrived in 1828; then finally a boy, George Thomas, in 1831. The family moved out of its temporary cabin to a stouter log house furnished in part with pieces bought from fellow settlers William and Margaret—"one bureau, breakfast and dining tables, two bedsteads, beds and bedding, one clock, one 15-gallon kettle."

George also bought from his brother a bay mare and colt, a "yoke of cattle," a cow, and two heifers. It was the modest start of what would be a large business in horses, mules, and shorthorn cattle.

George got his hands into everything—a partnership in a sawmill and a store, church affairs, mule trading, jury duty, road surveying, driving hogs overland to the stockyards at Madison, Indiana, on the Ohio River. In local politics he was a fervent and implacable Democrat, like most of the southerners in Hensley Township. He had an opponent, Avery Buckner, who competed with him in business and fought with him over the location of a road. They founded rival towns half a mile apart and battled for a post office, with Buckner getting his papers to Washington first and winning.

But the farm absorbed the cream of George's efforts. The Democrats asked him to run for office, but he turned them aside with a half-jest at his brother's expense. "Go ask William," he said. "He likes to hold office and does not like to work much."

At last boys were coming to help him—James in 1833, Isham Van Buren in 1837 (the summer after Little Van's election), and John in 1838. There was a last daughter, Rebecca, in 1843, and then five years later Matilda died—worn out by the frontier, a victim probably of one of its endemic sicknesses. (As late as 1850, the Mt. Zion Church in Trafalgar was closed for several months because of smallpox.)

In six months George was married again, to 20-year-old Martha Clark, the daughter of a neighboring farmer. Their first child, Marion, died in infancy—the only one of George's 15 children not to grow up. A second child, William Allen, was born in 1850 and then there were no more. Martha died in 1856, at the age of 28. Once more George found a new wife quickly, marrying Eliza

Prather who bore him six more children—Eliza, Emma, Dillard, Adaline, Henry, and Andrew.

Meanwhile, the frontier had washed over them and gone west. Roads were ending the early isolation of the settlers. The "great freshet" of 1847 carried away roads and bridges all over the Ohio Valley; marooned for weeks on their farms, people grew more conscious of the value of roads and rebuilt more strongly.

George's farm was growing to be a small Bridges duchy in its corner of Hensley Township. He sold a tract here, bought a larger tract there, until the farm reached more than 1,000 acres. A great-grandson, Albert Coppock, remembered hearing about that farm. It was a story, he said, of land "as far as one could see in all directions—and of horses—and all this wealth seemed to 'go with the wind' during and after the Civil War."

George's father, Isham, came from Kentucky for a while. George bought him a buggy with special springs to carry the old man's great weight, and built him a cabin near his own house. Isham loved children, and they would come to the cabin to play around him and hear his stories. (There is a rumor of a "silvery" daguerreotype of Isham, but it has never been found.)

In mid-century the railroad came, crossing George's home farm. He marked off lots in "Hensleytown" and became a "proprietor." There would be no more hog drives to Madison; the hogs, sheep, and cattle would go to market now in their thousands, by rail.

The railroad exacted its price, though. One day in the summer of 1852, while George and the older boys were away at a political rally, sparks from an engine ignited the fields behind the house. John, 14, frantically beat out the flames, but the smoke and heat damaged his health permanently.

Sometime about 1850 the family had left the log house and moved into a new two-story brick one. The house still stands, a mile west of Trafalgar. It was built of home-made brick; plowing still turns up bits of brick where the kiln stood and there is a hollow behind the house where the clay was dug.

In those busy and prosperous years, the larger troubles of the nation grew unnoticed at first, like a summer thunderhead rising behind a farmer intent on his plowing. When civil war came, it left George's family unscathed, for most of the Bridges boys were too old or too young to serve—and one or two of them may have escaped service some other way, perhaps by hiring substitutes. They were southerners, and the mood of many in Indiana then was "let the erring sisters depart in peace." Lincoln's election meant war, and Hensley Township was not Lincoln country. In 1860 and again in 1864 he got exactly 40 votes of the township's more than 290.

In the changing times after the war, George moved into new enterprises. He backed banks and took stock in return. He bought property in Franklin, the county seat. His cattle and mule business continued among the largest in central Indiana.

But the once-tireless energies had begun to flag (slowly, to be sure, for he fathered his last child when over 70). More and more the records show property disposed of with nothing new bought.

He still kept a tight rein on his land and family. Tracts were deeded to his sons, but he held the deeds, leaving the transfers to be recorded after his death. He made a will, carefully disposing of land, cash, and bank stock totaling—on paper at least—more than $100,000.

To his wife, Eliza, he left the home farm, $6,000 in bank stock, and $500 in cash. She also was to receive all the house furnishings, a variety of farm equipment, wagons, livestock, carpenter's tools, and "the watch now owned by me." To a woman who was apparently a servant, George left a set of household furnishings, some livestock, and "cubbardware" on condition that "she remains in my family during my life and conducts herself as she heretofore has."

To his children he left farms, cash, and bank stock. Each also was to get a horse, saddle, and bridle, and—at 21—either "an outfit for housekeeping such as I gave to my other daughters" or "an outfit for farming such as I gave to my other boys." Even grown, they remained his "boys."

On Aug. 22, 1872, his long pull in tandem with the century ended. The end must have come quickly, for his will was updated hastily and he signed it only the day before his death. Once more he signed with an X. Not long before, he had sold a town lot to his old compatriot, Henry Musselman, and Henry, too, had made his mark—the mark of the old settlers.

What sort of man was George? His daughter-in-law, Alice, remembered him as stern but always kind to her. A great-grandson—recalling his portrait seen in boyhood—thought of an Indian chief, and the high cheekbones suggest that faintly. He was a man of practical knowledge, at home in the mule barn, the saw-mill, and stockyard. He got on well with the rough men of his time; a granddaughter, Dell Bridges, recalled his son-in-law, Armstrong Alexander, as a "wicked man" who swore terribly, but George was his close partner in several enterprises.

He remained a southerner in spirit, as did many of his family for years afterward. They looked southward to Long Run and Floyd's Fork, in Jefferson County, Kentucky, as "the old home" and made journeys there, sometimes with great difficulty. (A few years ago, an uncle sent me a 1938 letter from my grandfather. "Auntie had word from the Kentucky folks last Sunday," he wrote, "telling her that Cousin Mollie had had a stroke . . . so she and I drove down last Tuesday and found all the folks there . . . ."

In their houses, coffee was "saucered and blowed" and the dining tables were loaded with old hen and dumplings, apple pie, salt-rising bread, and biscuits and gravy. (My father, recalling childhood visits to the Kentucky kin, said ham was served at every relative's. His mother, he said, joked that it was the same ham, taken from house to house.)

George's great-grandson, Albert Coppock, recalled this life many years later in writing of his grandmother, George's daughter-in-law. "Grandma often sang 'Dixie' and 'Little Brown Jug,'" he wrote. "Once in a while she smoked frog tobacco in a clay pipe—I'm sure it was not a corncob pipe. And when she sang, 'Look away, look away, Dixie land,' she was not singing because she was happy."

George was scrupulously honest, and one story of his honesty hints that he enjoyed a joke as well. Once he and a young relative had bought a herd of hogs and were driving them home. When almost to the farm, the younger man told George jokingly that George had cheated the seller by taking a pig he hadn't paid for. "Then we'll go right back," George said, "for I never mean to cheat any man." The younger man had a hard time dissuading him from the long trip back. One suspects that George saw through him all along, but enjoyed turning the joke back on him.

Here and there in the records is a suggestion of generosity and a certain largeness of gesture in George's life. Once he bought a plot of land far from his own farm. The seller was a widow and at the public sale George's price was "more than the appraised value and the best offer." When he had his grievance with Avery Buckner over a road, he presented his case to the county commissioners through Gilderoy Hicks, a lawyer—the only instance in many years of commissioners' records of a complainant being represented by counsel. (George lost, but the issue was later settled by compromise.)

Inferences from such frail evidence cannot be pushed very far, though. We are left finally with a little physical evidence to form our ideas of George Bridges—his house, a few records, his stern portrait, and the daguerreotype from which the portrait was made.

The daguerreotype has been lost, but it was reproduced 90 years ago in *Forsyth's History*. From it we see that the charcoal artist touched up his subject, for the face in the tintype is much older and gaunter than the one in the portrait at right. In this image, reproduced (below left) from the history, strands of hair escape control and there is a difference between the eyes, giving the face a slightly wild look. The vest, which the charcoal artist approximated with daubs of black, appears to have a floral pattern, perhaps indicating just a touch of the

dandy. The main impression,

though, is of an old man worn and strained almost to the limit by time and toil, but still staring indomitably ahead.

A HOUSE AND A GHOST

I went looking for my great-great-grandfather's house late in the afternoon of a sodden winter day, down a road I had never noticed. Many people had known about the house, but no one had thought to tell me about it, not even when, as a boy, I lived for a summer only three miles away.

That summer I often walked the tracks of the Big Four railroad into Trafalgar—escaping from gardening on my Aunt Laura Vandivier's farm, or to get a Nehi grape soda—without knowing that I could have followed the abandoned roadbed a mile farther west to George Bridges's farm and the house he had built more than 100 years before.

I had spent this winter day in a library, until I was restless and tired of old books. It was raining as I drove down the Mauxferry Road, which is only a county road now but once ran 100 miles south to Mauck's Ferry across the Ohio. It has always seemed to me a road backward in time, and now the car carried me southwest through the rain, past the farm of my boyhood summer, past 1900 in the farmhouse where my grandfather was born, through Trafalgar still lingering in the 19th century, and across the intersection where, in the 1820s, there stood a huge poplar blazed with three notches, giving the Three-Notch Road the name it carried until it became Highway 135 and an artery for the southward-reaching suburbs of Indianapolis.

From the Three-Notch Road, it was a short drive down an unfamiliar blacktop road and over a gentle rise to the spot where the maps in the library had told me I would find George Bridges's house—or perhaps, now, only an empty field.

But it was there, a huge, gaunt, beached-whale of a house, two-storied throughout its L-shaped bulk, its brick painted a peeling white, with a big apron of green porch roof along the front. The rain had stopped, and the setting sun had dropped below the clouds, dramatically lighting the shallow valley. Dark maples stood at one end of the house, adding to its brooding air; it was a place one might have chosen as the locale for a rural murder mystery, and indeed murder is supposed to have been done there.

The sense of the house's isolation, both in space and time, was heightened by its position far back from the road, on a fenced island in the fields, reachable only by a lane across a pasture. Though obviously occupied, the house looked that afternoon as though time had stopped there on Aug. 22, 1872, when George Bridges died.

I did not stop. George had taken perhaps two weeks in 1827 to travel here from the "old home" on Floyd's Fork east of Louisville. But I had to be back in Louisville that same evening, so I noted the name on the mailbox—Carl Lewis—and drove on.

Later I wrote to Lewis, explaining my interest in the house and saying I hoped to visit it the next spring. I didn't expect an answer and didn't get one, but Lewis was at least not surprised when my wife and I, with our three small boys, drove up several months later. He was a young farmer, stocky and full-faced, momentarily free of farm chores and willing to show us around. So we toured an ancient barn, the poplar timbers of which could have been hewed from tree trunks and pegged together in George Bridges's time. We saw the silo ring next to George's vanished mule barn, and looked across to the knoll above Barnes Creek—no more than a pasture ditch—where an old log house had stood. This, I knew, was where my great-grandmother, Alice Hunter Bridges, had gone to housekeeping, and where the crack beneath the door was wide enough, she said, "to sling a cat through."

Finally, we toured the farmhouse itself—Mrs. Lewis was away—and found it almost as vast and bleak inside as out. But one farm couple and two children could hardly be expected to fill or furnish a house built for 12 or 14, and so the rooms were sparsely appointed and some were vacant, with broken plaster and wallpaper hanging in shreds. Two empty rooms on the second floor, to which an improvised hall and back stair led, were the remnants of a World War II attempt at apartment-making for soldiers at Camp Atterbury. Lewis was a young man with a mortgage, trying to improve things by shoring up here and there, but farming obviously and rightly was his first priority.

The house was not well-designed. The rooms were big and square and—except for the "apartments" above—led to one another instead of opening off hallways. It was an ungainly, awkward house, full of space but not spacious. The few attempts at ornament fell flat in the vastness—the window cornice ends crudely carved in a pattern of concentric rings, the decorative woodwork partly masking the kitchen fireplace, an egg-and-dart cove molding around the living-room ceiling.

There was a sense of the house's having been scaled down over the years. Windows once much wider had been bricked up to the width of normal drapes and shades. Most strikingly, missing plaster over the front door revealed a hewn lintel fully a foot and a half above the present ample door. George Bridges was apparently a man who thought big, if not always with too fine a sense of proportion.

After we had walked through the house of this great-great-grandfather, I touched on the house's ghost—gently, since a man who must spend nights in a house with his wife and children may be sensitive to rumors of dark doings in its past. The caution was wise.

"Yes," Lewis said, "I've heard the ghost stories, and I don't want to hear any more about them."

I got the stories a little later from a neighboring farmer, Ogle Clark, a cheerful and talkative 80-year-old who, it developed, was a first cousin to my great-grandfather—and a man who, by being the youngest child of an old man's marriage was the nephew of my great-great-grandmother Martha Clark, dead in 1856, the second wife of George Bridges.

Mr. Clark said the ghost stories began with the tenure in the house of William "Bill" Jeffries, who bought part of the farm from the Bridges heirs in 1889. Jeffries supposedly murdered a cattle buyer who spent the night in the house, hiding his body in a closet that was never afterward opened. Then on his death bed Jeffries tried to gasp out a confession to his mother, who placed her hand over his mouth—here Mr. Clark gestured dramatically—and cried out, "God forbid! God forbid!" Pure gothic.

It was not clear who witnessed this scene. Mr. Clark did not claim it as fact, only as a story that had survived in the neighborhood. I had heard a similar story from my father by way of his grandmother, but it was placed earlier, during the time of George Bridges. In this version, a government messenger carrying gold to Madison, Indiana, stopped at the house and was never seen again.

Mr. Clark also recounted that early in the 20th century the house was occupied by a tenant, Jake LeVan, and his three daughters. The girls—Anna, Grace, and Bess—claimed to have met the ghost of Jeffries or the murdered cattleman on the stairs one night, and also to have seen Jeffries driving a phantom buggy on the Samaria road.

A cousin, Albert Coppock, who lived in the log house on the knoll as a boy, wrote me that "needless to say, I was familiar with the notion that there was something odd about the house. We children were afraid to go very near there, although all we knew about it was that the rooms were dim and dark and that strange noises were sometimes heard, especially in the dead of night."

I suspect that the imaginings of teen-age girls, amplified down the years by country gossip, have given Bill Jeffries a sinister reputation he doesn't deserve. By most accounts, he was a Christian gentleman, and his memory ought not to be burdened with a ghost.

But the stories persist, and not without some humor. In the 1920s, the ghost supposedly caused groceries to disappear from the kitchen table while the housewife's back was turned (they do that at our house, too, my wife says). And there is a story of a couple courting in the parlor who "heard the ghost" on the porch, and after clinging to each other for a while gathered nerve to go outside, where they found a skeleton—of an umbrella rattling in the wind.

And, finally, my Uncle Stephen faintly recalled hearing of bloodstains on the front steps of the house. On my last visit there, I left Lewis tinkering with a tractor, slipped around to the front of the house, and—feeling foolish and a little guilty should Mrs. Lewis be watching from inside—examined the steps.

They are worn by well over a century of weather and footsteps, perhaps a murderer's among them, but to my disappointment there were no bloodstains.

MT. ZION

In 1930, the remaining members of the Mt. Zion Baptist Church of Trafalgar met for the last time, and deposited three manuscript volumes of church records with Franklin College. It was a sad day—a final defeat after 86 years of defeats and victories. The members added the hopeful condition that the records be returned if the church should reorganize, but it did not. The building was torn down, and Mt. Zion became only a name and sometimes a line in an obituary, noting that the deceased had belonged "to the old Baptist church at Trafalgar."

Mt. Zion has a place in this story because George Bridges belonged to it for a time, and because his young second wife (my great-great-grandmother) argued with one of its pillars and was kicked out.

Neither George nor any of his three wives left a record of what they believed or how they stood on the vital issues of predestination and alien immersion. But we do know that Johnson County was a kettle of religions, boiling with all the conflicts, colorful personalities, and stubbornly held beliefs of the frontier. And we know that George and his wives were Baptists, and that to be a Baptist in that time was to be heir not only to an abiding faith, but to a social system, a way of life, and a vast number of what can perhaps best be described as family rows.

No one was just a Baptist—nothing as bland as that. Back in Kentucky after 1802 one might have called oneself a United Baptist, but some United Baptists were really Separate Baptists, with a history going back to the "Great Awakening" which had brought the church down to the common people before the Revolution.

Sometimes the Separates slid off and became "New Lights," extravagant apostles of every man his own Biblical interpreter. Over east in the Whitewater, elder Wilson Thompson was preaching to his "anti-means Baptists." To the west, the fiery Daniel

Parker of Illinois was telling his "two-seed-in-the-spirit predestinarian Baptists" that some men were literally children of the Devil, because the Devil as well as God had planted his seed in the human soul.

Over all, there raged the battle between primitive or "hardshell" Baptists and the missionary Baptists, who were sometimes but not always the same as "regular" Baptists. The hardshells stayed home and tended to their own affairs—they didn't hold with paid or educated preachers, or the "bloodsucking leeches" of missionary agents sent from the East to raise money for the heathen at home or abroad.

In retrospect, the missionary Baptists seem far more attractive, perhaps because they won. They favored an expanding church, trained and paid pastors, and a somewhat tempered theology. The difference was deeply philosophical and personal. As John Cady, the historian of Indiana Baptists, has pointed out, it was basically a difference between people who were introspective, suspicious, and defensive, and those who wanted to get on with the tasks to be done.

George, although a missionary Baptist and a task-doer, had a foot in both camps. His father's family—coming from a Church of England family in Virginia—probably tended toward regularity and a moderate outlook. But his mother was a Forsyth, and the Forsyths, besides being Scotch-Irish, were primitive Baptists and fiercely independent.

Their independence is evident in the curious story of the "Lying Baptists." Back in Kentucky in 1803 the Forsyths and their neighbors from Flat Rock church were at a log-rolling when an argument broke out over whether it was ever right to lie. Suppose, someone said, you were the father of five children and the Indians had just killed four of them and were asking if you had another child hidden. Should you lie to save the child's life?

Some were for truth at all costs. Others, including the Forsyths, were for lying. The argument was carried into the church and divided it, after which the "Lying Baptists" went five miles down the road and built their own meetinghouse.

Jennie Sturgeon Forsyth, George's first mother-in-law, was of this stubborn stripe. In her later years, when widowed, she moved to Johnson County and became a leader in the South Stott's Creek Baptist Church. There she was noted for belting out the hymns as the preacher lined them to the congregation. But she ran afoul of her orthodox brethren when she married a missionary Baptist.

They told her to choose between the new husband and the church to which her family belonged. But when she opted for church and family they refused to take her back, saying they could not have fellowship with a woman who refused to live with her husband.

In Kentucky, George Bridges's uncle, Benjamin Bridges, owned the farm where the Long Run Baptist Church had organized in the abandoned cabin of Thomas Lincoln, the future president's grandfather. The church expelled Benjamin for intoxication, but were reminded that he owned the church building, so they took him back—no doubt with much talk about "reforming the sinner within the church," a descendant suggests.

So George and Matilda Forsyth Bridges came to Indiana with a tradition both of religious loyalty and independence—a typical frontier mixture.

They were early members of the First Mt. Pleasant Baptist Church, which was founded in 1828 and survives today as that rarity, a healthy rural church. They left it eventually for Mt. Zion at Trafalgar but are buried at Mt. Pleasant, on a windswept hill behind the church, under a modest white limestone obelisk.

No one knows why they left Mt. Pleasant for Mt. Zion, soon after it was founded on June 8, 1844, in the District No. 1 schoolhouse near a corner of the Bridges farm. Perhaps the reason was simply proximity. There is no evidence of a schism in Mt. Pleasant at the time, and Mt. Zion's first pastor, elder John Reese, had pastored Mt. Pleasant earlier.

But there was, apparently, a split in the South Stott's Creek Baptist Church, where Jennie Sturgeon Forsyth had been excluded, first for marrying a missionary Baptist and then for proposing not to live with him. Many of Mt. Zion's original members came from this hidebound congregation. They included Frederick Ragsdale, William M. Clark, and his daughter Martha, who four years later would become George Bridges's second wife. Evidence of the split in Stott's Creek is that Mt. Zion was organized specifically as a missionary Baptist church, and in 1852 voted "to send the gospel into destitute places of the Association."

George was not among Mt. Zion's original 15 members, but he joined early enough to be one of its first three officers, along with James M. Cole and Frederick Ragsdale. Ragsdale was a pillar of the church. More about him later—enough for now to say that his name appears often in church records in connection with one dispute or another, and that the issues were invariably settled in his favor.

In August 1844 a committee was appointed to choose a permanent site for the Mt. Zion church, but its choice was rejected, and George was named to a new committee, which picked an acre of Stith Daniel's farm, in what was later Trafalgar. In November, George was named one of three trustees to obtain a deed to the lot. The position of trustee, Baptist historian John Cady notes, was at that time "neither essential nor important. It served only to meet the legal requirement of property holding." Soon a church building was erected, a frame structure 30 by 40 feet, which the congregation used until 1866.

Church minutes describe the business meetings held on the second Saturday of each month. The procedure was typical for the time, with opening "praise and prayer" and an inquiry into the "peace and fellowship" of the church. After that, any pressing matter or complaint against a member could be raised.

No area was off limits to inquiry. In 1846, brother Thomas L. Sturgeon confessed to intoxication and was forgiven by the church. In the same year, an eight-man committee was sent to investigate difficulties between the Franklin church and "some complaining persons"—former members. In December 1847 the meeting agreed to buy a stove. In 1850, Avery P. Buckner—a leader in the community and George Bridges's rival in many an enterprise—was "excluded" for allowing dancing in his house, but was later restored to fellowship. Not restored was Polly Beadle, excluded in 1855 "for bearing a bastard child."

Exclusion was common in that early day. Of the 15 original members of Mt. Zion, five were later excluded for a time and five dismissed. Of the church's 172 members up to 1860, 45 were at one time or another put out of the church for various transgressions, for "refusing to hear the church," or for "communing with the reformers."

This last charge meant going over to the new Christian or Campbellite church led by the brilliant, anti-creedal, and anti-missionary Alexander Campbell. In 1829, representatives of the New Light, German Dunkard, and Free Will Baptist churches had met at Edinburg, 15 miles east of Trafalgar, and united on the basis of Campbell's teachings. They soon had 15,000 adherents in a movement that would sweep like a fire through the established churches of the Ohio Valley.

George and his second wife were to be excluded from Mt. Zion, and in Martha's case at least, a dispute with Frederick Ragsdale was to blame.

Ragsdale was a founder and staunch member of the Mt. Zion church at Trafalgar. He was probably 60 or older at the time, the father of seven, "a man of many excellent traits of character, a true Christian," the Johnson County history says. He was a veteran of the War of 1812, having fought under Andrew Jackson at the Battle of New Orleans. In short, not a man to be lightly opposed.

On Ragsdale's complaint, Thomas Lynam had been "excluded" from Mt. Zion in 1845 and again in 1847, when the church found him "guilty of sin in accusing F. Ragsdale of lying and for saying he had as soon F. Ragsdale had claimed his horse and also for burning a flax brake [a flax-breaking machine] claimed and proven by F. Ragsdale." (The committee added the coup de grâce of "communing with the reformers," and indeed Lynam was to found what later became the Trafalgar Christian Church in his home the next year.)

On March 14, 1848, Matilda Forsyth Bridges died at the age of 41. On Aug. 16 of the same year, my great-great-grandfather George Bridges, now 48, married the 20-year-old Martha Clark— my great-great-grandmother.

By this time, however, he had left Mt. Zion for reasons unknown. A three-man committee had been sent in April 1847 to find out why he, his son-in-law Alexander Armstrong, and John W. Parkhurst had stopped coming to church. Alexander told the committee he had no desire to attend meeting, would not do it, and wished to be expelled. The church obliged. The committee made another effort with George, but he, too, was expelled in June 1847 for "absenting himself from and refusing to hear the church." He may have gone over to the Campbellites—there is a reference in a county history to a Mr. Bridges as one of the early members of Lynam's church.

"Refusing to hear the church" was a biblical term, linked with the "gospel steps" outlined in the eighteenth chapter of Matthew for solving disputes between church members:

> *And if thy brother sin against thee, go, show him his fault between thee and him alone; if he hear thee, thou hast gained thy brother. But if he hear thee not, take with thee one or two more, that at the mouth of two witnesses or three every word may be established. And if he refuse to hear them, tell it unto the church; and if he refuse to hear the church also, let him be unto thee as the Gentile and the publican.*

In May 1848 Martha's mother, Margaret Clark, was excluded for joining the Campbellites. In January, 1849, Martha herself became the subject of an absenteeism investigation, with sister Mary Sturgeon sent to call on her. Sister Sturgeon reported back that "Sister Bridges was hurt with sister Mary Forsyth and br. Ragsdale," and the case was continued with Martha "admonished to take gospel steps for a reconciliation."

There is no glimmer in the record of what the dispute was about, but there is some circumstantial evidence and something is known about the protagonists. On one side was Martha, with a grievance, newly married to a man already expelled by the church, with her mother gone to the Campbellites and her father also expelled at some point. She was a girl of 20, moreover, who had just become a stepmother of seven, including grown daughters, 23 and 20, sons 17, 15, 11, and 10, and a five-year-old girl. In addition she was three months pregnant with her own first child.

On the other side was Ragsdale, a man three times her age, of sternness and rectitude, who might have been upset by seeing this girl—whom he brought with him when he founded the church—married to an expelled member, and one almost as old as he was. Maybe he was just fed up with the Clarks and the Bridgeses, with their stubbornness and tendency to jump churches. Maybe Martha had been snippy—maybe, indeed, the whole business was her fault.

All we really know is that she was in church next meeting day, for the record reads: "The reference concerning Sister Bridges was read and taken up and she being present stated that she had seen sister Forsyth and satisfaction was obtained with her, but Sister Bridges failed to visit Br. Ragsdale and refused in church to have any communication with him."

This time the church appointed a committee of seven "to try to get sister Bridges and Br. Ragsdale together and labor with them to effect a reconciliation."

But it was in vain. At the next meeting Martha's brothers, Elisha and Absalom, were excluded, Elisha without a reason given, Absalom for "reporting that that was not true against Br. Ragsdale."

The church's resources of reconciliation were exhausted, the gospel steps all taken, and the story ends: "The reference concerning sister Bridges was attended to and she excluded for refusing to hear the church."

The Bridges homestead west of Trafalgar, as it appeared in 2010. When this essay was written, the house had been painted white for many years. Since then it has been sandblasted and the color of the original bricks restored.

THE NAME OF A ROAD

"WHAT WAS THE NAME of that road?" I asked Karen. "You know, the one that went south behind the Clark Memorial to the St. Francisville ferry. The Something Slab, because it was poured concrete."

She remembered the road, of course—we both grew up in Vincennes, Indiana—but couldn't come up with the name either. She said something telling: "That was a long way off, on the other side of town." She is a North Sider, and the Slab was at the south end of town, near Pearl City, where the mussel fishers lived in their riverbank hovels. An immense social divide.

In the days after our inconclusive talk, I tried out many names. Could it have been the Brevoort Slab? No, although the Brevoorts farmed hundreds, perhaps thousands, of acres along it. A famous picture from the 1880s shows teams of horses dragging up dirt for the Brevoort Levee, to protect their vast lands against the Wabash River. There were two Brevoort brothers, weren't there? Billy Brevoort and another, and in old age didn't they live in the Brevoort mansion at Sixth and Busseron in Vincennes—but in separate sides of the house, connecting doors sealed, because they weren't speaking?

This is how it is with home-town history. One thing leads to another.

But the Slab. It wasn't the St. Francisville Slab, even though it ended at a one-lung ferry, which could take one car at a time, slowly and slaunchwise, across the Wabash to the little town on the Illinois side. And it wasn't the St. Thomas Slab, even though the church of that name was a feature of the flood plain below Vincennes. Or the Purcell (pronounced PURR-sul) Slab.

I had my first auto accident on the Slab, turning too fast onto a gravel side road and nuzzling gently up to a tree. Several years later, Karen and I drove down the Slab to attend a church supper and then to "neck," in the quaint idiom of that day, along one of those gravel roads.

I went farther back. Around 1940, I found Vincennes and Knox County in a 1901 atlas at the home of my Great-Grandmother Bridges. There were names there that were new to me—Orrville, Red Cloud. Years later I looked for them, but whatever crossroad settlements had been there in 1901 were gone. Their names were not attached to the Slab.

And there was Bandmill store, far out on the Slab in a prairie of corn and melon fields. I went there once. I had come home from college and brought along Dr. Charles A. Deppe, my father's old biology professor from 1927. For some reason we went to Bandmill store—why he agreed to go, I don't know. He was an old man, and didn't have much to do, I suppose. We had a soft drink—perhaps an 11-Up (there was such a thing)—and came home.

But it was not the Bandmill Slab.

Nor the Dicksburg Slab, although the Dicksburg Hills were somewhere south of it, beyond the cypress swamp where White River joined the Wabash. Near that confluence was what my father called River Deshee, where water pooled around a flood gate and produced sizeable bass and crappie. River Deshee had other connotations, too. A little way west were the Deshee Farms, a collective where the federal government resettled poor farm families in the 1930s. "Little Russia," the natives called it.

But this was getting me no closer to the name I sought.

I would have to e-mail my sister. "This is urgent," I wrote. "If you don't know, call the Oldest Inhabitant and find out."

She made inquiries of local historians, but without success. Neither of my brothers could remember a road called the Slab.

But eventually I puzzled out that the name was probably just the Sixth Street Slab, because it was an extension of that street through the city.

A prosaic ending? Not quite, because as I searched, another and older name slowly returned from some quiet chamber of memory. The Cathlinette Road. It had always been that, hadn't it, before the graveling of county roads or the pouring of concrete? A traveler in 1816 had reported a "Canadien" village of Cathlinette (perhaps named for a saint) on what would be known as the Cathlinette Prairie. The village would have gone back to the days when Vincennes was an outpost of New France. And in 1779, George Rogers Clark had followed this Cathlinette path in his wintertime trek across flooded bottomlands to surprise the British at Vincennes and secure the Northwest Territory for the young republic.

And then the land surveyors of that republic had had to scratch their heads over the old farms, the "French surveys," that ran in narrow, undocumented strips across the Cathlinette Prairie to frontages on the Wabash.

I was satisfied and a feeling of peace stole over me. It was the Cathlinette Road, of course. My mind was at ease again.

IN SEARCH OF SCHNELL

SCHNELL HAS BEEN SILENT now for more than 50 years.

When I went looking for him, it was with no expectation of finding him, and this negative expectation was quickly fulfilled. After all, I didn't even know his first name, and our one encounter had been a conversation on a summer afternoon in the middle of the 1950s.

I don't remember why I visited him, in the forlorn New York Central depot where he was the freight agent and sole employee. Something to do, probably, with a story for the *Franklin Evening Star*, where I was the summertime cub reporter. I was reading *The Catcher in the Rye*, and wearing a baseball cap like Holden Caulfield's. Everyone I met seemed numinous and possessed of an unfathomed history. So I interviewed Schnell in his hot, dusty office, over his lunch of a sandwich unwrapped from waxed paper and a Thermos of iced tea. No memory of what we talked about remains, although just now it occurs to me that I knew him by initials—R.W. Schnell, something like that.

What I do remember, and have for half a century, is his anger. He was the angriest man I had ever met. Not dangerous or malevolent (or violent) in any way, but seriously, steadily, and committedly angry, with a dead level of bitterness I had not encountered before and have not since. Even his most ordinary comments seemed tinged with it, like a black border on a death announcement. This bitterness colored the way he talked about everything—the station, the railroad, his customers, the weather, his lunch. It was impersonal. I don't remember his unburdening himself of any disappointments, disillusion, or betrayals. In fact he said remarkably little about himself, which made looking for traces of him 50 years later futile from the start.

The station itself was long gone, jacked up and ferried across town to become the Chamber of Commerce office with a little railroad museum attached. On the site where it had stood, just off North Water Street, only a cracked and grassed-over concrete slab remained. The railroad itself was gone, though a few half-buried rails and fragments of crossties showed where it had run. When I walked over the vacant ground, I could see what I had forgotten, that tracks ran on both sides of the depot, one of them the "main line" of the New York Central or "Big Four" going up to Urmeyville, Needham, and Fairland, the other probably a switching spur to the nearby Pennsylvania (now Conrail) line. My grandfather had once been agent at this same depot. As I walked over the broken foundations, I breathed out "Schnell" a time or two, softly, into the silence. Not even the wind answered.

In the Johnson County Historical Museum, I found only one Schnell in city directories and telephone books of that time. In 1955, Lanna L. Schnell lived at 1151 Younce Street, phone number 1081-R. ("That number has changed," said a recorded message. "If you dialed five digits, please contact your long-distance operator.") She was not listed in 1954 or 1956. I imagined that she might be Schnell's mother. Somehow, Schnell struck me as a man who might be living with his (probably) widowed mother. Although he was by no means old, I had a hard time picturing him going home from the depot to a wife and children. Younce Street seemed about right for someone serving a year or so as a freight agent in this dismal backwater—it was within walking distance of the depot, in a down-at-the-heels neighborhood where a transient worker and his mother could have found a little house for rent, cheap. (When I finally visited the house, it was precisely as I had pictured it.) Yes. Let's say that Schnell lived with his mother. She would have packed the sandwich in waxed paper for him, and filled the Thermos of unsweetened tea.

At work, Schnell did not have much to do. His railroad was in its last days, with trains that ran only once or twice a week, carrying feed and implements to rural farm-supply businesses, maybe a load of coal now and then. Passengers were not even a distant memory. It was a scandal and a jest when one of the trains struck a car at a crossing near the depot; it was like two specks of dust finding each other in outer space.

Schnell may actually have been glad to see me—somebody to pass a little time with, a kid who might have reminded him of himself in more naïve days. But he did not "bend my ear" as the saying went. He answered my reporter's questions in that flat voice, with its freight of unaddressed sarcasm and rancid hopes, its distillation of bitter leaves.

I never forgot him. Years later I put him into a poem, "Freight Agent on a Branch Line":

> *Grown thin on the richness of it,*
> *sour on its savor,*
> *he nurses the sop of his hate*
> *beside the waybills*
> *in this out-of-the-way spot.*
>
> *Habitual food fuels*
> *his wrath at a caller, his look that curses.*
> *Such keen scorn could be admired*
> *for the fineness now of what whets it—*
> *even the furniture is afraid*
> *of this appetite, insistent as fly buzz,*
> *as wind sifting weeds on the siding.*
> *The taste*
> *is bitter, but he's come to love it.*
>
> *Lunch interrupts his feast, he takes*
> *a sandwich in oil paper, Thermos of tea*
> *out of a drawer.*

Later, in the vacant afternoon,
he sucks again the sumen of his rage.

This is not an especially good poem—it describes, but goes nowhere. "Did you mean *semen*?" another writer asked me. No, I meant *sumen*, an obsolete word for a cow's udder, or the fatness of something, its richness. A sacrifice stolen dripping from the altar.

I might have pursued Schnell a little further—could the New York Central archives still have employment records from 1955? I could perhaps have advertised for someone else who remembered him. But in a way I was happy not to do this, or to find out anything more about him. What biography I might have unearthed could not have told me more than I already knew. I found I was content to let Schnell go back (quickly, as befitted his name) into the silence.

It is a rich and populated silence. I am going there myself.

SEX IN THE CLOSET

WHEN MY WIFE AND I were still relative newlyweds, our friend Gwendolyn stopped by the house one day to change clothes in our closet. Why this was necessary I don't remember, nor on what trip of hers we were a way station. I also don't know why she chose to disrobe in the walk-in closet under the living-room stairs, instead of going to the front bedroom or upstairs to the bath. But it made a vivid impression on me.

Gwendolyn was a knockout blonde, and the wife of the pediatrician for our twin sons. We socialized with her and her husband, including dinners at their country home, where a pack of Newfoundlands ran through the house or bayed in the yard: visitors entered the house between pillars built from 100-pound sacks of dog food. The food—Gwendolyn's, not the dog food—was good and the conversation elevating. As I recall, her parents had been friends of Béla Bartók's.

But I had never lusted after her in my heart or anywhere else. Until now, when she was in our closet, peeling down to her undies. Any fantasy or plan of action was short-lived, however. I am many things, but stupid is not one of them. Had I yielded to some errant impulse, Gwendolyn would have decked me and stomped out. Karen would have filed for divorce, and our twins would have lost both their father and a good pediatrician.

But still, there it was, the image: Gwendolyn, naked or nearly so, in our closet, next to the twin stroller and the foldaway playpen.

I have thought about this scene over the years, when the conversation has turned to sex. I agree basically with the humorist (Thurber?) who described sex as too fraught with peril to be engaged in by actual men and women. Early in life, this attitude caused me to be regarded by friends as something of an innocent, and I was left out of various male trolling expeditions. My friends probably thought they were protecting me, or saving me (and themselves) from embarrassment. In fact, I wasn't all that innocent, just mildly repressed in the fashion of 1950s Indiana. I *did* have some idea of what went on (unlike the mystery of auto mechanics, where I continued to believe that the crankshaft went crosswise with a wheel on each end).

But sex was pretty much in the imagination, where it flourished and still does. Not long ago, one of those protective friends from youth remarked that he and his housemate, both in their 70s, were getting along fine, although "sex isn't a big deal anymore." The sex act maybe, I thought, but sex not a big deal? Have you put your funeral director on speed dial yet?

I did eventually get out of my imagination but remain convinced that lurid and hectic sex occurs only in novels and on Dr. Phil. Or that if it does occur in real life, it's apt to be more comic than cosmic. I'm sustained in this belief by a friend who has written entertainingly about being lured onto a night beach by a fellow partygoer intent on getting both of them out of their clothes and into the ocean . . . for starters. She went first and was attacked by swarms of blackflies, putting a quick end to romance. Reinforcing my belief are women themselves, who seem to recognize an innocent when they see one, and are invariably friendly, not seductive. There clearly are no pheromones at work here, or if there are any, they're not working very hard.

Still, there have been curious moments. Years ago, I called at my boss's house to talk with his wife about something—a charity, I think—and found the foxy Mrs. Boss home alone. We talked business for a few minutes, when the doorbell rang and she stashed me hurriedly in her bedroom upstairs. This struck me as slightly odd—there were plenty of rooms where I would have been out of sight, but the bedroom? Was I in a French farce? It was probably just my imagination in overdrive again. She came back, we finished our talk, and she showed me to the door.

Years later, I found myself alone in Taiwan, where there were plenty of attractive Asian women possibly not averse to spending quality time with someone from the mysterious West, or at least to practicing their English. But loyalty and innocence (and a certain sense of my own absurdity) came to the rescue again.

Peril came instead from an unexpected source—Oregon State University, which had sent a thirty-something intern to the office where I worked. Abigail and I hit it off, ate lunch now and then, and went shopping together. She was chatting cheerfully one day about her underwear and stockings, when I flashed on Abby, stripped, in my apartment, surrounded only by millions of Chinese. I wish I could say that firm resolve and marital fidelity kept me on the right path, but it was more the fear of having nobody to go shopping with.

Ah, the imagination! Gwendolyn is probably a gray grandmother by now. But if she came to my door today and asked to change clothes in the closet, my heart would still go pitty-pat.

A GREAT-GRANDMOTHER RECLAIMED

A FEW MONTHS AGO, I was putting together a CD with pictures of Karen's ancestors, to go with one I'd already made of Bridges family portraits.

There were some problems with this, since Karen's family—while they had saved many photos—had been less assiduous in identifying them, particularly the  ones from Denmark, pre-1900. This did not make them less fascinating. I could meditate for some time on the pictures of anonymous young men in uniform, leaning against desks or beside stone pedestals (like the youth at right) in various photographic studios of Denmark or northern Schleswig-Holstein, just before or just after this border area became part of the Kaiser's Reich. But one picture was different.

When I found it among the long-stored photos, it was a tiny daguerreotype measuring less than an inch square. It was damaged and got more so as it was removed from its resting place. The surface in many spots looked as though it had been burned. But behind the damage, a striking young woman was still visible. Her eyes were compelling—the photographer had caught the light in them, and they still gleamed after a century and a half.

I scanned the daguerreotype into my computer and repaired much of the damage in Photoshop.

But who was she? There was only the most circumstantial of evidence. She appeared to be wearing a formal, probably a wedding, suit. (This was long before the craze for white wedding gowns.) A farmer's daughter in Tønder, Denmark, would hardly have worn such a dress except to be married or buried in. The daguerreotype itself almost had to fall in the 1850s. Much earlier and such photos would have been experimental. Only a few years lat-

er and bigger, more polished photographs would have replaced daguerreotypes.

I printed the picture and hung it over my desk, to let it speak to me. And it did. The longer we looked at each other, the more I began to see Karen's father, Fritz, in the eyes, mouth, and cheekbones—the Petersen look. (I compared it with pictures from Karen's Thomsen ancestors, but there was no resemblance.)

Karen and I discussed it, and while she rightly noted that many people in Tønder even today remind her of her father, the facial features are too particular to ignore. Given everything, I decided, it had to be her great-grandmother, Johanna Christina Jessen, who had married Peter Petersen and given birth, on Sept. 22, 1857, to her grandfather, Ferdinand Jessen Petersen. The Petersen look was actually the Jessen look. A wedding date in 1856 seemed likely.

She was—and is—beautiful. It's a face that no doubt would thicken in a lifetime of farm and family labor. But at the moment the shutter clicked, she was radiant and young. Peter Petersen must have been a happy bridegroom indeed.

Muses appear when least expected, and at some point Johanna instructed me to write something about her. Here it is:

WEDDING PHOTO, CIRCA 1856

Johanna Jessen,
you look at me
across centuries.

I rescued your photo,
daguerreotype
scalded by time,

and now your eyes
are fresh again,
and your mouth,

keeping your vow
to all generations.

FERRYBOAT DAYS

UNTIL LATE IN THE LAST CENTURY, two ferries crossed the Wabash River near Vincennes, Indiana—the St. Francisville Ferry several miles below the city and the Russellville Ferry above it.

I've written briefly before about the St. Francisville Ferry, which was the better known of the two. My family used it now and then to visit friends in the village of the same name on the Illinois side of the Wabash. It was always an adventure for a child.

To begin with, the car breasted a little rise in a country road and then plunged straight down into the river—or seemed about to follow the road there. But my father always stopped in time and then, usually, we waited 10 or 20 minutes while the antique ferryboat came back from the farther shore. There must have been times when it was waiting for us on our side, but I don't remember them. The impression was one of waiting, in the languor of a summer afternoon, for a timeless process to unfold.

Usually we waited alone—this was not a much-traveled road. I think the boat carried only one car, although perhaps on high-traffic days that could extend to two. It was a ramshackle affair, with a "pilothouse"/engine room on one side, and was tethered to a cable over the river, which kept us from being swept away to New Orleans. The crossing took 10 or 15 minutes, and it would have been unthinkable to stay in the car—one had to get out and lean on the railing, to watch the Wabash dawdling its muddy way past.

And then there was the excitement of disembarking on the other side, with my father steering us expertly down the creaking gangplank, back on solid earth once more. And the superior feeling of seeing the drivers on the St. Francisville side, waiting to begin their own adventure.

My father was a veteran of highway travel, and told about driving through Tennessee with a friend in the 1920s in a Model T. They came to a river where there was not even a ferry. But there was a farmer with a team who offered to pull them across (for several dollars) after they had lifted the car's battery into the passenger seat. The "river" turned out to be a foot deep at most. "We were strangers and he took us in," my father said.

I crossed the Wabash at Russellville only a few times—that ferry, which was mainly to connect farm fields, didn't have the cachet of its southern sister. But there was a country tavern at Russellville where Karen's parents took us once for a very good catfish supper.

Both ferries shut down years ago, replaced by bridges or roads that diverted their traffic elsewhere. But I read a story recently about the Russellville Ferry. One day an overloaded farm truck sank the ferry during a crossing, and released several thousand cantaloupes, or muskmelons, to go bobbing happily down the Wabash toward Vincennes. The mussel fishers at Pearl City, behind the George Rogers Clark Memorial, quickly adopted a new business model, and for days everybody along the river had all the "mushmelons" they could eat.

III. Essays

Photo by April Knox, courtesy of the Columbus, Ind., *Republic*

Presidential candidate Barack Obama speaks at East High School in Columbus, Indiana, on April 11, 2008.

A FOOT SOLDIER FOR OBAMA
[SPRING, 2008]

THE LAST TIME I got involved in politics, it was 1968 in up-state New York, and "Clean Gene" McCarthy's local troops were bivouacked in our living room to hiss Lyndon Johnson on the telly. You could almost hear the air seep out of their esprit de corps as LBJ announced he wouldn't run again. Johnson you could hate, but Hubert Humphrey?

Forty years on, I read Barack Obama's *Dreams from My Father* and felt some of the old excitement stirring my 73-year-old blood. A literate president, what an idea! Then I heard his Philadelphia speech, "A More Perfect Union," and was hooked. Grabbing my credit card, I sent off $100 to the campaign, and on the next two Saturdays drove an hour to Bloomington (home of Indiana University) to register voters for Indiana's May 6 primary.

To be a Democrat in Indiana is doubly depressing. Not only do you know in advance that Indiana will go Republican in the fall, but even the Democratic primary is meaningless, since it always comes after the nomination has been decided in other states. But not this year. Hoosiers may be the ones to finally push Hillary Clinton's candidacy over the cliff—or they may revive it and send the whole circus gallywampusing toward a colossal train wreck in Denver.

If I sat at home, I'd never forgive myself. I like Hillary and think she'd be a capable president—but Barack Obama is a force I haven't seen in national politics since Bobby Kennedy. "A phee-nom," my ex-sportswriter friend Max would call him.

The two Saturdays in Bloomington were idylls. I teamed up the first afternoon with Ben (a doctoral student in sociology) and we knocked on doors nonpartisanly all over two apartment complexes, registering voters. Each of us took a block and then met to compare results. It didn't take much to make us happy, which was good, since these were student apartments—most occupants were either gone, still sleeping at noon, or from foreign countries. Still, we registered a handful and signed up some Obama volunteers.

The next Saturday was even better. It was a perfect spring day, with star magnolias blossoming around the apartments. What better way to spend it than talking to strangers and urging them to vote? (Disquieting at times, though. Two doors were opened by small children who were home alone.) This time my partner was Sydney, a grayhead living on Social Security. She mixed Obama politicking with her registration pitch, lectured one student for watching Fox News, and took me home to her apartment for a lunch of toasted cheese and tomato soup.

The Bloomington Obama forces seemed well organized. They had their own downtown headquarters, and had signed up hundreds of new voters. But the registration drive ended, and I was tired of driving a 100-mile round trip. Why wasn't anything going on closer to home?

It turned out something was. A few days later, the candidate himself came for a "town meeting" at Columbus, 20 miles to the south. My $100 had gotten me on the Obama Internet, which I was checking out one afternoon when an announcement flashed up: free tickets for the town meeting would be handed out starting in an hour. Karen and I jumped in the car and drove to Columbus, where a hundred people were already in line. The line (outside a theater) had stretched to nearly two blocks before the tickets finally arrived by car—delayed, an Obama organizer explained, because the printer had died halfway through the job.

Two days later, tickets in hand, we drove to Columbus East High School where by 9 a.m., about a thousand people were already in line for Obama's 11 a.m. appearance in the school gym, the Orange Pit. (The crowd reached 2,500, newspapers reported.)

We got upper bleacher seats, with a good view of the arena-style speaker's platform. Others were being prodded to higher seats, but a friendly Obama usher said, "I'll leave you two here, for mobility reasons." Actually, Karen and I are still quite upwardly mobile, but gray hair can be an advantage.

Barack gave a stock stump speech, with his familiar lines about the need to reform health care and about "pain trickling up." Only once or twice did something else peep through. During the question session, an elderly woman put a young black up to asking about Social Security. Barack caught on instantly, and chuckled—a throaty "heh, heh, heh" that (it suddenly flashed on me) came straight from some long-ago African uncle. And he called on one youngster who blurted, "How do you like Columbus?"

"Is that your question?" Barack asked. "I like Columbus fine—you were just taking a star turn, weren't you?"

"He has a sense of humor," Karen said on the drive home.

Later that day the storm broke over Obama's "elitist" comments to a California audience about small-town Pennsylvania. At 4 p.m. Kitty, the CNN anchor, was pounding the point relentlessly. "Stay tuned and we'll tell you more about Obama's *stunning* comments." After half a dozen repetitions of *stunning*, I was remembering why I hate TV news.

A day or two later, the Obama Internet invited me to join a "township team" in my own area. I did, and was directed to a meeting in Greenwood, just north of my home. Nate, a young field organizer, gave us a basic pitch and apologized for a certain frazzledness—he had just taken over from Kali, who had caught mono and gone home to Ohio. "Campaign organization is an oxymoron," he said.

The next weekend, I went back to Greenwood to knock on doors and this time blatantly urge ballots for Barack. Others had some depressing experiences. (Greenwood was a KKK stronghold in the not-so-old days, and one canvasser reported meeting a die-hard.) But my encounters were all pleasant. One man was vehe-mently anti-Clinton—"a conspicuous liar," he called her. Another was just as soured on Obama, who he said has "no integrity," be-cause he didn't walk out on Reverend Wright's sermons. My list of names and addresses had been targeted at registered Demo-crats, and I had several undecideds or leaning-toward-Obamas, all of whom I faithfully recorded, with their responses, on my can-vasser's tally sheet.

One man, about my age, was not on the list, but was in his yard. "What's your business here?" he asked. It turned out that he not only was enthusiastic about Obama, but wanted to give me money on the spot for his campaign. (I took his name and address so Nate could contact him, but there may be a problem. He couldn't remember his house number and had to go ask his wife.)

Oddly, in my nonrepresentative microcosm of voters, there was not a single Hillary loyalist.

Foot soldiers need a little R&R, so Karen and I have invited my fellow canvassers to a party at our house this Tuesday night, to watch the Pennsylvania results come in. I don't expect more than half a dozen, but Karen—a better crowd predicter than I—is already planning food and figuring out how to move the bedroom cable TV to the living room.

A lasting impression: the Obama campaign has organized it-self superbly through the Internet, a little less efficiently through its fallible human troops on the ground. My local newspaper gave a large front-page spread to the Clinton effort, but hadn't been able to locate the Obama side until I put the editor in touch. What's really fueling the Obama drive is the army of people who have fallen for this candidate and taken time off from their lives to do something about it—and to send money. More than a hundred attended the opening of the Bloomington headquarters, which surprised the organizers and forced the ceremony outside. Leo-nard Pitts, the columnist, says Obama's opponents have made a fundamental miscalculation: "They're running political campaigns—he's leading a movement."

Will all this frenetic activity mean anything in the end? At the moment, Barack has a 5 percent lead in Indiana. We may yet be a pivotal state for a resurgent Hillary. Or by May 6, a Barack win or near-win in Pennsylvania may have reduced Hoosiers once more to an afterthought.

"Had there been a battle? And was it Waterloo?" asks a foot soldier in a Stendhal novel. My bit of soldiering is lost in the ruck of this vast, exhilarating, boring, frustrating, endless, and inspiring campaign. But as I sit drooling in the chimney corner (perhaps just before the 2012 election), I can at least say to the enthralled children at my knee that I once did "see Obama plain. . . . How strange it seems, and new!" (And if you recognize that quote, keep it to yourself, or it will tag you as a hopeless elitist.)

OUT ON OLD ROAD 44 [FALL, 2008]

On the campaign trail, today is State Road 44 day for me.

I've driven (or been driven on) Road 44 most of my life. It's a twisted strand of two-lane road that goes uphill and down, around right-angle turns, from Franklin southwest to Martinsville, Indiana. When I was a kid, it was the only way to get from our home in Vincennes, in the state's southwest corner, to my grandfather's home in Franklin. I loved the curvy, up-and-down road as much as my father hated it. When he was running our car on wartime kerosene, the hills of Road 44 were murder on the engine, and he had to stop every so often, at places like Bud and Mt. Nebo, to let things cool.

Many years later, I came close to losing two of my children on Road 44. David, with his brother Colin as a passenger, took one of the curves too fast on an icy day and did a 360 in the middle of the road.

My great-great-grandfather is buried in the Mt. Pleasant cemetery, beside Road 44.

In all that time, I've never really looked at houses along the road. But today I'm looking at (and for) houses, armed with an address list supplied by the local Obama campaign. It's a gorgeous fall Sunday afternoon in Indiana, but Road 44 is as cantankerous as ever. Just finding houses in these boondocks is a challenge, and I skip one address because the house is surrounded by police cars and units of the Trafalgar Volunteer Firemen (yes, that's what's on the side of the trucks—no gender-equality nonsense about "firefighters" here).

At the next house a woman wipes sweat from her brow as she explains that she's been out trying to keep the grass fire next door from reaching her family's barn. "We're for Obama," she says— but it's clearly not the time for a political discussion.

As always, driving Road 44 is enough to make a driver lose his religion. Numbers on mailboxes are small, scanty, and confused. Which side of Centerline Road is No. 1865 on, anyway? And do the numbers run up or down? Traffic is much heavier on Road 44 than in my youth, so I have to be careful turning on or off it. And careful about backing from a driveway onto a road where a curve or the crest of a hill may be only 50 feet away.

The drama only begins with the road. At No. 611, a woman closes the door firmly in my face when she sees my Obama button. "You're at the wrong house," she says. And down the road at No. 570, I bounce the car down a rough and pitted gravel drive to a house that appears wrecked and abandoned, despite two pickup trucks, a yard strewn with trash, and a hose snaking out an open door into the bushes. No one answers my knock, so I leave an Obama leaflet in the door and move on.

A little further on I make a turn into a wrong address. I hear gunfire, and see—a little way off—three or four men firing rifles behind a barn. It seems a good time to move out smartly and find the right address. (When Sarah Palin spoke to 20,000 people near

Indianapolis last week, a sign in the crowd said, "Guts, guns, and Sarah.")

Sometimes the reception along Road 44 is friendly. At No. 874, a woman and her two teen-age sons invite me in for a half-hour discussion about politics. She's leaning toward Obama, she says, but is worried because friends are telling her he's Muslim. And what's Obama's position on gun control, she asks. (Answer: No problem with hunting and recreation, but he's tired of kids being killed on the streets of Chicago—or Indianapolis.) Her 15-year-old son, a non-voting McCain supporter, peppers me with questions (good ones) about Obama's experience and his tax proposals. "Tell me something you like about McCain," he says, and this is easy—his personal courage, his integrity, his sense of humor.

Down the road, at No. 808, Johnny Rees talks long and thoughtfully about the campaign. He's a Republican and the father of four, who drives 80 miles to a job where his employer is cutting back hours in the economic slump. He says Christ turned his life around in the 1990s, and he's taught a young people's Sunday School class just this morning. He wishes Obama were more firmly against abortion, but the economy is moving him toward supporting him anyway. He listens to news on NPR as he drives to and from work. Race doesn't bother him, he says—"my family never was that way." And he adds, "The first black president—that would be something. Maybe then we could put that subject behind us." As I leave he says, "I haven't said this to anybody but you, but I think I probably *will* vote for Obama."

What with the long discussions and searching for addresses and trying to keep from getting killed on Road 44, this is not a very productive day on the campaign trail—at least not in numbers of voter contacts. After four hours, I've knocked on 13 doors and talked to eight voters—two are for Obama, two are leaning toward him, three are for McCain, and one is undecided. That's very close to the distribution among the hundred or so people I've talked to over the last month. It mirrors almost precisely what the polls in red-state Indiana are saying. It's going to be a very close election here—if Obama can pull it off, he'll be the first Democrat since Lyndon Johnson in 1964 to do so.

It's after 4 p.m. now, and time to quit. The Indianapolis Colts come on in a few minutes against Green Bay, and nobody in Indiana wants to talk politics while the Colts are playing.

At home I tally up the statistics. I'm halfway through probably the toughest address list I've had from the campaign—a lot harder stumping than in subdivisions, apartment complexes, or compact city blocks. Yesterday I knocked on 24 rural doors, with 14 voter contacts. The breakdown so far on this list: six strongly for Obama, three leaning that way, seven strongly for McCain, two undecided. It seems a long way from Sarah Palin's 20,000 fans or the 100,000 who turned out yesterday for Obama at the Gateway Arch in St. Louis.

Tomorrow, I'll try to finish the list—Road 44 is done except for two houses I never found, but I have 21 addresses to go on country roads with names like W 100 N and S 75 W. Overall, I'm at 363 doors knocked (plus a couple of hundred in the primary), and I'd like to get to 500 during the next two weekends. Then, please God, this marathon will be over.

'HEY, LOOK HIM OVER!' [FALL, 2008]

Birch Bayh came back to Indiana this week, and Karen and I went to see him again.

The last time was Dec. 10, 1962. Karen was a 21-year-old student at Indiana University in Bloomington. I was 27, with the largely mythical title of Sunday editor for the Vincennes, Indiana, *Sun-Commercial*. We were getting married in three weeks. Bayh was 34 and had just upset Indiana's veteran senator, Homer Capehart, in the November election.

We were interviewing both Bayh and Capehart, separately, to get their reflections on the just-ended campaign, which had taken place amid the Cuban missile crisis. It was a government-class project for Karen, and a Sunday feature story for me. Capehart had entertained us at a leisurely fried-chicken lunch on his farm near Washington, Indiana. The visit to Bayh in Terre Haute was more hurried—the moving van for Washington, D.C., was at the door, his wife Marvella served hot dogs in the living room, and their son Evan, 6, was underfoot and trying to unpack boxes.

Looking back, the interviews were hardly the stuff of history. Capehart wryly conceded that the Democrats had outhustled the Republicans, and that Bayh's incessant campaign jingle had been "catchy"—"Hey, look him over, he's your kind of guy. His first name is Birch, his last name is Bayh."

Bayh said he might have lost if the missile crisis had gone on longer—as it was, he scraped by with a margin of 30,944 votes out of more than 1.8 million cast. And he conceded that the Hoosier electorate was probably getting pretty sick of that jingle.

But for Karen and me, the whole project was swathed in the glamour of youth, love, and politics—our first joint venture. She got an A on her paper, I got my Sunday feature. Bayh went on to serve three Senate terms, during which he distinguished himself as a sponsor of the proposed Equal Rights Amendment and legislation to give 18-year-olds the vote. He campaigned briefly for president in 1976, a bid put aside four years earlier during Marvella's losing fight with breast cancer.

Now, on a sunny fall morning, he was back home in Indiana, making some campaign stops for Barack Obama. Karen and I went to hear him at Franklin College.

Bayh is 80 now, and the years have been good to the Shirkieville Slicker, as opponents once called him. He talks and walks more slowly, but the face of a political "comer" has weathered to that of an old Hoosier farmer. (He ran his family's farm as a young man, but for years has been a Washington lawyer and lobbyist). He stayed behind the podium for about a minute, then came out to meet his college audience, shed his coat, and walked around like a professor prowling a classroom.

He said he was meeting Obama in Indianapolis the next day, but laughed at the idea of the younger man's seeking his advice. "He talks to the real Senator Bayh," he said—that's Evan, former Indiana governor and then senator, who for a time was on the Obama vice-presidential "short list."

His own advice for whoever wins this year's election—"I don't say this lightly, but they'd better pray."

Bayh did not quite escape the old man's failing of telling one story too many, but the stories were good and one was aimed at the students present. He told, movingly, how he had rallied a bare majority of senators to defeat an unqualified Supreme Court nominee, in large part because Harvard law students had exhaustively researched the man's dubious record. "We stopped that guy," he said. Your work and your vote count, he told his audience.

When he was finished taking questions, Karen and I chatted with him. He did not, of course, remember us, although he contrived somehow to not quite admit that fact. He did remember the house and the move to Washington. Karen had brought her old government term paper along, with its A grade and the prof's comment: "A very fine job in all respects." And Bayh sat down and signed the paper himself: "Still doing a great job, Karen! + + A"

After the talk he walked over to the new Obama headquarters (climbing three flights of stairs to get to it). He told a few more stories, including one he hadn't told Karen and me in 1962—how President Kennedy had phoned him after his narrow victory and called him "you old miracle worker." As he spoke, the afternoon sun streamed in the window behind him, throwing the furrows of his face into shadow. For a moment, he looked 34 again.

END OF THE TRAIL [NOVEMBER, 2008]

Nothing is more over when it's over than an election (except pregnancy, Karen says, and then—like elections—there's a whole new set of problems).

It's hard to believe that less than a week ago I was furiously involved in a 14-hour get-out-the-vote campaign, which was actually the wind-up of a furious four-day GOTV campaign. I now live in a presidential blue state, at least for the next four years. The air seems fresher somehow.

But it was just as close as the polls predicted. Obama won by a skimpy 23,000 votes out of 2.6 million cast. As it turned out, he didn't need Indiana, but that was fine. We were one of the last four states to be declared, at 2 in the morning. By then I'd gone to bed.

I've been trying ever since to figure out what really happened, especially here in Johnson County. My beatific vision that our little red corner of the state might somehow turn blue was dispelled. I'd been seeing a lot of people on doorsteps who were voting Obama, and they seemed enthusiastic about it—no Bradley Effect that I could discern. But among the not-at-homes, the no-commenters, and the quickly closed doors there turned out to be a solid Republican majority. Johnson County is still part of the "ring of fire" around Indianapolis.

But looking beyond that, the story gets more interesting, if you can stand a few statistics. The county voter turnout (including a huge early vote) went up from 60 percent in 2004 to 64 percent this year. Bush took the county by 75 percent to 25 percent for Kerry. McCain managed only 63 percent to Obama's 37 percent. The raw numbers are also interesting. Rounded very roughly, 6,500 more people voted than in 2004. Obama got 8,700 more votes than Kerry did, and McCain got 2,200 hundred fewer than Bush. So in a sense, Obama got all the new voters and 2,200 of the old ones.

Those are faulty statistics, of course, since they don't take into account a bunch of variables. But in a rough way they're exactly right. Obama outperformed Kerry, and McCain underperformed Bush. That was the story of the night all over the state. Gary, Indianapolis, and Evansville didn't have to do it all—our rural counties also helped out.

How that came to pass is part of the larger story of the fascinating Obama campaign.

The primary here was a home-grown effort, operating mostly out of a city park in the northern part of the county. The Obama campaign supplied direction with an overworked college student or two, and it clearly had some idea that Indiana might be worth attention. Obama himself—in the effort to head off Hillary—had already begun making what became nearly 50 visits to the state (compared to two or three by McCain). Hillary won the Indiana primary too narrowly to give her any help, and I figured my campaigning was done—Indiana would be red as usual in November.

But the Obama campaign kept chugging. It opened a real office, with a roof this time, at the north edge of the county. Then, amazingly, it opened a second one, in Franklin. This was a sort of stealth office, because it was unpaid space in another business—and the Republican building manager wouldn't allow any advertising or signs. Still, it was a place to operate from, where Oliver Harwood, the Obama operative, could stay up all night and put together "walk packets" for volunteers. (Oliver was on a year's rustication from Cornell and just back from playing soccer for an Italian league.) I was happy because I could campaign close to home, instead of making the hour round trip to the northern office. I think Obama ended up with 44 such offices in the state, compared with about half a dozen for McCain. In effect, the Obama organization took over for our moribund Democratic county committee.

A lot of money certainly was spent, just as McCain complained. The handouts and door-hangers for volunteers were glossy, up to date, and changed weekly. We had lists of targeted voters to call on, although these lists were somewhat slapdash and not always up to date. For Nov. 3 and then for Election Day itself, the door-hangers were different, and personalized with the polling places of the prospective voters—I found this fairly amazing, in views of the complexities of four-color printing and split runs.

I finished up my door-knocking on Saturday and Sunday, having reached a total of 600 doors since September plus several hundred more in the primary. For Monday and Election Day, Oliver put me in change of the volunteer walkers. I sat all day in the office, handing out packets, logging the lists back in, and making sure each volunteer was profusely thanked.

Not everything went as planned. Lists and door-hangers had been prepared for parts of the county so remote than even I barely knew where they were. "We're going to get to every one of them!" Oliver exclaimed. I knew better, but played along—on my tally sheet these were grouped as "Outer Darkness." Oliver gave up about noon and had the phone bank call them instead.

There was also something called the Houdini Operation, at three polling places where Republican shenanigans were feared (although none developed). The Obama camp had poll book watchers at these, who were also supposed to listen for voters' names as they signed in, then phone these to a central location. In turn, someone there would notify our local office so that we could tailor our voter contacts minute by minute and not call people who had already voted. This was too much! The plan broke down and was abandoned by 10 a.m., but just the fact that someone had thought it up and given it a try was awe-inspiring.

Probably the weakest part of the effort was a shortage of volunteers. Some of the better ones were working the polls. I was stuck in the office doing bookkeeping. People wandered in on no particular schedule, had packets and maps thrust into their hands, and were shooed out the door.

I got to the office at 4:45 a.m. to get the packets organized in some rational way. Rich, my chief assistant (from whose computer business we were operating), arrived an hour later and spent the next two hours trying to wake up. "I never knew 5 o'clock came twice a day," he groaned. But he and his buddy Mike eventually got moving and by 3 p.m. had covered five walk/drive areas all by themselves. By then I was down to one undistributed packet (other than the abandoned ones in Outer Darkness), and so went to work on Rich and Mike to do one more run.

"There are two voters up on Graham Road who are sitting home wondering why nobody from Obama has been by," I told them. "As Graham Road goes, so goes the nation." Pissing and moaning, they went back to work. (There are some parallels here with motivating reporters.)

And then it was all over and gone, like Shakespeare's great globe itself, without a wrack left behind. I don't even have a souvenir Obama button, having given mine away to an eager voter on the last day. Already it's hard to remember what I was doing last Saturday, and everything else is fading—all the campaign craziness, the punditry, Tina Fey, the hate mail from the Republican state GOP, and the idiocy of our local county clerk (in charge of ensuring a fair election), who was caught leaving fliers on her employees' desks, describing Obama as "a young black Adolf Hitler." Ah, Indiana—you may look blue for now, but you've still got a lot of red in your veins.

P.S. The day after the election I got a nice e-mail thank-you note from Barack for all my work. We are on a first-name basis now. I think I'll apply for a post as chargé d'affaires in some small, warm country.

TEN WEEKS WITH THE CIRCUS
[A SUMMER IN WASHINGTON]

IN MAY 1993 I started on what would be a 15-month odyssey—the first ten weeks as a "faculty intern" copy-editor for the Scripps Howard News Service in Washington D.C., the remaining time as a senior editor for the Free China Journal *in Taipei. What follows are excerpts of letters from the time in Washington—starting with my arrival at Apt. 7-B in a rooming house at 2126 R St. NW, not far from Dupont Circle. The letters, unless otherwise noted, are to Karen. I've adapted the title of the series from James Otis's Victorian classic,* Toby Tyler or Ten Weeks with a Circus, *about a boy who runs away from home. The items are arranged chronologically within sections, but not overall.*

ARRIVAL

(May 21) So where exactly am I? Imagine me sitting at a card table in a most oddly shaped room, since it has (by my best count) at least six walls. It is very much the broom closet that Kelley [the usual occupant, daughter of a colleague at Franklin College] described, but quite adequate. It is roughly triangular, about 11 feet at the widest point and narrowing to six feet at the closet end. A good place to store arrowheads. Two windows (these are second-floor ones) look out over shady, busy Florida Avenue.

Furnishings: a ramshackle chest of drawers, a cement-block-and-boards bookcase, a small fridge, a boom box with a large collection of tapes, a wok, a radiator (certainly unnecessary in a D.C. summer), and a window fan (which will be highly necessary). Finally, there is the card table at which I'm typing and the "sofa" on

145

which I'm sitting, which folds out into a very comfortable futon/bed. This is much better than I expected, so I am a happy camper. There is also the telephone and a TV with the tiniest screen I've ever seen—no more than five inches on the diagonal. In short, a typical grad student's room.

Well, not quite. A huge Chinese Communist flag covers most of the wall above the futon. At least I think this is what it is. At any rate, it's bright red and has five stars in the corner.

By pulling the card table to one side of the room and hoisting one side of the table over the radiator, there is room to unfold the futon/bed. My big worry had been that I might have to fold up the card table in order to sleep, but no worry. Everything fits. I will be very happy here for the next 10 weeks (or at least as happy as I can be without you on the premises). . . .

Kelley left me adequate space, but her stuff still fills half the closet, and there are mementos everywhere, from the Mexican sombrero on top of the wok, to the photos on the mirror, to the little bunch of dried roses tacked to the top of one window frame. I feel something of an intruder and will try not to disturb the ambiance too much. However, your photo is now on the dresser and my books are spread out on the shelves.

Moving out from the room (this is the Marcel Proust approach—start with the writer at his table and expand to the wide world) there's a narrow, fairly dark hallway with the bath at the far end. Stairways go down from the center of the hall in both directions, one of them ending in a small entrance hall with a table where mail is laid out. Old chromos on the walls, Italian scenes. This whole place looks a lot like European hotels we've stayed at—much like Athens, a step up from Henry-the-Whatever in Paris.

The other staircase leads to the first floor and then on to the basement kitchen, a cheerful room with a big table and all kinds of equipment. There seem to be about 12 apartments in the building's three floors.

The house is a slightly shabby (no, a lot shabby) gray brick, on a narrow street (R) shaded by maples and a big locust. It's in the sharp angle created by R and Florida, right where we placed it on the map. The Ritz-Carlton is about three blocks away, on Massachusetts Avenue. This is not the Ritz-Carlton, but the neighborhood is lovely. Much shade (very southern), the brick sidewalks undulate gently, the houses have an air of gentle decay.

I am on Third World Embassy Row, with Mali just next door, Tanzania and Brazil on the next corner, the Mariana Islands a block over, and the Republica Dominicana Embajada a few steps beyond that. A little further on, 22nd Street ends in a tiny park with steps and a lion's-head fountain at the top, gushing into a pool. Two women were eating their lunches there when I passed this afternoon.

As I was returning, a Lincoln Continental pulled up at the Mali Embassy and the driver handed out a distinguished gentleman who flowed up the steps and in the front door. It must have been the ambassador—no one else could have given such an impression of carrying the weight of Africa on his shoulders, and so gracefully. (The car license was QT 001.)

There will be a lot to explore around here. A galley of Inuit art is just across the street, and the Phillips gallery is around the corner. A high-toned restaurant, "Nora," is cattycorner, but since entrees start at $20 I do not expect to be patronizing it much. There are many, many flower stands. I need a vase. Have found the Metro stop over on Connecticut. Also a bookstore that looks good (just looking). Tomorrow, I'll push farther out, locate Scripps Howard, and maybe do some sight-seeing.

HOUSEMATES

(June 20) First, something about the "housemates" (they actually refer to themselves that way). Kelley and Marianna said I would like them, and I certainly have—just some very nice people, who seem to have adopted me, to have accepted me as an older version, but basically okay. (Part of this may be the mystery element—"What IS he typing all the time?")

The ones I see most often are George Harrell, Tim Yarling, Nicole Fleck (Kelley's friend), and the Aly Khan brothers, Fuad—the writer—and his younger brother, Saad. Pakistanis. Tim is the house manager, who keeps getting my free parking permit renewed—this week he went to a different police station, which should be good for two more weeks, plus a two-week renewal. By that time, he will have been forgotten at Police Station #1 and he can start the cycle over there. (Not much record seems to be kept of these permits—at any rate, I'm now parked for the week just a couple of doors down the block on R Street.)

I haven't quite figured out what Tim does for a living. He and George (sort of his assistant manager) do a lot of serious long-distance running; I see them mornings in running gear with their numbers pinned on, going off to wherever the weekend's event is. Yesterday it was about 10,000 runners on Pennsylvania Avenue doing a "run for the cure" for breast cancer. Tim and George finished in the top few hundred.

Tim looks to be about 30. George is in his early 20s—holds a couple of jobs including one as a gopher for a law firm (he is a law student). Also works as a weekend volunteer at the Phillips Collection; hence his help in getting me the cut-rate membership. I believe he told his bosses that I was his father. A good guy and a wicked sense of humor—he and our Mike would play off well together.

I realized yesterday that there is a kind of test to be passed as a housemate, and the story goes back about a week to a supper gathering in the kitchen one night at which one of the house residents (Gary) made some fairly mild but still pretty offensive sexual innuendoes directed at Nicole, who said nothing but went on eating. Nobody else said anything—I'm thinking, "Gary, you're a real jerk." More recently, however, I was in on a conversation in which Gary was pretty much read out as a housemate—sort of "how did we ever let this guy in?"

So I think the housemates are a good bunch and am pleased, even honored, to be a short-term member. A sort of "adjunct housemate"? It's always nice to find friends in a new place—I heard someone hailing me in the bakery yesterday morning, and it was Nicole, who came over to chat about her weekend trip to New York. When I went over to the Phillips yesterday, George was on the information desk—think I got points for actually using the membership that he went out of his way to get for me.

There are other housemates seen now and then. Mateo is in and out. Deb, Jenny, Teri Thomas, Steve Martin (no, not that one), and Ilona, who does plies on the rail by the front step. A couple I never see, but they apparently pick up their mail.

A NIGHT OUT

(June 20) The essay on the housemates was by way of introduction to last night's excursion to *Much Ado About Nothing*. Five of us started out about 6 p.m. with picnic lunches—Tim, George, Saad Ali Khan, moi, and Alisa, whom Tim and George had met on yesterday's run. We rode the bus out to Carter-Barron, got there too late to picnic in the park, rendezvoused with several other friends of George's, and took over a small block of seats.

Picnic lunches were then served, with Alisa carving up a loaf of bread and some of the hottest cheese I've ever eaten. The play began. So did thunder—rolls and rolls of it. And then came the rain. Umbrellas went up everywhere, a festive sight, and the audience hunkered down for a rain delay. We did, too, and someone produced a bottle of Chablis.

After 20 minutes or so, the rain got worse and the performance was cancelled, but none of our group seemed in any hurry to leave, and there was still Chablis left. We eventually cleared out with the last stragglers, and a group decision was made to go to a bar in Adams-Morgan and drink beer. George's friends had someplace else to go, but the housemates plus Alisa got back on the bus and headed for A-M. Along the way it was decided to skip the bar scene (this is really not a serious drinking crowd), buy a six-pack, and go to Alisa's apartment. Which we did—a nice place, and she turned on "the A/C" in our honor. (Nobody says "air-conditioning" in Washington—it's always just "A/C" and critically important to life.)

Tucked under the apartment door was a copy of "Lies of Our Times," the muck-raking critique of the *New York Times*. Points were made by yrs truly with Alisa, who was surprised, I think, that an old person would know about a sort of counter-culture magazine.

Turns out that Alisa is rather seriously counter-culture herself, professes anarchism, and believes society is threatened by a giant conspiracy of 300 special interests—we stopped just short of getting to the Trilateral Commission and the Bilderbergers, but would have gotten there eventually. All this from a wisp of a girl who looks like she ought to be enrolling as a freshman at Franklin College—in fact she's employed on some sort of EPA waste-management project.

I did what I generally do—recommended reading matter, including Bill Greider's *Who Will Tell the People?* Also promised to try to find her a copy of an old *St. Louis Journalism Review* with its annual article on the "10 best-censored stories of the year." Here is where you come in, love. Go see John and/or Ellen [at the journalism school] and find the *SLJR*—should be one in Ellen's back-copy file in 022. If you can find it quickly, bring it along when you come to Virginia, and I'll pass it on to the anar-chist-in-training. (Youth, it's wonderful, isn't it? Fin-de-siècle idealism.)

George helped the discussion along by putting on his law-yer's hat and professing to believe that officials *should* lie to the public—"after all, how else can you get anything done?"—and got the desired rise out of Alisa. All of this very congenial and funny.

Alisa's roommate showed up *mit* boyfriend and the four of us left (one beer apiece having been drunk) and walked home through Adams-Morgan at midnight, with some very strange people on the street. The café scene was in full blast (this is the party area of Washington). It went by too fast for me to absorb much, but I did notice some women (?) without a whole lot on except knee-high boots, doing some sort of performance on the sidewalk. It wasn't Indianapolis, Edna.

[I liked Alisa, wanted to talk to her some more, and invited her out for coffee. She showed up as scheduled, but by the time we had ordered, a host of housemates and friends had piled into the coffee shop, and it turned into a group event. It was fun and I was happy to see them—but I had a distinct feeling that we were being chaperoned!]

STARTING WORK

(May 24, to Colin) Your pappy is now a card-carrying member of the Washington press corps. One of the things I did on the first day of work was to go over to the Capitol (with a guy from Scripps Howard) and get a press badge that admits me to the Senate and House galleries and adjacent telephones and work space. I'll probably never be actually working over there, but I am ACCREDITED!

The S-H man actually took two of us over—the other person was Marjona Duering, who works for PAP, the Polish version of Associated Press, and who is at Scripps Howard through June on some sort of fellowship. She is just a couple of years out of school and even greener in Washington than I am—very nervous but being brave. English passable but not great. She's likeable, though, and will do fine.

They kicked a poor intern, Jennifer Maddox, out of her desk for me, but she was very gracious about it—and in fact will only be here another week or two. She's a Smith College graduate of a few months back, who apparently just showed up and was hired. We swapped stories about college newspapers—she was news editor for the paper at Smith.

Scripps Howard seems (on the basis of one day's experience) to be a good place to work. Pleasant, modern office on the top floor (10th) of a downtown office building. People were very helpful, came around to introduce themselves and say, "Be nice to my copy." The office is a mixture of editors and reporters, pretty much like any city newsroom. Physically, the place is about the same size as the *C-J* newsroom, which means nothing to you but will to Mom. About the same number of people working there, too.

I saw a senator! In fact rode the little Congressional subway train with him—Dennis DeConcini of N. Mex.

The office uses an Atex computer system, same as the *C-J*, so I felt right at home. There are some new commands, queues, directories, etc., to learn, but basically nothing I haven't encountered before. Should be fully up to speed in a day or two. I edited half a dozen longish stories today, which was probably more than they expected me to do.

Got there at 8:30 a.m., as per instructions, and found only two other people in the office. One of them steered me to the coffee pot, and in a few minutes some other staffers showed up and got me started on the computer. Worked along until about 2 (with time out for the trip to the "Hill," as we say here in Washington), and then went out and got a hot dog from a sidewalk stand. There are some restaurants in the neighborhood (the "Lunch Box" seems popular). But a hot dog is usually enough for me. There doesn't seem to be any going-to-lunch culture in the office; people seem to drift in and out on their own schedules. Neither does there seem to be a lot of socializing in the newsroom, at least among editors.

As in most newsrooms, copyeditors are a solitary bunch who come in, do their work, and go home.

Am seeing a little more of the seamy side of Washington— Monday brought out a lot of panhandlers, who thrust paper cups at people as they go by. Most (me, too) just go on by. One homeless person was wrapped up in a blanket on a bench near Dupont Circle as I walked to work this morning. Aside from a few things like that, the parts of Washington I see are pleasant and people are friendly—not the hard edge one encounters in New York.

(May 25) My immediate boss, Al Thompson, has about figured out I'm not a rookie—told me this afternoon to go into the directory and pick out what I wanted to edit. I seized on one about a new book which proposes that Nazism was rooted in some teachings of Luther. It was 1,500 words and Al suggested "under 1,000, if you can." Kein problem, Herr Oberdienstfuhrer, 955 it is. Hope that's close enough.

Other copyeditors besides Al and me: Mark Wood, who toils at his desk but says little; Pam Reeves, a lovely lady who has a son Colin; and managing editor Dale McFeatters, a big, funny, slightly raucous sort—I like him a lot. All in all, a happy crew. The running banter today was about a pompous columnist who called in to complain about "what that girl on the desk did to my copy." The "girl" was Pam, who was given a hard time and who says, "Just wait!"

(May 26) I'm now three days into the Scripps Howard experience, and it's going fine. Most of what I did today was whacking good long stories into good shorter ones. Al threw me a 4,200-worder, a novel by wire-service standards, and I reduced it to 2,450 without losing much information or flavor. I hope the reader will not even know I was there. Spent part of the morning doing the weekly digest of editorials—a chore but easier than trying to figure out what the *Frankfurter Allgemeine* was saying, back in UPI days.

Chatted with the White House correspondent, Ann McFeatters (Dale's wife), for a moment today. Told her I liked her use of
"unfired" to describe the rowback on the White House travel office. She said she debated between "unfired" and "defired."

I tune in on a lot of conversations—fun to hear reporters talking about their frustrations with covering high-ranking officials.
It's not much different from listening to reporters gripe about the
mayor and the city council.

(May 27) Today I learned how to use the telephone system!
And how to make printouts! And heard Dan Thomasson, the chief
editor, bawl out a hapless reporter!

Thomasson is not much in evidence, but obviously reads the
wire—and came out this afternoon to complain that a political
story had a dull lead and would never be read. The offending reporter was summoned and said he wrote a flat lead "to be fair."
"Fine," Dan said, "except nobody is going to read it. Punch it up."
It evidently was an Army-related story, because he added, "If I
was the Army PIO and read this, I'd think, 'Fine, this guy isn't
going to give us any trouble.'" Dan has the good old wire-service,
beat-the-competition mentality, and as a wire-service vet I totally
agreed (although as an ethicist there might be an occasional
qualm).

There is simply all the difference in the world between
watching Washington from Indiana and watching it from Washington. Politics and government are in the air in the most immediate, vivid way—in part because the newspapers and other media
hang on every development and in part because reporters are
strolling in and out with word on what happened 10 minutes ago
at Sen. So-and-So's news conference. Mary Diebel walked by this
afternoon and remarked, "I just came from the food fight between
the Supreme Court and the Library of Congress." This was over
the release of Justice Marshall's papers, which has been a big
brouhaha here—I don't suppose Indianapolis has given a damn.

I can see how easy it is to slip into the Beltway mentality. The big news tonight will be what happens with Clinton's budget bill—the local media are whooping it up as Clinton's last chance to avoid a failed presidency. There's a real attitude that he's lost it (if he ever had it)—but no doubt a favorable vote will reverse all that.

If I were to take up Washington corresponding, I'd certainly want to carry around a supply of Elmer Davis/Hoosier-type smart pills and take them frequently. I could get tired of the politics-as-a-game mentality real quickly.

Chinese lessons start next Wednesday.

MR. GREAT KNOWLEDGE

One of my aims in Washington was to start learning Chinese, in preparation for going to a job in Taiwan at the end of the summer. Therefore I signed up for a course at Wong's Chinese Language School and Boxing Academy in a distant part of the capital.

(**June 2**) Had my first Chinese lesson today with Master Yang (actually a young guy who's a student of comparative religions at the University of Maryland and is doing this on his summer break). Seems very nice and has a beautiful speaking voice. He also has a certain sense of fun—he drew the character for rice today and commented that it bears some resemblance to the Union Jack, which is known among Chinese as the "rice flag." I'll have to spring that on Yu-long [Prof. Yu-long Ling] at the first opportunity.

Lessons will be at 6 on Thursday and 2:30 on Saturday; I've already explained that I'll have to cut the last Saturday in June, but all seems flexible. I was the only student today, so this may turn out to be tutoring. I have the feeling that Master Yang and Gina, the business brains of the operation, may be flying by the seat of their pants. Anyway, it's a nice house with big airy rooms and polished floors on which, I suppose, martial arts are conducted at other times. Master Yang is a Taipei native and actually knows of the *Free China Journal*.

It takes about 20 minutes to get to school from Scripps Howard. Down the street to the Farragut subway stop and then about seven stops to Potomac. Coming back I can get to Dupont Circle with an easy transfer at Metro Central, a cavernous place with two enormous intersecting tunnels. It feels like Moonbase Alpha. Coming up at Dupont is an experience; the escalator is even longer and steeper than the "rabbit hole" near our hotel in Rome. The Metro appears to be a very deep subway in spots.

This was the day I felt I turned the corner at Scripps Howard. Edited like a demon all day, made no mistakes (that I know of), and I think impressed Al by knowing that Malcolm Baldrige is spelled without a second "d." (He didn't know it.)

(June 5) Master Yang gives no quarter. He's a good teacher and also a purist who doesn't much like going through the English transliterations. So we're already starting to go directly from Chinese characters to the spoken word.

He drilled me today for 20 minutes on the numbers one through eight, jotting the Chinese characters on the board and having me pronounce them. And not just in order—oh no, he mixed them up! This is the way to do it, of course—look at the character and say it, without mentally translating, either into the English or into the English transliterations ("pin-yin"). But my tongue was hanging out by the end of the lesson. He seemed pleased and complimented me on my memory and pronunciation.

He also had worked out a Chinese name for me, as follows:

貝 浩 聞

This is pronounced (roughly) "Bay How Wun," and it means "Mr. Great Knowledge." Obviously, Mr. Yang is a fine judge of character. He is a purist in other ways, too, and insists that the Chinese characters be drawn in precise ways, up and down, left to right. If the strokes are not made just that way, "you're not really writing Chinese," he says. I am impressed and will try to be worthy of my new name. (I am not to be the only student in the class; a second person will be there for Saturday afternoon's session.)

Chinese has driven everything else out of my head.

My fellow student is a Karen, and her pronunciation makes mine look good. She's a college graduate of a year or so ago, now working in some civilian job for the Navy while she tries to get accepted for law school. Nice kid who reminds me of a lot of Franklin College students. Kiddie Karate was running late today, so Gina shunted us off to a basement room, saying, "I hope you don't mind cats." There were about four very pretty ones.

(June 13) Mr. Yang loaded me up yesterday—I was the only student who showed, so he piled it on and I learned a lot. Can now say, "My brother doesn't have 237 boxes," in case the need for that ever comes up in conversation.

> *I was of course, pretty "set up" about being Mr. Great Knowledge and mentioned that fact several times after arriving in Taipei. A friend finally took me aside and said, "You know, Bill, those characters can be interpreted another way, as Mr. Know-It-All."*

AN EDITOR'S LIFE

(June 7) This was the day I earned my pay at Scripps Howard. Went in before 9 and did solid editing until 6. College teachers aren't used to honest labor. Much of the day was routine work, but toward late afternoon the library began coming through with my child-support project stuff—about 15,000 words all run together in one humongous piece with lots of garble. This was retrieved off the DataTimes network. I got the pieces separated, found they had sent a lot of stuff I hadn't asked for, and made a start on cutting the package down to 3,500-4,000 words.

(June 9, to Colin) As I told Mom on the phone just now, they've made me a sort of projects person, when they have some huge pile of copy that needs to be whipped into a manageable package for the wire. They try to offer clients one such package every day—I noticed that for next week three of the six packages are ones I put together. That's fine—I'd rather do those kinds of projects than piddle around with a bunch of little stories or gardening columns.

(June 14) Have acquired another project, editing material from something called the Russian Daily News Wire. This is a group of Russians and Americans (ex-spooks?) who are trying to make it in the news business. Dale McFeatters agreed to distribute some of their stuff over our wire and was regretting it, I think. The Russians write not the English so good. Enter your husband, who just <u>loves</u> to unmangle copy. I rewrote their first piece (on the political situation in Kalmykia). They loved it, Dale loved it, and I now have the job regularly. Should be fun.

I'm getting to like the Scripps Howard crew a lot—even if they don't talk a lot or lunch together. Pam Reeves is very nice— I've been given the desk next to her at least for this week. She was on the phone to a child at home this afternoon: "No, I told you no, and you do what I say, and that's the end of the discussion." Told her I'd heard <u>that</u> conversation before.

(July 3) Funny story. Robert Packwood (the senator of sexual-harassment ill fame) is in trouble again, for sending letters to Jewish constituents intimating that he also is Jewish (with references to "our" homeland, etc.). He's actually a Unitarian. Dale McFeatters's comment: "Maybe the Unitarians are the lost tribe?"

(July 10) People's faith in copyeditors is touching. Andy Schneider walked by yesterday and said, "What county is Athens. Ga., in?" Mr. Great Knowledge didn't know! He does now. It's Athens County, and he'll never forget it.

(July 11) It's been good to have the Scripps Howard experience as a trial run for the "real world." Demanding as academia is, in some ways it's a soft touch. I'll go to Taipei with renewed confidence that I can hold my own in the workplace. This reminds me of a skirmish at SH recently—short, fairly friendly, but pointed—between ME Dale McFeatters and Joan Lowy, the Congressional reporter:

> **Dale:** Joan, when will that story be done?
> **Joan:** I'm working on it.
> **Dale:** Well, Joan, I need to sked it—can you give me an idea of when it will be in and how long?
> **Joan:** I <u>said</u>, you'll get it when I'm done with it.
> **Dale:** (Loudly, to the room) Deskers, Joan says her story will be in when she's damn good and ready!

As I sit here free-associating, I'm reminded of a book review I edited last week by the Washington rep of one of our client papers. The review was awful—pompous, stuffy, badly written. The author ended by indulging himself in some pedantry about "the American tendency" to stick "up" on the ends of verbs, "as in that piece of second-rate hymnody, 'Rise Up, O Men of God.'" That happens to be a grand hymn, and the idea of singing "Rise, O Men of God" is absolutely silly. I asked another editor how he handles this reviewer. His response: "I try to avoid him. He writes pretentious crap."

(July 12) A good day at the great metropolitan news service. Not too strenuous—handled 23 stories, somewhat off the peak pace of about 30.

Handled a review of a new coffee-table book about U.S. presidents and baseball. The reviewer says William Howard Taft threw out the opening-day ball "like a sea lion throwing a javelin." Isn't that wonderful?

(July 17) Dale McFeatters called the staff to the daily meeting yesterday with, "Let's go conspire. Time to plot and scheme. Time to spin gold out of flax." You would like Dale.

Vignettes of Washington

(May 30) The cookout last night in front of the house was fun. Joe, a former house manager, had invited a young couple who are friends of his. They brought along a friend of *theirs*, visiting from New York. A Belgian couple showed up (he's interning at the World Bank). Several house residents arrived, including Tim the manager with chances on the Indianapolis 500. A good time had by all—lots of hot dogs and hamburgers done over the grill, pop, ice cream, pasta salad, etc., etc. This was all set up on the sidewalk in front of the house; passersby simply walked around us. Only hazard was an occasional hit from the huge mulberry tree in front of the house, which litters the walk and steps badly.

Note from yesterday: As the 1st Baptist service began, I was startled to see two flag-bearers coming down the aisle, one carrying a Chinese banner (just like the one hanging over my futon). But there hadn't been a coup; it was just the start of a long procession of national flags, in honor of the pentacostal message to go into all nations. If you ask me, 1st Baptist puts on too many airs.

(June 7) Still living in the glow of the Phillips Collection today. Mentioned the open house to Pam Reeves and she suggested a couple of other good exhibits—her husband is an art writer. Also talked some today with B.J. Cutler, the editor who does so much wandering around the office. He's a former correspondent in Russia and the ex-editor of the Paris *Herald-Tribune*—knew Henry Shapiro in Moscow, my old boss Bill Long, and other UPI stalwarts. I think he walks to meditate—he seems like a gentle, philosophic man (as Uncle Bill once described John Hurst Adams on the *Franklin Star*.)

(June 8) On the way home today, two women, in their 20s, breezed by, and I heard one of them say, ". . . and when he went to Moldova, it was just another example of . . . ." And then she was out of earshot. Now I'll wonder all evening why anyone would go to Moldova, and what it might be an example of. Impetuousness? Insensitivity? Of course she may just have been discussing foreign policy, but I don't think so—there was a definite note of personal grievance.

The beggars are everyplace, with paper cups, asking for "friendly change." Most are not aggressive, but I decided I could not go through the summer and brag about never having given anything. So I plunk down a quarter for the fellow outside the Chesapeake Bagel Bakery each morning, when he's there. (He doesn't come out in the rain.) So I salve my conscience.

I have a squirrel (or a chipmunk) in the oak tree outside my window. Also a lot of spatzies—they probably like the mulberries. I learned a new name for sparrows yesterday from a story on the wire—LBJs, Little Brown Jobs.

(June 17) Woman at the bakery today ordering "a poppy and veggie" to go." Translation: Poppyseed bagel with vegetable spread. Roses are gone, having given way to marigolds, shasta daisies, and a beautiful big clump of hollyhocks just down the street. Dupont Circle changes with the time of day; in the morning there are homeless wrapped in blankets and sleeping on the benches—coming home this afternoon there were lots of people playing chess on permanent tables, plus what appeared to be a bicycle tour taking a break.

(July 2) Friday! Three-day weekend! The housemates will be barbecuing out front Sunday afternoon—I'm invited to that and to trail along afterward for the fireworks on the Mall. BYOHD (Bring Your Own Hot Dogs).

(July 5) I mentioned on the phone talking at the 4th celebration with the Burmese woman who works for the Japanese bank, but didn't tell you that she was trapped for two hours in the World Trade Center, on about the 40th floor. [Note: This was the 1993 bombing.] She said they assumed fire but didn't know if it was above or below them. She suffered some smoke inhalation.

The 4th was a beautiful night in Washington. We walked past the lighted White House. The lawn between the huge trees was also lighted—by hundreds of fireflies. Looked like our back garden.

(July 9) Disaster! Catastrophe! Major threat to stability!

Somebody broke the house coffee pot last night—I just found the pieces in the trash. I think my departing contribution to 2126 will be a new one, even though not many of the housemates drink coffee. Even if only *one* does, I'll have saved that one from a caffeine fit.

I plan to go visit a new print exhibition at the Phillips, which has just replaced the Van Gogh-Lautrec-Picassos. Was happy to see that my less-than-enthusiastic view of August Vincent Tack was agreed with this week by a D.C. art critic, who described "his billowy, too-sweet abstractions, which are displayed in virtually no other museum in the world." (The critic did give the Phillips high marks for its loyalty to its founder, who was ga-ga about Tack.)

(July 10) Had a pleasant after-work drink yesterday with Maria Marron, the other intern. We kicked Scripps Howard around, good and bad points. She's quintessential Irish—a nice brogue and says "Mother Divine!" for emphasis. We're both down to three weeks at S-H, then she's off for Texas.

(July 11) The weather is a little more bearable today—I went out to church in shirt sleeves. As I walked down 17th Street, a clamor of bells broke out. I thought it might be change-ringing, but it was more like Venice on a Sunday morning, just a lot of loud, crashing, joyful bells. I followed them to the Foundry United Methodist Church, then (in a churchy mood) went on to 1st Baptist, where the service ended with one of my favorite hymns, Slane ("Be Thou My Vision")—when I shuffle off, I want that sung as a finale by a real go-to-hell contralto. . . .

What's wrong with people? An interesting article came across the desk last week, proposing that because we lack community every minor slight becomes an assault on one's identity. On the other hand, maybe it's just the hot weather. About 2:30 this morning, over in the wild-and-woolly Shaw neighborhood, 400 people were in a tiny dance hall with no air-conditioning. Somebody bumped a 16-year-old and he shot five people, two of them critically.

(July 12) Home to a mostly unintelligible but clearly obscene phone call on the answering machine—woman's voice. This _is_ the age of equal opportunity, isn't it?

UNTOLD STORIES

Letters can tell a day-to-day story, but they tend to dwell on the personal and lack wider context.

My summer with Scripps Howard was also the first summer of the Clinton administration, but the only two major news events I find mentioned in letters are Clinton's push for a balanced budget and "Travelgate," an investigation of alleged irregularities in the White House travel office. A sensation of the summer, the suicide of White House Counsel Vincent Foster on July 20, is not mentioned at all.

Although Bill Clinton had been in office only half a year, much of the press corps seemed ready to write him off as a failed president—which struck me as slightly premature. On June 14, I wrote: "Watched the presentation of the new SCOTUS justice today, including Clinton's temper tantrum at Brit Hume's quite reasonable question. Ann McFeatters came in later and said Clinton apparently just couldn't take any sour note being introduced in his big day. Ann says he still has no understanding of why the $200 haircut was such a big deal—the prevailing feeling here certainly is that he's in way over his head. But of course this is just those terrible journalists talking."

Although Clinton had some notable failures, like health care, he passed his comprehensive budget reform act without a single

Republican vote (remind you of anybody?), presided over the longest peacetime economic boom in U.S. history, was re-elected in 1996, and left office with a budget surplus. Monica Lewinsky had not yet been heard of.

There were other contexts, including family ones. Our son David married Connie Godwin in June at Hampton, Va. Karen and Colin flew out and I drove down for the event. Later Karen and Colin came to Washington for several days before flying back to Indiana. (Karen then returned in late July to see me off for Taiwan and drive the car home.)

There was the context of a host of friends, relatives, and colleagues who wrote letters (this was before the days of widespread e-mail) and formed a support network that helped keep me afloat in Washington and Taiwan. But of course one person was key to this.

As I edit technical books these days, I've become aware of a certain cliché of acknowledgments—the obligatory bow to the writer's wife or girl friend, with emphasis on her love and patience. Like most clichés, it's true, and I don't doubt the sentiment. But a line or two hardly seems adequate credit for what I know has gone on. And I know it because it is the story of my life.

From the day the possibility was raised of an extended absence from home, Karen's attitude was "go for it." And while I went for it, she stayed home and saw Colin through his senior year in high school, kept our bills paid, and thawed the pipes after the coldest night in Indiana history, 36 below on January 16, 1994. (I was grouching, meanwhile, about temperatures in the plus-50s in Taipei.) When she came to visit in February 1994, she lugged a toaster oven all the way across the Pacific so I could bake bread and apple pies.

And most of all, she wrote letters—nearly every day. She disparages her skill at that, but they were the most welcome letters I've ever received—a lifeline I could not have lived without.

In this series of sketches, I've quoted only a few of the letters that went from 2126 R Street in Washington to 920 Walnut St. in Franklin, and none of those that came back. Among those un-quoted are love letters, intended only for the recipient. She and I were both getting our minds around the idea of our first substantial separation in more than 30 years of a close marriage. It is not a unique situation—military families, to name only one group, deal with such separations routinely. Had she not supported the idea, I could not—would not—have run away from home to places that opened the world to me in new and surprising ways. When we talk about this time and congratulate ourselves on the strength of our marriage, we both add "but let's never do this again." I have noticed that she invariably says it first.

I looked carefully through all the Washington letters to see if there was one I could include that would somehow catch the flavor of our time apart, without being soppy about it (I don't mind being soppy, just not for publication). And I think I have found one. It was a note written on June 30, just after Karen had gone back to Indiana after the wedding, and it goes like this:

"Dearest Kit—You're not even home yet, and I already miss you and feel blue—will pull myself together and write a note so you'll have something in the mail (probably after July 4).

"Came home and blew myself to an Italian dinner over on Conn Ave (not the place you saw, I think). Came back to the room, unpacked everything, unwrapped my new underwear, and rolled it. See how despondent I am?

"It was wonderful having you here—Colin, too. My life has a big hole in it when you're not close. I'll now begin marking off the days until the end of July."

When these selections were first assembled (for my blog) it was May 2010, and we were preparing to go back to Taipei—together this time. We planned to stay at a hotel not far from my top-floor apartment near the Taipei Jade Market. We expected to buy a little jade, have supper at the restaurant where a celebrating party popped a champagne cork into Karen's coffee, and walk hand-in-hand on Renai-Lu, where on Valentine's Day, 1994, a Chinese girl turned and handed Karen the red rose her boyfriend had just given her.

In the spring of 1994, after Karen had gone home from her month's visit, I wrote a brief poem called "Sign":

The Chinese sign for "listen"
includes eye, ear, and heart.
I will listen better now,
my dearest, hearing you with my eyes,
seeing you with my ears,
knowing your heart
by heart.

FORGOTTEN WRITERS

FORGOTTEN IS RELATIVE, of course. None of these writers is totally forgotten, by everybody (although one may come close). Treatises are occasionally written about them, and one or two may have societies of aficionados. One might certainly argue that Laura Riding is not forgotten at all. But they are, shall we say, quite a distance from the New York Times *best-seller list. Still, there's something about each that I like or that intrigues, and this is my effort to keep them visible a little longer.*

A NOTE ON LAURA RIDING

I encountered Laura Riding years ago in a poetry anthology, where she was notable by her absence. The compiler wrote that she had refused to allow her poems to be republished.

Well! Such reticence certainly got my attention, and I went looking for her (in pre-Google days) without a lot of success. She had renounced poetry in the 1930s and, although still living (at that time), seemed to be in deep seclusion. I found a novel she had written, *A Trojan Ending*, which struck me as peculiar and not very good, at least as a novel. Maybe as something else . . . .

Then several years ago her collected poems were reissued and I bought a copy. Good stuff, though heavy going. About that time, the poet died, in 1991 in Wabasso, Florida. Several years later still, I picked up the poems again, got more interested, and found a critical study, which supplied some biography. I put some of this together in a sketch for a literary friend, as follows:

"Riding, neé Laura Reichenthal, led an unusual life, even by the generous standards of literary behavior. A brilliant young poet in the 1920s, she had a formidable mind and a perfectionist spirit, both of which she turned to the pursuit of truth. Human beings are distinguished by mind alone, she believed, and discovering truth is the mind's only worthy activity.

"In 1929, after a strange lover's quarrel (four people seem to have been involved), she stepped from a fifth-floor window in Paris, broke her back, and was unconscious for days. Recovering, she considered that she had 'died' to the senses, and that her 'unreal' or spiritual life had begun. In the early 1930s she moved to Mallorca with the writer Robert Graves and built a circle of disciples, all of whom she eventually alienated by her uncompromising views. One of these followers, T.J. Matthews, has described her:

> *Laura's was the most brilliant mind I had ever encountered. Her brilliance, or mental force, was so dazzling and lightning-like that there was something frightening about it.*

"The same writer also took a snapshot of her appearance at this time:

> *When she was in full regalia her dignity matched and enhanced her costume, and I can't remember anyone thinking it laughable or even eccentric that on these occasions she was crowned by a tiara of gold wire that spelled LAURA.*

"In the early 1940s, having written a series of striking poems, she renounced poetry as inadequate for her pursuit of truth. Poets falsify everything, she believed, because they depend on the sensual world rather than on pure thought. She married another truth-seeker, Schuyler Jackson, and they spent the rest of their lives isolated in Florida, selling grapefruit for a time and writing a dictionary that was to pin down forever the precise meaning of English words.

"Periodically, she wrote about this work—but in such prolix and difficult prose that the reader wonders about her mental state.

When she died at 90, the dictionary was unpublished (unwritten?). The literary world had virtually forgotten her, or was only just beginning to rediscover her. She won the Bollingen Prize in 1991 for her poetry.

"Riding has no biographer [Note: Since this was written she has acquired several], but Joyce Wexler has written an acute critical study, which notes that Riding's answer to the question 'What is truth?' resembles 'other attempts to describe spiritual reality to men comfortable in physical reality.' Wexler regards Riding's later life as a tragedy—the kindest thing one can say, she suggests, is that Riding never lost her stern moral vision, or her hope that others would rally to the true and the good as she saw them."

Having written this small (and fairly uninformed) vignette for my friend, I probably should have stopped. But T. J. Matthews's descriptions had captured me, and I got several of his own books, which was a mistake. He turned out to be one of the more unpleasant writers I've encountered. He had known Riding and her circle intimately in the 1930s, and none of those "friends" fared well at his hands. Riding, in particular, came across as a vicious character, a sort of intellectual dominatrix. Matthews's final memoir was one long whine over his wasted life and spoiled talent. I dropped his books back at the library and fled. I had started assembling notes for a memoir myself—now I ripped these out of the notebook and destroyed them.

But it's hard to leave totally a literary enthusiasm, and when it turned out that Riding had finished her great lexicographical work—and that it had been published in 1997 by the University of Virginia under the editorship of William Harmon—I obtained a copy. It is not light reading or easy to summarize—in fact to attempt such a summary would do the writer grave injustice. But I can perhaps safely say that *Rational Meaning: A New Foundation for the Definition of Words* is an extraordinarily complex effort to make language behave and express not nebulous fields of meaning but intense, precise, and focused points.

169

I was encouraged that she spoke favorably of George Crabbe, the author (1816) of *English Synonymes*, as "a heroic battler in the cause of distinction of meaning." I like Crabbe myself, and have made use of his efforts to distinguish between such words as "courage" and "fortitude."

But Riding clearly was thinking of more than fine shades of dictionary definition. The deep waters swirled over me when I reached page 298 in *Rational Meaning* and read: "In treating of terms, one needs to keep a firm balance between consciousness of their relative unimportance in respect to words proper, and their importance to this unimportance."

A little further on, Riding seemed to express her own motivation with clarity, writing that "partial knowledge, partial consideration of words' meanings, partial definition in people's minds as entire definition—this produces equatings of meanings that are very seriously destructive to rationality of thought."

In the last years of her life, Riding received some overdue recognition of her place in American letters. And since her death, a lot has been written about her, and there is no longer any difficulty in finding as much as the student wants to read.

A critic, Helen Vendler—who was not enthusiastic about Riding—wrote in a different context about the "casts" of poets, using the fly fisherman's term. Some poets have a short cast, she said, and are comprehended and recognized in their own time. Others, like William Blake, have a cast that is not appreciated for many years, perhaps for centuries.

That thought, applied to Riding, strikes me as an admirable caution.

BORROW'S 'BELLE'

I've always thought that Women's Studies departments were missing a bet by not doing something with Belle Berners, the heroine of George Borrow's two novels, *Lavengro* and *The Romany Rye*.

Belle, described somewhere as "the splendid road girl," first appears near the end of *Lavengro*, Borrow's veiled autobiography of his life with gypsies. Belle is not a gypsy but has been consorting with them when she first encounters the author, during a rural traffic jam:

> *Dashing past the other horse and cart, which by this time had reached the bottom of the pass, appeared an exceedingly tall woman, or rather girl, for she could scarcely have been above eighteen; she was dressed in a tight bodice and a blue stuff gown; hat, bonnet, or cap she had none, and her hair, which was flaxen, hung down on her shoulders unconfined; her complexion was fair, and her features handsome, with a determined but open expression.*

The writer and Belle eventually go off to live side by side at a camp in a "dingle," where one of the most extraordinary love affairs in literature develops—perhaps the only time a courtship has been pressed through the lover's strenuous efforts to teach Armenian to his sweetheart.

"Sweetheart" is the wrong word. Belle is too independent and forthright to qualify for that tepid word. And there is absolutely no hanky-panky in the dingle—the couple meets over their campfire to drink tea and talk—and conduct increasingly frustrated lessons in Armenian. Belle has her own enterprises and is often away. And yet over weeks (or months, the time frame is uncertain), a sort of idyll comes to pass in the dingle: it becomes clear that these two people are in love, although both are too shy and too self-sufficient (or just stiff-necked) to admit it. The romance, if one can call it that, ends when Belle cuts it short and leaves to emigrate to America.

Borrow, a 19th Century English novelist, fits into no category. His books are hodgepodges of information and incident—

everything from horse-training to learning Chinese—and they are marred for modern readers by a violent anti-Papism. But for a reader willing to slow down and dawdle with the author along old English back roads, they have their delights, of which the first is Belle Berners.

D'Annunzio: The Flame of Life

When Gabriele D'Annunzio is remembered at all, it's as a picaresque figure from the World War I era—leader of the 1918 "Flight over Vienna" (to drop propaganda leaflets) or "duce" of the briefly independent city-state of Fiume in 1919-20.

"Poet, journalist, novelist, dramatist, daredevil," Wikipedia calls him, and he was all of those. Mussolini paid him off to keep him out of Italian politics, and borrowed some of his own tactics from him—the Brown Shirts, the balcony speeches, the florid rhetoric. As a result, D'Annunzio has come to be seen as a sort of proto-Fascist, a view which has some truth to it, but ignores his merits as a writer. (How serious a Fascist was the man whose charter for Fiume called music the fundamental principle of the state?)

D'Annunzio, born in 1863 to well-off parents, began as a child prodigy and before 1900 had compiled an impressive list of literary achievements—volumes of poetry, novels, plays, and trenchant journalism. In 1894 he began a celebrated love affair with the actress Eleonora Duse, which went on more than 15 years. His interest in aviation began when Wilbur Wright took him up for a spin in 1908, during one of Wright's tours to sell his airplane to European governments.

D'Annunzio's best writing was behind him by then, although he continued to write until his death in 1938.

One of his books has followed me through life. This was his *Il Fuoco*, of *The Flame of Life*, published in 1900. The Modern

Library edition was in my parents' library (along with such works as *The White Monk of Timbuctoo*), and I still have it.

The book is in two divisions, and the titles hint at its exalted and somewhat superheated nature: "The Epiphany of the Flame" and "The Empire of Silence." The setting is Venice and the main characters are the poet Stelio and his beloved La Foscarina, standing in for D'Annunzio and Duse. La Foscarina, the author writes,

> *. . . gathered into one deeply conscious glance all the beauty scattered so divinely through that last hour of the September twilight. In the dark, living firmament of her eyes the neighboring garlands of light, created by the oar as it dipped in the water, seemed to encircle the fiery angels that shone from afar on the towers of San Marco and of San Georgio Maggiori.*

And a page later:

> *A sound of applause burst from the Passage of San Gregorio, echoing along the Grand Canal, re-echoing in the precious discs of porphyry and serpentine adorning the house of the Darios, that stooped under their weight like a decrepit courtesan under the pomp of her jewels. The royal barge was passing.*

That kind of writing wouldn't get very far in the post-modern era, but lovers of Venice will understand the impulse. And the description of the Palazzo Dario (above right in a 1974 photo) is, in fact, absolutely accurate.

THE BLIND SEER OF AMBON

Georg Eberhard Rumphius is not a name likely to be fresh in most people's memories. This will be the briefest of sketches, mostly to remind myself not to forget about him.

It draws upon a note I wrote in August 2008 to my son Karl, asking him to do a little research. (This is not an uncommon request, since he is a librarian, and I firmly believe that all librarians get up each morning in the hope that they will receive an inquiry from me that day—why else bother getting up?) I wrote, with some abridging and editing:

"What I need is a little research on Georg Eberhard Rumphius (or Georgius Everhardus Rumphius, 1627-1702, the 'blind seer of Ambon,' as he's sometimes styled). I'll send along the titles of a couple of articles. The main one may or may not be titled, *The Ambonese Curiosity Cabinet*, but I know that it's by Tim Flannery, in the 12/16/1999 *New York Review of Books*.

"So what's this all about? It goes back to 1999 when Flannery wrote his review of Rumphius's masterwork (that's the *Curiosity Cabinet*), which was the fruit of a lifetime of scholarly labor on the island of Ambon in the Dutch East Indies. In 1999 it had just been printed in English for the first time, in a lavish edition selling for about $250. I was so captivated with Rumphius's story that I talked Ron Schuetz [the Franklin College librarian] into ordering a copy of the *Cabinet*, so I would have easy access to it. Presumably it's still in the library, unless some sub-sub put it out on the 10-cent table.

"The story behind it is an astonishing one of scholarly persistence. Rumphius went to the Far East as an agent for the Dutch East Indies Company, but there wasn't a lot to do on Ambon (now the Indonesian island of Amboina) except study natural history. There was a lot of that, though, and Rumphius got busy with observations and drawings of flora and sea life.

"Then about the time he was done, the MS was destroyed in a fire. Then he went blind from glaucoma, but kept on working with the help of his wife and assistant. Eventually the rewritten manuscript went off for publication in Holland.

"This time the ship was sunk by French privateers and the MS lost. But Rumphius had learned his lesson and had made a copy. Eventually this did reach Amsterdam, but for some arcane geopolitical reason the government wouldn't allow it to be printed. In fact it didn't get into print for about half a century after Rumphius's death.

"Had I world enough and time, I'd write a biography of Rumphius. His book is magnificent, but there may not be enough personal information about him to sustain a 'life.' In fact the *Ambonese Curiosity Cabinet* may be most of what remains of this toiler in the uttermost parts of the sea."

OUIDA: A GOOD EYE

No one reads Ouida anymore, which is a shame. When I went looking for her in the Louisville Free Public Library a few years ago, the book I wanted had to be brought up, shrink-wrapped, from a distant cellar. She doesn't rate a mention in my old Bartlett's.

Ouida was really Maria Louise Ramé (although she preferred de la Ramée), born on New Year's Day, 1839, in Bury St. Edmunds to an English mother and a French father. Over a long and colorful working life, she wrote more than 40 novels, children's books, and collections of essays and short stories. Among the best known was *Under Two Flags*, a story of the British in Algeria, which was filmed several times, including in 1922 with Rudolph Valentino and in 1936 with Ronald Colman and Claudette Colbert. Ouida died broke in Italy in 1908.

The book the library exhumed for me was *In a Winter City* (1876). In it she describes her heroine, Hilda Vorarlberg:

Lady Hilda was beyond all dispute the most beautiful woman of the rooms, she threw them all into the shade as a crown diamond throws stars of strass.

And she describes society women who

shriek over their gambling as the dawn reddens over the Alps, and know no more of the glories of earth and sky,

*of sunrise and sunset, than do the porcelain pots that
hold their paint, or the silver dressing-box that carries
their hair-dye.*

Romantic, flamboyant—but a good eye.

THE MYSTERY OF WILLIAM VAN WYCK

In a fat manila envelope on my attic shelf reposes Copy #9 of
Savonarola, by William Van Wyck, published in 1927 by Edward
W. Titus "at the sign of the Black Manikin, 4 Rue Delambre,
Montparnasse, Paris." It was inherited from my Uncle Bill, who
was a friend of Van Wyck's in Paris at that time.

Back in October, 2007 (could it have been that long ago?)
Karen and I had the Great Book Sort-Out, to reduce our inventory
to manageable size. Many of these books came from Bill's after
his death in 1984—some of them we had read, some we knew we
would never read. We needed our house back.

So Karen checked, as I recall, more than 1,200 volumes on
the website for AbeBooks, and then we drove a hard bargain with
a bookseller. (Well, perhaps not all that hard. He was more than
fair to us, and we didn't expect to get the full AbeBooks price, so
it was an amicable transaction.)

Bill had several books by Van Wyck, and we let them go.
Among them was an expensive Chaucer set he produced, with art
by Rockwell Kent. But I hung onto *Savonarola*. AbeBooks listed
only one other copy for sale, #10, which it priced at $600. I held
mine back from the sale, not so much for the value, as because it
was a genuinely rare book. Only 10 copies were printed, and it
tickled me to have one of them. My copy has a humorous inscrip-
tion from Van Wyck to Bill: "This here is the genuwine edition of
ten copies of the book published by one Tight Arse of Paris." I
liked keeping it as a memento of their friendship. Besides, I
thought, I might actually read it.

There is a mystery about Van Wyck. Who was he, anyhow, and what happened to him? He published a number of "art" books in Paris, but nothing about him personally shows up on Google, and he's not in any authors directory so far as I've been able to find. He seemed simply to disappear after the "lost generation" years. A William Van Wyck did publish a biography of Robinson Jeffers in 1938, which sounds like a subject that might interest my man. But I haven't followed up that slim lead yet.

I suspect he may have been a grandson of Augustus Van Wyck, who was a noted jurist in New York and ran for governor there unsuccessfully in 1898. Augustus died on June 9, 1922, leaving $500,000 to his son, William, who by my hypothesis would be the father of the young Bohemian in Paris. (My son Karl, who is my chief research assistant in such matters, checked probate records to discover the bequest.) If my supposition is correct, it may explain why young Bill was able to spend a rather large sum for that time in publishing very fancy books in extremely limited editions.

I probably could track him down. Amazon's "Open Library" offers an edition of *Savonarola* published by E. Benn in London, 1926. There's probably a Van Wyck family association, and *Savonarola* is dedicated to a sister, Jessica. Somewhere in the literature of the Lost Generation his name should be recorded. I wish I'd asked Uncle Bill, but Van Wyck wasn't on my radar then.

At one point, I wrote about Van Wyck on my blog. It may be that Google's spiders, in their relentless march through the world's websites, will browse my site someday and eventually put me in touch with a Van Wyck scholar. But I love a mystery. And I can wait.

UNDER A SPELL

I HAD THE EXPERIENCE recently—extremely rare—of being under a spell. It happened this way.

I had gone out walking in late afternoon along Hurricane Creek, a small stream running through parkland and behind housing developments in our small town. The legend is that the creek was named for a windstorm in pioneer days, but this may be false etymology. Roaring Run, another fast-running creek, is described in an early document as "the hurricane."

A city "greenway" trail follows Hurricane Creek from a parking lot, past tennis courts and softball fields. It then plunges into woods briefly, before emerging beside a retaining pond with a view of distant homes. Then it takes another turn through trees, meets the creek again, and ends a few yards further on at a school. I have walked it many times—from the parking lot to the school and back takes just 40 minutes.

On this summer afternoon I was alone on the trail. The creek had flooded recently and the usual walkers and cyclists hadn't yet returned in force. At the last stretch of stream before the school, nine ducks were feeding in a line along a barely submerged sandbar. I stopped still on the trail and regarded the scene.

The stream was perhaps 15 feet across, bordered on the far side by a dark patch of trees. Trees behind me cut off the view in that direction. The ducks, in their mystic number, floated in the shallows or stood exposed in the slight wash of water over the bar. Ducks are much larger birds than we usually notice. Paddling in a stream, their bodies are mostly submerged, but standing on the bar, these still seemed surprisingly plump, with swelling breast feathers modeled in painterly fashion by the muted light.

As they poked at the bar, it occurred to me that the recent flood must have been good for them, dislodging all sorts of edibles. No wonder they were fat!

It also struck me that there was something odd about the scene. It was too ordered and the light too perfect. I had never seen this many ducks, of the same size, stationed in a line along this stretch of river. The day held its breath. In the far distance a car moved silently along a hidden road, like a continuity violation in an old film. What would happen next?

Nothing dramatic, certainly. After a few minutes, five ducks broke away from one end of the line and floated downstream out of sight. A few minutes later they returned and joined the line again. After a while, a duck at the farther end paddled off upstream for 15 or 20 feet, and all but two of the others gradually segued after him. The two dawdlers continued feeding at the lower end of the bar, until—perhaps realizing they were alone—they too paddled off to rejoin the line.

Two bicyclists burst out of the woods and whizzed by me, disturbing the ducks not at all. But whatever spell there had been began to ebb. These were simply ducks, feeding along a half-submerged sandbar. I turned and walked back down the trail to my car in the parking lot.

I guessed that I had spent half an hour watching the ducks. I know, from experience in Zen sitting, that I tend to *underestimate* the passage of time. But half an hour seemed reasonable. When I reached the car, I checked my watch. Forty-five minutes had passed since I left it—just five minutes more than my usual time on the trail.

A Winter with Stendhal
1.

I HADN'T PLANNED to start a major reading project in January, but Mike and Amanda gave me a new journal for Christmas, and it was imperative that I do something with it.

Understand that this isn't just a spiral-bound notebook. It's a magnificent handmade volume, bound in real leather and secured by a leather strap that wraps around it a full three times. It has creamy pages, with deckled edges. The kids purchased it at the Rivoaltus "legatoria" on the Rialto Bridge in Venice. Wow!

I knew I had to mess it up quickly, or it would lie on a shelf untouched for years. So it's now the Italian Journal, to be used for notes on a re-reading of Stendhal's *The Charterhouse of Parma.*

This is at least my third time through *Charterhouse*, and I needed to read it on the 10-pages-a-day plan, so that I would really read it this time, not just romp through the story, lusting after Gina, the hero's delectable aunt. It also seemed like a good way to get through the depths of winter.

For those who don't know Stendhal's classic, my translation (by Richard Howard) provides a synopsis that could hardly be improved on. Daniel Mendelsohn writes in the *New York Times Book Review* of Aug. 29, 1999:

> *At first glance, the bare bones of Stendhal's story suggest not so much a literary masterpiece as a historical soap opera. The novel recounts the headstrong young Italian aristocrat Fabrice [or Fabrizio] del Dongo's attempt to make a coherent life for himself, first as a soldier in Napoleon's army and then, more cynically, as a prelate in the Roman Catholic Church; the attempts of his beautiful aunt Gina, Duchess of Sanseverina, and*

her lover, the wily (and married) Prime Minister, Count Mosca, to help establish Fabrice at court, even as Gina tries to fend off the advances of the repellent (and repellently named) Prince Ranuce-Erneste IV; Fabrice's imprisonment in the dreaded Farnese Tower for the murder of a girl friend's protector and his subsequent escape with the help of a very long rope; and his star-crossed but ultimately redemptive love affair with his jailer's beautiful (and, it must be said, rather dull) daughter, Clélia.

Howard, in his own afterword, notes that Stendhal "engages your complicity, and for that you must be all attention." Reading at 10 pages a day—no more, no less—enforces that attention. As this is written, I've just followed Fabrizio through the battle of Waterloo. And for the first time—with attention—I've figured out the time frame in which he moves, as well as the astonishing number of horses he runs through (five in three days). Of course I found again the memorable question he asks when it's all over: "Had what he had seen been a battle and, furthermore, had this battle been Waterloo?"

But I've realized only now how close the puzzled Fabrizio came to the center of the action. Stendhal places him at one point on "the sunken road," which a bit of Googling reveals as the main line of the main French-British conflict. No wonder he almost, but not quite, saw the Emperor Napoleon ride by.

So my wonderful journal is filling up with ragged, messy notes and comments on *Charterhouse*, Waterloo, and Stendhal himself, including the remark by Jean Délecluse on his intelligence and its gaps: "It is like a bullet hole in a flag. The flag keeps on flying, but through part of it you can glimpse the sky beyond."

"What's the book about?" Karen asked. "Oh . . . . life," I replied. It was pleasant later to find Dan Mendelsohn saying the same thing.

I'll get to Gina presently.

2.

THIS IS WRITTEN at roughly the halfway point of my current reading project, Stendhal's *The Charterhouse of Parma*.

The hero (anti-hero), Fabrizio del Dongo, is safely tucked away in his prison, the Farnese Tower, on a somewhat trumped-up murder charge. Gina (the Duchess Sanseverina) and her lover, Count Mosca, are just beginning to figure out what to do next, beyond bribing everyone in sight at the Tower. Gina has just explained to Mosca that she has never betrayed him with Fabrizio, that she loves her nephew simply as a pure soul. And that she will have to break (or appear to break) with Mosca in order to effect his rescue.

This is at least my third reading of Stendhal's classic, and the first reading "with attention," in translator Richard Howard's phrase. I've taken notes! I have the entire sequence of events clear before me. But I know not a bit more than in previous readings why this story fascinates or what it is really about.

Stendhal wrote it at white heat, in 52 days. He wore out his secretary, and anyone who tried to call on him was told that he had gone hunting, as indeed he had—the hunt being, in some way, for the human soul.

Balzac made the novel's success, by praising it for its virtues while all the time suggesting that it would have been even better rewritten as a novel by Balzac. Stendhal responded appreciatively, but clearly he wasn't about to adopt Balzac's suggestions for improvement. *Charterhouse* is what it is, whatever that may be. It may take a poet-translator like Richard Howard to divine what Stendhal was up to—there is some evidence that Stendhal himself did not entirely know.

As a poet, I'm struck by Howard's observation that "towers, platforms, windows, heights, imprisonment, flight, divination, hiding, vision: these images and themes weave the novel together."

And also that there is "nothing fixed" about the novel or its author. "The man was a human question mark," Nietzsche said.

In his wonderful commentary at the end of Howard's translation, Daniel Mendelsohn recalls Jean Giraudoux's 1926 novel *Pella*, in which a dead comrade asks the narrator to summarize, in a word, the theme of *Charterhouse*. In a word, because "with the dead there are no sentences."

The word, Mendelsohn says, is "life."

3.

A FEW DAYS AGO, I finished my reading (third reading, actually) of Stendhal's *The Charterhouse of Parma*, using the tested 10-pages-a-day plan. This plan is a sort of Zen discipline—I knew that over a 50-day span from Jan. 12 to March 2, there would be a time each day between early morning and midnight when I'd be immersed in Stendhal's tale of love and court intrigue in a 19th century Italian principality.

Earlier parts of this essay have described the strange appeal of this book. This is just to wind up a few loose ends. I promised to write about Gina, or the Duchess Sanseverina, who to my mind may be the most engaging woman in literature. Gina is enamored of the young hero, Fabrizio, but it's a platonic affair because Fabrizio has fallen for Clélia Conti, the daughter of his jailer in the Farnese Tower. Clélia is a nobler but much duller character than Gina—thus illustrating Stendhal's belief that we are imprinted by love, and that the process is irrational.

We meet Gina as a teen-ager, giggling at the shabby attire of a young Frenchman, Lieutenant Robert, who becomes Fabrizio's unacknowledged father. By the time the novel really gets going, after the Battle of Waterloo, Gina is the mistress of Count Mosca, the brilliant adviser to the Prince of Parma. Gina and Mosca are both eminently practical politicians. Perhaps the most delicious moment of *Charterhouse* is when Mosca suggests to Gina that she secure their fortunes and continuing relationship by marrying the ancient Duke Sanseverina-Taxis. Part of the arrangement will be that the Duke receives a coveted honor but agrees never to set foot again in Parma.

"But you realize that what you are suggesting is utterly immoral," Gina exclaims.

"No more immoral that many another thing that is done at our Court and at twenty others," Mosca replies.

So the deed is done, to everyone's satisfaction including the elderly Duke's, who showers his bride-in-absentia with money and a palazzo.

But much as Gina appreciates and even loves Count Mosca, her heart of hearts is set on Fabrizio, and when he is imprisoned (more or less wrongly) for murder, she exerts all her considerable charm and influence to get him freed.

Eventually she does, but the price of the bargain is an agreement with the new and callow Prince of Parma that she will give herself to him. Later, she argues and schemes to get out of this pact, warning the Prince that if he holds her to it she will leave his kingdom forever. The none-too-bright Prince insists, and thus gains what must be one of the most unsatisfying conquests in the history of love. Stendhal handles it discreetly in a couple of sentences:

> *Dismissed by the indignant Duchess, he [the Prince] ventured to reappear, trembling and altogether wretched, at three minutes to ten. At ten-thirty, the Duchess stepped into her carriage and left for Bologna.*

Gina pines for Fabrizio from afar, but he has been reunited with his Clélia, who has taken a vow to the Madonna never to see him again. She attempts to honor this by meeting him only in the dark, although the vow is already riddled with violations.

Fabrizio's love for her is true, though, and she has redeemed him, giving him an understanding at last of what love really is.

One of the novel's most poignant lines is Clélia's whisper to him out of the darkness of her garden: "Come in here, friend of my heart."

The Charterhouse of Parma, to which Fabrizio finally retreats, is famously not mentioned until the last three paragraphs of the book. But an argument can be made that it has been foreshadowed from the beginning. At the end, Stendhal sweeps all his characters off the stage except Mosca and the Prince. One explanation is that his publisher insisted on a shorter book. But I can't help feeling that this is just a characteristic Stendhalian abridgment—he has already, at several points, erased years in a sentence, to keep his tale moving.

So now I'm done, at least until the next reading. My paperback copy of Richard Howard's translation is wrecked, with one whole section fallen out and pencil scrawls on every page. The first 70 pages of my wonderful leatherbound journal from the Rialto Bridge in Venice are now filled with notes and a synopsis of the book. Thanks, Mike and Amanda, for the gift of the journal—I love you guys.

What's next? I think it will be alternate readings of James Morier's *Hajji Baba of Ispahan* and Sven Hedin's *My Life as an Explorer*—both from roughly the same part of the world. The first is an old favorite and the latter a Christmas present from my "adopted" granddaughter, Amber. But not today and not at 10 pages a day. I've had enough Zen reading discipline for a while.

SARAH RUDEN'S 'AENEID'

BEFORE READING The Charterhouse of Parma *on the 10-pages-a-day plan, I had tried something a little different for another reading project. The three short essays below appeared on my Green Market Press blog in the summer and fall of 2009.*

1.

(July 27) When this appears, I'll be 20 pages or so into a new translation of Vergil's *Aeneid*, by Sarah Ruden. I've adjusted my usual 10-pages-a-day system to five pages—in part because things are busy here just now, but mainly because I want to linger over Ruden's words. Her translation is exactly 295 pages of verse— astonishingly, line for line from Vergil—so I should finish up on the weekend of Sept. 19-20. I will, too. The system hasn't failed yet and has gotten me through the *King James Bible*, the *Decline and Fall of the Roman Empire* (both volumes), the *Iliad*, and *The Tale of Genji*.

The amended five-page plan also worked earlier this year with Robert Fagles's translation of the *Aeneid*, which I read with a Latin pony in hand.

Ruden's *Aeneid* is special to me, and not just because of Garry Wills' ecstatic review in the *New York Review of Books*, which called it the best English poem written on Vergil's classic since John Dryden's. No, Ruden is special for another reason.

Nearly 20 years ago, she and I were both contributing to the *Plains Poetry Journal*. It was a good if slightly quirky litmag and the contributors were competent poets—but Ruden was a genius. Here's a small sample:

THE STUBBLE BURNING

I have lost my friend. The semi trucks out there,
Their far sound in the desert of the air.
The field, the smoke dissolving in the clear
Evening above the refuse of the year.
The house, the children shouting on the lawn,
Their rhyming menaces. My friend is gone.

After reading her for a few months, I wrote a fan letter, addressing it to the Harvard classics department where she was a graduate student in Latin and Greek. I was shy about scraping acquaintance so didn't include a return address—not too surprisingly, I didn't get an answer.

It doesn't matter. To me Sarah Ruden is a pre-eminent example of early promise fulfilled. If you want me for the next two months, I'll be in the *Aeneid*, reading her again.

2.

(September 2) With a really fine book, it's a good idea to read it through a second time, right after the first.

With that in mind, I'm marching through Vergil's *Aeneid* for the second time this year. (The start of this enterprise was reported on July 27.)

The first time was tough going. I used Robert Fagles's excellent translation and Latin ponies supplied by my son Karl and Candace Moseley, wife of the Franklin College president. Moseley, a Latin teacher, has been a continuing encouragement.

The second time, with a new translation by Sarah Ruden, has been easier. I have the story down now, have reclaimed a little of the Latin, and can enjoy the excellences of Ruden, a "scholar poet," as Garry Wills calls her. Ruden's translation, the first major one by a woman, follows Vergil line for line, which makes reference to the original easy.

Ruden is modest about her work, and writes, "When the target language is English, with its strict word-order rules, to approach Vergil's effects is beyond fantasy, but monotony is always within reach."

She avoids it most of the time, and now and then shows a flash of the lyric genius that I loved in her poems when I first read them 20 years ago. Here's Aeneas telling about the Trojan decision to let the horse enter: "Had heaven willed it, had we all been sane." And the fury Allecto reporting her mischief to Juno: "Here is your conflict, sealed by dismal war."

Ruden is direct and colloquial when that's called for. After Juno dismisses her, Allecto "left the steep sky for her home in Hell."

Candace has asked what Ruden's translation owes to her being a woman, and it's hard to tell—which may be testimony to her skill as an impartial translator. I think she handles Vergil's women a bit better than Fagles does. Male translators probably tend to be dazzled by Queen Dido. Ruden gives Dido her full due, but with a hint of the wry and practical—one member of the sisterhood commenting on another. I'll have to think some more about this and see what she does with Lavinia, Aeneas's Italian bride.

At five pages a day, I'm now well past halfway and will finish in a few days. Another report then.

3.

(September 26) I finished reading Sarah Ruden's new translation of Vergil's *Aeneid* on schedule last weekend, and this is a brief final report.

Ruden's *Aeneid* is a joy to read as an English poem, just as Garry Wills said it would be, in his article for the *New York Review of Books*. I went back recently and re-read Wills's review. This time I paid more attention to his remarks about the "Harvard school," which he says tends to re-interpret classical authors as slyly trying to weaken the underpinnings of authority. Its effort to recruit Vergil to this cause is wrong-headed, Wills believes—while Vergil may write with a certain sadness about the cost of founding an empire, he never doubts that the cost is worth it. Ruden doesn't try for a postmodern Vergil, and it obviously pleased Wills to be able to praise her. After all, she's a graduate of that same Harvard classics program!

As I read Ruden and Wills, I thought how much we still live in the afterglow of Rome, from the words of our language to the laws that shape our societies. Hard to see this sometimes in our frantic, media-obsessed world, but the underpinnings are there. Jove spoke truly when he promised that Aeneas's heritage would last forever.

Any reviewer ought to make one quibble, to validate his praise. Wills objected to the line, "As Rhoetus drove past, making himself scarce." The book's one clinker, he called it. I added a couple of my own, but it would be captious to list them. Three weak lines out of 9,895 is hardly an indictment.

And there are some marvelous lines, like this one:

All of us who laid waste to Troy have paid
Horribly for our crimes throughout the world.

Now and then Ruden achieves something that eluded another excellent translator, Robert Fagles, as in her rendering of "oculos dejecta decoros"—"her fine eyes, cast down"—to describe Lavinia, Aeneas's bride-to-be. Fagles translates it as "lovely Lavinia with downcast eyes," which makes her beauty seem only ordinary.

Candace Moseley, my mentor on this project, asked if Ruden's translation owed anything to her being a woman, and I think—as in the above—she has an especially keen appreciation for the women of the *Aeneid*, including the chief of them, the implacable Juno.

I hope Candace won't demur at that "mentor" above, even though we've simply exchanged a few e-mails. At several points her comments and her much deeper knowledge of Vergil have crystallized something for me. She observes in one message that "War is ugly and without glory in the *Aeneid*. Wounds are grotesque and pitiful. Vergil is writing in a Roman world that was sick of war, especially the civil wars that had raged for more than a century until Augustus ushered in the new golden age."

Another comment sent me back to re-read Aeneas's dream of Hector, in Book II. It's worth quoting Ruden here, not only because (as Candace notes) Hector's appearance is in such pathetic contrast to Homer's depiction, but also because it's very fine Ruden:

> *I saw a desolate Hector in my dreams,*
> *Streaming with tears and black with dust and blood.*
> *His feet were swollen with the thongs that pierced them*
> *When he was dragged behind the chariot.*
> *How different from that Hector who returned*
> *Wearing the plundered armor of Achilles*
> *Or hurled our Trojan torches onto Greek ships!*
> *His beard was dirty; dried blood caked his hair.*
> *He had the many wounds he got defending*
> *His city's walls. And in that dream I wept . . . .*

I've now read the *Aeneid* twice this year, in different translations. I'm glad to have done this but am not ready to start on a third, just yet anyway. "It cost so much to found the Roman nation," wrote Vergil (and Ruden). Worth it, no doubt, but Christmas is coming and I'm ready for a season of peace.

CHATEAU DE TURNIP

1.

(September 1) John Moore didn't write many books, but in William Hart of "crackbrained" Brensham he created a character for the ages. William dominates—is—*The Blue Field*, Moore's love letter to English village life of the mid-20th century.

Hart is an old reprobate, no question, but among the most endearing in literature. In youth he was a roisterer, a "bruiser," given to wild brawling and cries of "Thee carns't touch I—I be a descendant of the poet Shakespeare!" William was also a superb wainwright, gardener, and (when finally too crippled to go down to the Horse and Harrow) a maker of wine from any kind of fruit or vegetable he could grow—which was about anything.

Several years ago, sensing that the day might come when I couldn't get to the pub either, I decided to follow William's example and start my own wine cellar. The pear tree at the bottom of the yard had outdone itself that year, so I began.

Please understand, any oenophiles out there, that I've never intended to be good at this. Home winemaking exemplifies for me the maxim that "not everything worth doing is worth doing well." I got some plastic wastebaskets, muslin, and baker's yeast, and was in business. An old book on winemaking by H.E. Bravery (just the name for this enterprise) was my guide.

I threw the chopped-up pears in the wastebaskets, added water, sugar, and yeast, put muslin over the top, and went away for 14 days. By winter I had some still-potent but pretty good pear wine. (I did take steps against contamination, having as a child made five gallons of elderberry vinegar by accident.)

In the years since, I've made pear/cosmos blossom wine, peach brandy, wheat wine, carrot "whisky," persimmon wine, and one or two other things that took care of a garden surplus. A gallon of blueberry wine is ripening nicely at the moment. It's an astonishing bluish-red, but probably a little too sweet. It doesn't matter. You shouldn't drink very much of any fruit wine, if you want to totter to bed in a reasonably straight line.

This summer an attack of fire blight diminished the pear crop, but the garden has thrived as never before. I can almost hear William Hart's priapic genius laughing over it. And I have a turnip surplus.

2.

(September 11) So I had a turnip surplus, and some general directions on root wine from my mentor, H.E. Bravery, author of *Successful Winemaking at Home*. Alas, Mr. Bravery did not think too highly of the idea of turnip wine. He wrote:

> *Turnips and swedes—I have heard of people who have made something with these roots, but I must confess that friends and I who have carried out trials with them have been forced to conclude that while they might make good wines, we have not had much success with them, and we have decided that with so many other kinds of materials available it is hardly worth wasting time trying to evolve a reliable recipe for each of these roots.*

Easy for him to say, he didn't have the turnip surplus.

Sometimes one has to do something for the sheer hell of it, so I began. While Mr. Bravery gave no recipe for turnip wine, he did have one using mangel-wurzels, a mysterious British vegetable, defined by the *Oxford English Dictionary* as a sort of giant beet, "cultivated as a food for cattle." That sounds something like a turnip, doesn't it?

I pause to confess that my record on substituting one ingredient for another is not good. This goes back to childhood, when I found myself out of baking powder while making cookies. But I did have some tooth powder, which looked a lot like baking powder. Surely it would work as well. (This is known as the triumph of hope over experience.) The cookies were a failure, although years later a friend said I had missed my chance at fame and fortune: "You could have marketed them as Billy's Dental Biscuits—'Eat Cookies and Clean Your Teeth at the Same Time.'"

Anyway, Mr. Bravery's mangel-wurzel recipe looked simple and generic enough to apply to almost any root. And it had the advantage of getting rid of the turnips early in the process. After a brief soak in boiling water, the resulting turnip broth was then combined with chopped-up oranges and lemons, mixed with sugar and yeast, and left to ferment for 10 days.

I did this, then squeezed the remaining juice from the fruit and added enough sugar water to fill up a gallon jug. A gallon of turnip wine is now stowed away to finish fermenting.

Before plugging the jug (with cotton balls and Saran wrap), I decanted a small quantity of the unfinished wine. I can say that it is indeed on its way to wine, with more of a fruit than turnip taste, which is all to the good. I can also say that in its present halfway state, even a small beaker would knock your socks off. With luck the extra sugar water will temper it a little.

I doubt, though, that it will ever be a notable vintage—no Chateau de Turnip, I'm afraid. Mr. Bravery warns that all roots are best used in their withered state after a winter's storage. By that time they've lost some of their starch, and the wine will clear. My turnip wine, while an interesting shade of yellow, is very murky and may never settle properly. In extremity, such wine can be drunk, but it's a little like drinking mush.

3.

(August 4) Nearly a year has elapsed since Turnip Wine 1 and 2, so for the benefit of anyone keeping track let me recap.

Back last September I wrote about William Hart, the hero of John Moore's delightful book *The Blue Field*. Hart had been a battler in youth, but old age eventually caught up with him.

Here I digress for a moment to quote my favorite verses on this subject (by James Ball Naylor and possibly others):

King Solomon and King David
Led merry, merry lives,
Had many, many lady friends
And many, many wives.

But when old age crept over them
With many, many qualms,
King Solomon wrote the Proverbs
And King David wrote the Psalms.

To return to William Hart. As it became more difficult to totter down to the Horse and Harrow, William decided to make enough fruit and vegetable wine to last out his life. This seemed like a sensible precaution, so I determined to do likewise. Beginning in 2002 with some passable pear wine, I went on to peaches, persimmons, wheat, and some delectable carrot whisky. Last summer tested the outer limits, though, with a gallon each of pear, blueberry, parsnip, and turnip wine. The turnip wine was a leap into the unknown—even my literary mentor, the aptly named H.E. Bravery, had advised against it. And indeed the first decoction looked like yellow mush.

But there's good news (good, that is, if you happen to like high-octane fruit and vegetable wines). Everything, including the turnip wine, cleared beautifully in the attic over the winter and spring. When I got back to it a few days ago, the turnip wine was the gold of old pirate treasure. The parsnip was slightly yellower, but still glowed as the light fell through it. The pear, as always, had a good color, and the blueberry was something else—a deep carmine shot through with blue underlights.

But what about taste and potency? Karen has been known to use words like "paint stripper" when discussing my vintages. And as I decanted the wine into bottles, Colin asked that a sample be set aside in case the coroner needed to test it later.

Oh, ye of little faith! Amazingly, all of it tasted pretty good, at least by my standards (which are low but not abysmal—I drew the line after an unfortunate experience with Walmart's bottom-line vintages). The blueberry was exceptional—even Karen had to concede that the flavor was okay, although she did add that it was a tad strong and perhaps should be drunk "in thimblefuls." That's probably not a bad idea. Those who think that fruit wines are mild and genteel will discover otherwise when they try to stand up and walk.

Anyway, I now have around 28 bottles of wine put away. Oh, I'm going to keep warm this coming winter!

However, my effort to emulate William Hart and sock enough away to see me into eternity is not getting anywhere. In fact I'm drinking it about as fast as I make it. Maybe I need to plant some more fruit trees. Or expand the turnip patch.

DEAR PATHETIC SLOB

I DON'T KNOW YOUR NAME, although I might be able to find it out. I got a good look at your car. But I prefer to think of you as "Order 381, Register 3, Franklin Taco Bell, 5:27 p.m., 5/04/01."

You drove past my house on Walnut Street a few minutes after that. As you passed, you extended your hand from the car window and flicked a little plastic baggie into the middle of the street.

I was on the front porch, waiting to go out to supper myself, and I got to wondering what gift you had left for me and my neighbors. Kittens, I thought for an instant, but happily it was only taco trash. I walked over and picked up the baggie, surprising a motorist not used to seeing a man in a suit out trash-picking on a lovely Friday afternoon.

I'm not sure why your casually bestowed trash interested me so much. I'm used to finding pop cans, beer bottles, and fast-food litter on my lawn. But those are impersonal. They just show up, like crocuses in spring. But I saw your very human hand, and the graceful arc it gave the baggie, like Jalen Rose sinking a 10-footer.

Inside the baggie, I found the receipt for your snack. It told me you had eaten "2 B-BFSP" at a cost of $3.38, "1 Mild" at no charge, and "1 PEP-32" for $1.29. With the 24-cent tax, the bill came to $4.91 at the Drive-Thru window. "Thank you for eating at Taco Bell," the receipt said.

"And thank you for throwing your trash on my street," I said.

But now my journalist's curiosity was piqued, and I wondered what else I could find out about you from your trash. You know how we journalists are. I carried your baggie to my garage and went through it, piece by messy piece. (Hope you don't have any loathesome skin diseases, Slobbo, or you'll be hearing from my lawyer.)

Your meal turned out to have been two Fiesta Burritos with Mild Border Sauce. You used one packet of sauce; your companion used two. Or maybe it was the other way around. You left some sauce on the wrappers and a couple of wadded-up napkins, which I unfolded carefully. It made me feel very close to you, Pathetic Slob, almost intimate.

But the most interesting things in the baggie were what you didn't consume or soil—11 unopened packets of Mild Border Sauce, weighing 3cwt each and containing water, tomato paste, vinegar, spices, salt, xanthan gum, one-tenth of 1 percent sodium benzoate (as a preservative), and natural flavoring. "Packaged exclusively for Taco Bell Corp., Irvine, Calif."

Eleven packets. But why not, since they were free? The preservative wasn't all that necessary, since you decided in the four blocks between Taco Bell and my house to chuck them into the street.

There were also a couple of unused napkins.

I washed my hands very thoroughly.

A story in the morning paper says Earth is losing its "scrubbers." The tiny hydroxl radicals that have destroyed atmospheric pollution for millennia are slowly declining in number. The planet's fragile atmosphere is undergoing profound change, the story says, and may have crossed a threshold that threatens its self-cleansing ability.

But why should that surprise us? We are dirty creatures, who dump and discard and foul the beautiful blue planet on which our children and children's children might have lived in health and happiness for all time. We foul the world, but the world begins on Walnut Street.

It begins with me, too. We are partners, Pathetic Slob. Too many plastic baggies, too many soiled napkins, too much Mild Border Sauce. I don't throw it in the street the way you do, because I had a mother who taught me better. But it piles up, it piles up.

Do you know about the Nut Room? It's a theoretical problem in which a room is filled with nuts in their shells. You are allowed to eat them all, but you have to leave the shells in the room. The joker is that you can't eat them all, because a time comes when you can no longer find the nutmeats among the shells.

That's the kind of Nut World we're creating. Think about it your next time in the Drive-Thru. I'll think about it, too—and about you, Pathetic Slob, my brother, sister, friend.

WHY I HAVE WOOD FIRES

HAVING A WOOD FIRE gets rarer and rarer. It's a lot of work, beginning with finding the wood and getting it to your house.

Brown's Tree Service dumps mine in the back yard, but I have to stack it. The chunks are dirty, full of splinters, and usually the wrong size. I have a fine fireplace, wide and deep with a strong draft, and made safe now after once setting the house on fire. But the wood still must be lugged inside on a wheeled cart, and I'm always forgetting and having to trudge out into the snow for a couple more pieces.

I also have to buy bundles of kindling at Kroger's. What the tree service brings is not kindling—these are splitter-riven fractions of logs. Getting them to burn, even with kindling, requires a fire-starter brick and oversized matches. The whole process is long, messy, and expensive. And afterward there's fireplace clean-out and ash disposal.

So why bother, especially since much of the heat goes up the chimney and there are nagging environmental concerns? My friends have gas fireplaces, which are cleaner and more efficient—a neighbor has an especially classy number called "Fire 'n' Ice," which splays a minimal gas flame across a shimmering bed of crystal. It's fire and nice, if somewhat antiseptic.

I think my refusal to give up wood has something to do with the nature of fire, which changes things. These hanks of ash, black walnut, and cherry are being consumed, giving up their energy in different ways. Each produces a different fire—I especially love hackberry, which is tough, stringy, and burns a long time.

My friends' gas logs are the same now and forever; nothing gives itself up to the flame. "To build a fire you have to throw yourself in," a poet writes, and I have spent labor, time, and love on this fire, in a way my friends haven't.

This doesn't make me a better person—maybe the opposite. A wood fire is an extravagance in a world where whole continents are being stripped of fuelwood by those who need it just to stay alive. My fire pollutes the air and contributes to global warming. So I rationalize—it's only a small fire, industrial burning and fossil fuels do infinitely more damage, the tree service's removals would go to waste if I didn't burn them, I'm not doing anything illegal. All the arguments of privileged luxury.

But the fire is beautiful, and I'll warm my bones at it a little longer before they go into the long cold. I began tonight's fire with two oak billets laid on the kindling. When they had burned down a little, I threw on a wide slab of ash and watched Sasha Cohen do miraculous things on the ice from Torino. Now, at the end of the night, the TV is off and the fire is working on a curving chunk of hickory, a natural firebow bridging a deep bed of coals. Soon I'll have to poke and turn it some—a wood fire has to be tended if you want it to become ash and your fireplace not to be filled in the morning with half-burned ends, like cigarette butts.

At the moment, not a lot is going on with my fire. A few flames at its back show the firebow is still burning, and as I write a sudden gust of fire springs up from the log's near side and a splinter at the top spurts into flame, then subsides. And, oh! something just popped and a galaxy of sparks flew up the chimney! A new show every minute! The preacher who said man is born to trouble as the sparks fly upward was writing beside a wood fire.

My fire is about as safe and trouble-free as an indoor one can be. But when the fireplace was built, the builder skimped secretly on its construction, and a dozen years afterward—late one night— I noticed a thin thread of smoke issuing from a dark corner of the firebox, beneath which the floor joists were burning. The fire department put the blaze out quickly, and a new contractor rebuilt the firebox with yards of concrete beneath it and the adjoining floor. I could launch a rocket now from my hearth.

A wood fire has a history. Early in life, it's brisk and enterprising, a cheerful force. It could do anything and spends itself gaily. It has a stable middle age, fuel and fire in balance. An old fire burns from within, paying out its energy in flickering coronas. The firebox, once bright, takes on a darker look, and the shadows deepen. In an old castle, this would have been the hour of despair and treachery, of movement behind the arras and the doing of things not to be thought of in the bright day.

Absorbed in this, I've let my attention wander from tonight's fire, and when I look up it's aged and become quiescent. No more shooting flames, and the coals have darkened significantly. Time to poke and stoke—except that I won't stoke any more tonight. It's nearly midnight and time to turn off the room light, get a last cup of decaf tea, and sit by my fire as it fades slowly, until I close the glass and iron doors, slip off to bed, and let the last embers fire my dreaming.

BUYING A BOARD

IT'S HARD to buy a board anymore.

I found that out during Fourth of July week, when I went looking for boards to repair my front porch, so that I won't be sued by a door-to-door salesman who steps through the rotten spot. It looked like a simple matter—a few 8-foot, 1x4-inch pine boards, tongued and grooved.

The boutique lumber store didn't have such things, and the clerk had no idea what I wanted. So I drove up the road a few miles to a mega-lumberyard, which also didn't have boards. Or so the clerk said, although I suspect he just didn't want to deal with a small-order, walk-in customer.

It got me thinking about lumberyards, and how there almost aren't any real ones left. By real ones, I mean those where a kindly old man in a feed cap says, "Yep, I think we've got some of them fellers." At least three pretty good lumberyards have closed in the Franklin/Greenwood area during the past few years. They all sold boards, and could produce them without making me feel I had requested teak planking for a man-of-war.

Some would even let me go back in the shop, against regulations, to watch the circular saw whine through the boards and to breathe the friendly scent of sawdust.

Lumber and I go back a long way, even to before my birth. My father, in pre-OSHA days, spent much of his youth hanging around Bryant's lumberyard in Franklin, where he learned about boards and eventually how to shape them into beautiful furniture. I have the pine chest he built about 1920 because he spotted a lovely "figure" in a board, probably at Bryant's.

Many years later he built a desk from mahogany boards as a wedding present for my wife and me. Over many moves and kids it got battered, but we turned it over to some furniture craftsmen who spent most of a year restoring it with love and care to its original condition, if not a little better. Halfway through the process, the Head Craftsman observed that the desk was "in about 1,300 pieces." "Just so you get them all back in," my wife said. "You'll never know," the H.C. replied.

Once, my father got the job of removing a pipe organ that Vincennes High School had installed in its new gymnasium, built in a fit of euphoria after the Alices won the 1923 state basketball championship (important validation for a team named after the heroine of a novel, *Alice of Old Vincennes*). The organ had deteriorated badly, and my father couldn't find a buyer to restore it. So he sawed the 16-foot redwood pipes into boards and paneled the inside of a house with them. I've wondered if the tenants ever hear ghostly music in the night.

My father taught me very little about boards, but in his eighties we began building clocks together. One day he had trouble putting in a heavy screw, so he got a bar of soap and greased the threads. "Where did you learn to do that?" I asked. "Oh, it's just one of the things a Bridges knows," he replied. "Then why didn't I know?" "Your mother's influence," he said, without missing a turn of the screw.

My wife and I had the first argument of our married life over lumber—or more accurately over my desire (at an estate sale) to buy a handsome armoire fashioned from walnut and poplar, set over against her wish to have rugs in the house. "That thing," she said, "is not even all one kind of wood—it's a *half-breed*!" I won, but it was a hollow victory. We were telling the story to my stepbrother, David, several years ago, and he began laughing. "This argument isn't over yet, is it?" he said.

Our children grew up with the armoire, and one of them recalls being on a class trip to some historic home and seeing a sim-

203

ilar one. "Oh, look," he cried. "A half-breed!" "A what?" his classmates chorused.

He told us about it accusingly afterward. "I thought all those things were called half-breeds. I didn't know it was just a family term. You might have told me before I embarrassed myself in public!"

Over the years I've bought a lot of boards—to build a fence around a back yard, to repair a porch ceiling, to make a kitchen counter, to fashion a sign for a friend's cabin in Minnesota. Finding boards was never a problem, until now.

There is a happy ending, though, to my search for a board. After failing all over Johnson County to find a lumberyard that sold boards, I began telephoning. Eventually, my wife and I drove to Shelbyville, to the place that once had sold us old-fashioned wood shutters, with working louvers.

The clerk wasn't wearing a feed cap, but he was of an age to know about lumber. He was friendly, helpful, and had 1×4 pine boards, tongued and grooved, in stock. It cost $20 to have them delivered to Franklin, but it was worth every bit of it.

HOW TO USE A CHINESE DICTIONARY

FIRST, find a dictionary.

Mine is the handsome *Far East Chinese-English Dictionary*, published in 1992 by the Far East Book Company, Ltd., of Taiwan. I bought it at the Caves bookstore on the North Road in Taipei, while I was living and working there in 1993-94. My copy is stamped in red as No. 203481.

I had an idea of becoming fluent in Mandarin, but that dream went glimmering.

Still, I get the dictionary out now and then when I want to look up a character. And recently I used it to "back translate" into English a Chinese version of one of my own poems, translated by a Taipei friend, France Yu, and published in the Taiwan *Journal of Dentistry*.

But this is not explaining how to use the dictionary—and to explain requires another short detour, into the mysteries of Chinese orthography. Chinese is one of the world's oldest written languages, evolving from ancient marks on tortoise shells and "oracle bones." It is a "broken" syllabic language; the Chinese character stands for a sound rather than being a pure hieroglyph. Several of these characters may go together to make up a word. The characters (letters) are based on 214 radicals or roots, which is what makes it possible to have a Chinese dictionary.

Not that this makes anything easy. Some radicals are extraordinarily complex. Radical 214, "ywè" (flute), is a large character in itself and combines with only two other characters in my dictionary. Other radicals are hidden within their characters, so only a fluent reader can see instantly where the word will be found.

And then there's stroke count. Under each radical, my dictionary arranges characters in ascending order of count. (I believe the most complex Chinese character has 64 strokes.) Counting strokes might seem easy, but it's not, at least for a Westerner. Certain conventions dictate the count—unless you know this code, you may count a character and be several strokes high or low. It has to do with the action of the brush—the actual stroke used by the calligraphic artist.

Discouraging? Not entirely. The *Far East Dictionary* has helps for Westerners. To begin with, it numbers every character in its 1,759 pages, from 1 (yī) to 7,331 (yù). The characters themselves are in large type and easy to scan.

In the front of the book is a list showing each of those 214 radicals (along with any variants) and the page on which its characters begin. So if you can spot the radical, you're now down to looking at perhaps 3 percent of the 7,331 characters. If you know the stroke count, you can narrow this still more. There is also an index listing every character under its radical, although this type is rather small. A good magnifying glass helps.

But suppose, like me, you're a rotten stroke counter and spotter of radicals. The dictionary offers help here, too. In the back, there's the Mandarin Phonetic Symbol Index. There are also two lists of all 7,331 characters arranged phonetically by their sounds in English—the U.N. Mandarin Phonetic Symbol Index and the Gwoyeu Romatzyh Index. (My dictionary omits the famous and formidable Wade-Giles Index, for which I'm grateful.)

If I have heard the word pronounced, I can go to one of these lists and with luck (sometimes a lot of it) find the anglicized word and next to it the Chinese character I'm looking for, with its number in the dictionary.

How does this work in practice? Here, in brief, is how I tackled France Yu's translation of my little poem, "Birds of Taiwan," in 43 Chinese characters.

The title was easy. France had stuck to "Taiwan Birds" ("niǎo"). Her opening words also followed my scheme. But then, as good translators do, she moved away from a slavish translation of the original and created her own fine poem in Chinese, based on mine but unique.

A few characters I knew. I could spot the radicals in others and find the words in the dictionary. But then I came to two characters that baffled me. I could locate one of them and get the phonetic "kāi," which is character No. 6,533 in my dictionary. But "kāi" is an extensive character with definitions that go on for several pages. So I wondered if it was paired with the second character in my puzzling phrase? Yes, it was. The full word was "kāi-kěn," meaning "to open wasteland to farming."

With the phonetic for this second character, I could then go to the lists at the back of the book to identify "kěn" as character No. 883, under the radical "tǔ" with a stroke count (I think) of 12.

Some characters were tougher. I recall marching for a long time through all possible permutations of the sound "zhi," trying to guess what the creators of the phonetic indices were thinking of.

In the end, I found all 43 characters and could read France's fine translation and even speak it aloud in Chinese. And this all took only two days of solid work.

Since writing this, I've encountered a more serious problem that illustrates another translation pitfall. France had sent me a poem of her own to translate—53 characters, so it was slightly longer than "Birds of Taiwan." The poem was about space and (appropriately, as it turned out) time. My translation, titled "The Little Trees," is in the preface to this book.

The first 12 characters gave up their meaning quickly. Then I hit character 13. It looked easy, with a stroke count of about 12 and an easy choice of radicals. I tried all of them, but none included my character. Hope rose briefly with character No. 4309 in the dictionary; it bore a slight resemblance to my No. 13, but the radicals didn't match.

So I launched what cryptographers call a "brute force" attack—overwhelm the problem by checking every possibility. I looked at all the characters from nine to 15 strokes. No luck. This infernal character had no radical and wasn't in my dictionary! By this time two hours had passed.

I finally found the character in the vocabulary list of an old textbook: "syi," meaning "thin, slender, delicate." But I still didn't know where it was in the dictionary. And now the phonetic indices let me down—there was no such character under "syi." Or under "ji," "shi," or "xi." Then my eye fell again on No. 4309, under "xi." Since I now had a definition, I went back, and there it was: "thin, slender, delicate." The poem text had used a variant of the radical that wasn't shown in the dictionary.

I penciled it in for future reference. The next day I located my handy *Guide to the Chinese Writing System*, which identified both versions as radical 120, the "silk" radical. "The student should learn to recognize both forms," it said helpfully.

Yes, indeed.

IV. TALES

Illustration by Colin Bridges

GeeGee Dapple at work on his Remington 16 in Silk Willoughby, Lincolnshire. Readers of Murder in the OED *will recognize the object beside the typewriter:*

> *It was a rather frightening Jenny Haniver. . . . There was no note, and as GeeGee picked up the creature he saw that it was only an ordinary skate, or small marine ray, anamorphosed by someone with a sharp knife and needle into the dried and wrinkled doll that now grinned satanically up at him. It was not, as he had hoped, a true* Myliobatus noctula."

—*From Places & Stories*

The cat in the window is Fowler, whose specialty is mice, and who resolutely refuses to join all those other cats in current detective fiction who help their masters fight crime.

THE HANDS OF ESAU
[A GEEGEE DAPPLE MYSTERY]

CHARLES GEORGE GORDON DAPPLE—GeeGee to his friends, and the Tall Terror to generations of copyboys on the *Lincolnshire Reflector*—was singing happily, to a tune of his own devising, what he liked to think of as "The Editor's Hymn:"

> *I stand a wreck on Error's shore,*
> *da-dum, da-dum, da-dum . . . .*

He gathered up the contents of his letterbox and marched toward the kitchen, where morning tea—a ritual of his solitary retirement from the newspaper to the village of Silk Willoughby—was waiting.

> *Where is the promise of my years,*
> *Once written on my brow?*
> *Da-dum, da . . . .*

Hullo, what's this?

The song broke off as GeeGee weighed on his right palm an envelope with the London return address of *The Literary England Poetry Annual*. The envelope was lighter and thinner, he noticed with surprise, than the one containing five poems that he had posted five months ago, in answer to an advertisement. He opened it with slightly more haste than usual and took out two rejected poems and a letter.

"Congratulations, Mr. Dapple," the letter began. "The editors of *Literary England* are pleased to inform you that three of your poems—"Silk Willoughby Summer," "February Evening," and "Nightscape"—have been accepted for publication in the next *Annual*. You will receive . . . ."

211

A veil of discretion should be drawn over the scene of a poet's first acceptance, especially when the poet is a retired newspaper editor of more than 60 winters, with a reputation in Lincolnshire journalism for skepticism, sobriety, and scholarly calm. Let it be said that GeeGee recovered more quickly than some. Within minutes he was able to finish reading the letter from Hubert Arthur, editor of *Literary England*.

"You will receive a complimentary copy of the magazine," it said. "Your presence is also requested in the magazine's chambers, Great Russell Street, at 7 o'clock on the evening of June 17, during which, it is hoped, you will read one of your accepted poems. A prize of 100 pounds will be presented to the author of the best contribution to the *Annual*."

So it was that on a balmy June evening, GeeGee found himself in a dusty, first-floor hall in London, on a low dais behind a standing microphone, facing the predicament of anyone six feet or taller who has ever followed a five-foot-tall speaker to the platform. Twenty seconds of battle with a balky adjusting ring brought the microphone to the neighborhood of GeeGee's chin, and he heard himself reading:

NIGHTSCAPE

Great constellations riding on the night
are anchored in our failing human view.
Our reckonings err, by a parsec or two;
our eyes confuse the new and ancient light.
So we make neighbours of two stars that keep
cool distance in the universal deep . . . .

When he had finished, GeeGee sat down amid warm applause from his 20 fellow poets. He was followed to the platform by a short and tubercular youth wearing a primrose boutonniere, and a second Battle of the Microphone was fought. Other readers came and went, until at last Mr. Hubert Arthur, rotund and beaming, stepped forward to announce that the anonymous but distinguished jurors had awarded the Grand Prize of 100 pounds to Lady Hyllerie Thomas for "Swallows."

The applause this time was more than warm. Lady Hyllerie, whose name GeeGee vaguely recalled, had been a sensation from the moment the audience glimpsed her mane of auburn hair, Grecian features, and snowy shoulders rising from the perianth of an aquamarine evening gown. Now she inclined her tall beauty above the fortunate Mr. Arthur, accepted the magazine's cheque, and said a few soft words, lost to everyone beyond the first row of chairs. A camera flashed, and the evening dissolved into the rattle of teacups and literary chat. It was, GeeGee reflected later as he prepared for bed in his hotel, a little world of its own and a long way from Silk Willougby.

Yet not such a long way, he discovered two days later upon opening his *Reflector*. Also on the night of June 17, he read, thieves had broken into the home of Lord Edmund Thomas on the north edge of Lincoln and had stolen a wall safe containing nearly a million pounds worth of jewelry, including the Star of Madras diamond. The theft had occurred while Lord Edmund and Lady Hyllerie were in London attending, respectively, a meeting of his company's directors and a literary reception.

The thieves had entered through a window, cutting the glass expertly to avoid an alarm. They then had removed the small safe in its entirety from the wall behind a sliding mirror. The break-in had been discovered the next morning by Lady Hyllerie's personal secretary, who had helped the Thomases board the train to London the previous day. The jewelry was fully insured, the story concluded.

GeeGee considered the incident as he drank his morning tea at the kitchen table. He now clearly recalled Lord Edmund and Lady Hyllerie—a handsome young couple whose names and pictures appeared from time to time in the *Reflector*.

Something stirred faintly in GeeGee's memory. He reached for the telephone on the worktop, rang a Sleaford number, and waited for his sister to make her slow progress to the telephone under the stairs. At 89, GeeGee reflected, Vicki might be England's last unalloyed Victorian. Her name, Victoria Regina Dapple, matched the décor of her home and the moral convictions forged during 30 years as headmistress of a girls' school. She had raised the four orphaned Dapple boys; one reason GeeGee had stayed in Silk Willoughby after his wife's death was to be next door to Sleaford, without being quite next door to Vicki.

The voice that finally said "Yes?" somehow conveyed in that syllable a disdain encompassing not only the telephone but the whole of the modern world.

"Vicki," GeeGee said, "I know you detest the telephone, and I try not to ring you oftener than once a month, but I have an odd question . . . .

"Charles." The rusted murmur at the other end silenced him firmly. "You may forgo the tedious apologies. You ring me at least once a week, and I'm grateful. Also, no question of yours could possibly surprise me. You have been asking them since you were five years old, and your brother Raglan put you up to asking me whether all things were possible to God, and, if so, whether He could make a stone bigger than He could lift."

"As I recall, you successfully avoided answering," GeeGee said, "but this question is easier. I seem to remember your saying something once about Lord Edmund Thomas's wife, Hyllerie. Something that happened when her grandparents were sending their children to your school."

There was a long pause. "Yes, well." Vicki's voice was like a whisper from across the galaxy. "You must already have realized, Charles, that there is something very wrong with that business in the *Reflector* about the stolen jewelry. Hyllerie Thomas was a Millborough. The Millboroughs lied for each other. When I had Hyllerie's mother as a student, she could lie like a bishop."

214

GeeGee posed his own doubts the next day to an old friend, Inspector Wilfred Crabbe of the Lincoln police, who received them and GeeGee skeptically in his office. "Something peculiar about the robbery?" he repeated. "I hardly think so, old chum— although the insurance company would dearly love it if we could find something."

"Unfortunately for the company, everything looks very straightforward. Nobody in the house. Housekeeper had been let go two months back. Lord and Lady Thomas turned on the window alarms and locked up before they left, and everything about the break-in itself was tickety-boo. Footprints under the window and all that. The safe was small, but it took metal torches to cut it loose from the steel wall moorings. Very professional. The insurance lads would like to show that the jewelry wasn't properly protected, but that safe was proof against any amateur. Those gents cut it right out of the wall. It must have taken them half the night."

"You don't suppose his Lordship might have hired some safecrackers and split the take with them, do you?" GeeGee suggested.

"Not bloody likely," Crabbe replied. "Who's going to turn over nine-tenths of a haul like that after doing all the work? And there would always be the threat of blackmail. Sorry, but this one looks like a straight heist."

"And you're sure the jewelry was actually in the safe?" Gee-Gee asked.

Crabbe sighed. "The secretary saw Lady Hyllerie put it in earlier in the day before they left for the station. Lady Hyllerie was showing her a weakened clasp that had finally broken. The jewels had been in the family for generations, and the secretary knew them as well as she knew her own bracelets. Anyway, one could hardly mistake the Star of Madras in that famous silver brooch."

"And the secretary?" GeeGee persisted.

"Sixty-eight years old and a pillar of rectitude," Crabbe replied. "She had worked for Lord Edmund's mother, and Lady Hyllerie took her over after the mother's death. Also, she had an airtight alibi. Twenty minutes after the train pulled out with the Thomases aboard, she was drinking tea at her daughter's house, and she was with the daughter and family the whole night."

"Somehow I suspect that Lord and Lady Thomas have equally good alibis," GeeGee said.

"They do," Crabbe replied. "Lord Edmund met with the directors of his company early in the evening—they're going through a bad patch right now, I'm told—and then about 10 p.m. he and Lady H. came back to their hotel, the Regency, where they're well known. Room service took champagne up about midnight. Hyllerie had been at some sort of literary tea fight earlier, while her husband was at his meeting. We talked to the editor whose magazine threw the party, and he confirmed everything—even gave us a picture of Lady Hyllerie receiving an award."

Crabbe rummaged through the welter of papers on his desk and produced a glossy print of a familiar scene—Lady Hyllerie accepting a check for 100 pounds from Hubert Arthur, the editor of *Literary England*. A sloppy photo, GeeGee thought, with the microphone obscuring her chin, though not her décolletage. A *Reflector* photographer would have done better, or he would have answered to Charles G.G. Dapple.

"I don't see how she could have a better alibi," Crabbe concluded, "unless you were at the party and saw her yourself."

"As a matter of fact," GeeGee said glumly, "I was and I did."

In the post next morning was GeeGee's complimentary copy of *The Literary England Poetry Annual*. He read over his poems and those of Lady Hyllerie Thomas. Without the sensational gown, "Swallows" struck him as no more than ordinary.

Two days later, GeeGee became a Literary Figure. His morning *Reflector* carried a headline, "Lincolnshire Poets Honored," above a small, inside story about Lady Hyllerie's award. Next to the story was the picture Crabbe had shown him, with a credit: "Photo by courtesy of *Literary England*." There was nothing slow about the magazine's publicity department.

The last paragraph read: "Charles G.G. Dapple, editor emeritus of the *Reflector*, also had poems chosen for inclusion in the *Annual*." At the very moment, GeeGee thought wryly, some former colleague at the *Reflector* was probably tacking the cutting on the paper's bulletin board and appending a bawdy comment.

Ah, well, what did they know, the Philistines? Doomed to labor in the muck of daily journalism, what could they understand of the creative air in which the contributors to *Literary England* lived and moved and had their being? GeeGee thought of those contributors as a lonely and rather brave band, toiling in isolation until the magazine brought them together from across England. Even then, he thought, they might have remained almost strangers had not Mr. Hubert Arthur bustled about, praising their work, introducing them to each other, and posing them for the photographer. And of course the stunning Lady Hyllerie had thrown everyone else into the shade.

GeeGee examined the *Reflector*'s picture again. It was an excellent likeness of Lady Hyllerie, even to the mole on her right cheek. GeeGee had noticed it during the reception: the only blemish on an otherwise perfect face. He would have liked to have seen the whole face again, with that perfect Grecian chin . . .

At that moment, GeeGee knew, with awful clarity, that he had been a fool, and that no matter what his former colleagues were scrawling across the cutting on the bulletin board, it was no more than he deserved. He rang inspector Crabbe and spoke earnestly and confessionally with him. Crabbe was decent enough not to laugh, at least until he got off the phone. When the inspector called back two days later, his tone was matter-of-fact.

"You were quite right, GeeGee," he said, "but how did you happen to notice the microphone? Nobody notices things like that. It's just part of the background—or foreground, in this case."

"You damn well notice it when you're my height and can't even say thank you without adjusting the thing," GeeGee replied. "Hubert Arthur had just announced the check presentation, and he's a short, round little chap. When Lady Hyllerie came up to accept, she didn't use the microphone, because it was too low for her. And when she spoke, nobody could hear her.

"But in the photo, the microphone was level with her chin. So the photo couldn't have been of the actual presentation."

Crabbe cleared his throat with a sound like a lorry shifting gears and described his interview with Lady Hyllerie.

"She's an accomplished liar," he said, "and she gave us the full treatment. How dare you suggest such a thing about us of the upper classes, and all that. As though she hadn't grown up as a butcher's daughter in Grantham.

"She caved in, though, when we showed her the blow-ups of the picture Hubert Arthur gave to us and to the newspaper, and of the same shot taken by the photographer at the reception. Arthur squealed on the photographer, who was quite happy to give us his undeveloped reception film.

"The difference in microphone heights stuck out, of course, but there were some other differences—a few age lines makeup couldn't hide and a little difference in the cheekbones. The mother is more classically beautiful than Lady Hyllerie, although they did their best to look exactly alike, even to the mother's putting on a mole to match Hyllerie's.

"The disguise was quite good enough to fool the Regency staff. Lord Edmund and his mother-in-law were drinking champagne to celebrate the success of the scheme about the time Hyllerie was finishing lifting the safe at the house."

"Genesis 27:22," GeeGee said. "The oldest con—the voice is Jacob's but the hands are Esau's. That explains why the mother didn't use the microphone."

He paused a moment before adding, "But didn't you say the robbery was a professional job?"

"It was, very nearly," Crabbe replied. "Lord and Lady Thomas had been working on the safe supports with torches for weeks—ever since they sacked the housekeeper—and covering the work with quick-drying plaster during the day. All Hyllerie had to do was cut the last quarter-inch and drag the safe to her car. Then it was off to a fence who could dispose of the safe and get the jewelry to the buyer. The cash plus the insurance settlement would have just about saved Lord Edmund's business."

"You've got to hand it to them for nerve," Crabbe added. "A year of planning. Soliciting poems and printing an issue of a phony magazine. Sending out the publicity picture of the real Hyllerie getting the check. Drawing everyone's attention to 'Lady Hyllerie's' smashing gown and having the real Hyllerie walk around outside the house in men's shoes. They were cool customers."

"But who in the world was Hubert Arthur?" GeeGee asked.

"A professional actor and a cousin of the mother's," Crabbe replied. "The photographer knew something was up when he shot the scene in the empty hall with Arthur and Lady Hyllerie—then came back and shot an identical scene a week later at the party. But they paid him well, and Arthur seems to have had something on him about phony passport photos."

GeeGee looked wistfully across the kitchen table at his copy of a very rare publication. "It seems a lot of trouble to go to," he said, "and someone could have tripped them up at any time."

"Yes," Crabbe said, "but the important thing was to make the lie big enough—to have an alibi no one would even think of questioning. They didn't want us or the insurance company to begin doubting."

"And you know these struggling literary sorts," Crabbe added. "Desperate to get published, touchingly grateful when they are, not inclined to ask questions." There was the faintest ghost of a chuckle as the inspector hung up.

GeeGee picked up *The Literary England Poetry Annual* and slipped it into a drawer. A scrap of song flitted through his head once more:

Where is the promise of my years,
once written on my brow . . . .

He remembered that the lines were by Adah Isaacs Menken, an actress known mostly for appearing on stage half nude and strapped to the back of a horse. She also wrote poetry.

"Nightscape" wasn't half bad, GeeGee decided, and it hadn't really been published. It might be just the thing for *Pumpernickel: A Poetic Potpourri*. He turned to his typewriter and began to type and hum.

ENDINGS

HE DIDN'T KNOW HOW he ended up doing it. Teach some-body to write? Teach your grandmother to suck eggs. It can't be done.

But here he was, late at night, reading bits of a story as it came in over e-mail. "Send me something," he had said, foolishly, to students at the reading, and now it was coming in piecemeal at 1 a.m. A love story, of course. Ragged, raging, as if the writer had broken up with the girl earlier that night, as he had, probably.

Too close to life, not enough distance, artless. And yet . . . . "Look," he wrote back, "why don't you . . . ." And in 10 minutes, just as he was about to turn in, the paragraph came back, shorter and sharper. He got himself another cup of coffee and wrote, "OK, tell me more. Where is this going?"

At 4 a.m. he had a complete draft of a short-short, about a thousand words (987 by his computer counter). Still rough and the ending needed work, but there, by God, there.

"Where are you?" he wrote. And when the answer came back from a few blocks away, "Meet me at 5 in Alta's—we'll finish up there." Then he threw cold water on his face, threw on a coat, and trudged to the café. He hadn't pulled an all-nighter in years.

The writer—he remembered him as a face in the second row (there were only three rows for a barely known writer)—was there ahead of him. They ordered breakfast—biscuits, gravy, all the things he wasn't supposed to eat. Then they went to work.

By the time the sun came up, the story was polished and there was an ending—not quite the one he would have written, but an ending, cleansed of the writer's first anger and pathos, pointing to something, to a possibility not a conclusion.

221

On the way home he passed Maggie's house. She was on the porch in a ratty bathrobe, picking up the paper. He'd seen her only a few times, over dinner, over coffee in her kitchen—two old people, their lives spent.

"My God, you look awful!" she said. "Get in here before the cops pick you up for vagrancy."

She tried coffee first, but he was coffee'd out. So she put him to bed, in what he saw even in his stupor was a handmade bed, with roped bedposts topped by delicately turned pineapples.

"My husband made it when we got married," she said. "He didn't have any sense either. Go to sleep. When you wake up, we'll talk."

HILDA TO THE RESCUE

I HATE PEOPLE who tell me their dreams, especially when I want to tell them mine. So I'll keep this short.

I've called this meeting, see, and it's 4:30 on a Friday afternoon, and I have to inspire this gang of bright and talented people to go out and conquer the world, or sell more hair goo, or pull a Broadway play together, or something—and it is not going well, as you can perhaps imagine. Everybody is talking at once, planning their weekends, whatever. But most of all they are demanding chocolates. Where can I get chocolates on a Friday afternoon, before things go completely to pieces?

"Somebody get Hilda!" a cry goes up. "We can't have a meeting without Hilda!" And in a moment Hilda appears. She is a big, surprised-looking woman who has evidently been taking a bath because (1) she's wearing a bathrobe, and (2) she's puffed up exactly like a giant sparrow who's been dousing her feathers in a bird bath and is about to shake herself and rain all over everybody. And she's wearing boxing gloves—big red Everlasts. And her arms are full of boxes of candy.

"Here, you turkeys," she shouts, "have some chocolates!" She begins throwing the boxes at everybody in the room. "Have some chocolates, and then dammit listen up, because this is important!"

And they do, and it's the best meeting I ever ran.

THE GLOVE COMPARTMENT

HECTOR WAS THE HEAD DOORMAN at the Fairmont Hotel on Massachusetts Avenue NW in Washington, D.C. He was a commanding presence—six-feet-four, 250 pounds, wearing a brown cloak stitched with a red "F" and a hat with gold braid to shame a Bolivian dictator. A *generalissimo* of the curb, whose two-fingered shriek could halt a ton and a half of charging taxicab almost within its own length.

Ramon was a rabbitty little man who drove an independent cab and patrolled the streets around the Fairmont. The first few times Hector ushered guests into the cab, he had misgivings, but the guests returned with good reports. "What a great guide," one said. "He must know everything about Washington." A grandmother from Chicago said, "He's the nicest cabbie I ever met."

After that Hector relaxed. Eventually he talked to Ramon and got his cell-phone number. He didn't call him for every guest— the ratty cab would have repelled some of them. But if it was a historian visiting the Library of Congress, or a family from Nebraska, or an art student walking over from the Phillips Collection, he'd push the button for Ramon. "Fare for you, buddy," he'd say, and Ramon was usually there in a minute or two.

Gradually, Hector learned a little about Ramon. He had no friends or relatives, it seemed, and lived in a rooming house at Florida and R streets, diagonally opposite the Nora restaurant. But the Nora was too expensive for Ramon, who took most of his meals at the Voyager Café and Bar, in a little shopping center tucked behind the Burkina Faso embassy, two blocks from the Fairmont.

Hector, whose only family was a son in San Pedro, began showing up now and then for lunch at the Voyager. He and Ramon discussed Washington, mostly—odd guests and odder passengers, the foibles of politicians. Now and then Hector let Ramon use the employees' toilet at the Fairmont, or shared coffee in an efficiency apartment the hotel provided him for being on call at any hour. When Hector's son was hit by a drunk driver, Ramon drove him to Reagan International in record time. "No charge, friend," he said, waving aside Hector's money.

It was over a beer at the Voyager that Ramon first mentioned the glove compartment, diffidently, as though unsure how his friend would react. "Something funny is going on with my glove box," he said. "Sometimes it glows."

"So?" Hector murmured, not really listening. "Yeah," Ramon went on. "Sometimes when I look in there it's like a furnace—all gold light and stars. "Well, don't burn your hand," Hector said, and Ramon reassured him: "It's just light, not heat. And it never happens with someone in the cab."

After that, Ramon returned occasionally to his gentle fantasy. "My glove box was really jumping last night," he might say, or, "I could hardly get the door shut—the whole box was full of stars." And each time he mentioned the glove compartment, a look of beatific peace stole across his face. "I must be the luckiest person in the District," he said.

Hector stopped trying to respond and never asked to look in the glove compartment, but over the months it began eating on him.

One crystalline night in December, Ramon drove up to the Fairmont without being called. "Gotta take a quick dump," he told Hector. "Watch the cab for a minute, friend."

Hector didn't consider what he was about to do. He just walked to the passenger door and opened the glove compartment.

There was no radiance, no fiery furnace. There *were* stars—crude black ones that Ramon had painted on the gray cardboard with which he had lined the box. In an instant, Hector saw the depth of his friend's delusion and knew something had to be done. He slammed the glove box and the door a moment before Ramon came out of the hotel and climbed into his seat.

Hector drew himself up and walked firmly around the cab. Ramon, looking puzzled, rolled down the window and Hector started in.

"Look, buddy," he said, "we've got to talk *seriously* about this glove box craziness. *I looked in the glove box.* There's nothing there but junk you painted yourself. This is psycho, man! I can't send guests with a crazy person—sooner or later you'll start telling them about stars and glowing lights, and they'll be jumping out of the cab in Adams-Morgan, and who knows what will happen to them there? You need"—he reached for words and drew Dear Abby—"professional help!"

Ramon sat slumped and silent. Hector was halfway to the hotel entrance when he heard the engine start. But he didn't see the cab glide off down Massachusetts Avenue, leave the pavement, and rise, clearing the bare trees on Dupont Circle, before shooting straight up and dwindling in an instant to a fourth-magnitude star just south of Rigel in the constellation Orion.

SAMARKAND AND BOKHARA

For the mole on her cheek,
I would give Samarkand and Bokhara
                                        —Hafiz-e Shirazi

ROM WAS, AS USUAL, more than a couple of jumps ahead of Galindian customs, having backdoored its computers in an earlier life. Now those computers were telling the spaceport drones that the shiny interplanetary hopper loaded with contraband sapphires was really a third-class rice hauler from the agricultural planet of Gu. There were advantages to total automation.

Still, he hadn't been able to give up the human touch entirely, so tonight in the glittering bar of the Galindian Crowne Plaza he would hand off to an intermediary the codes that would allow his cargo—already loaded by the drones in a Level 3 transporter—to continue toward whatever its destination might be. The transfer of his fee into a secure and untraceable account would take place at the instant the codes were punched in. He would be gone, with a new name, his presence on Galindia not even a ghost in the computer.

The intermediary was late. Rom decided to give him 10 minutes before switching to an alternate system with a new touch point and codes. Meanwhile, his eyes shifted to a party of six women and a man at a nearby table. From their appearance, the women were slaves from Transvaliana, and not unhappy about it either, smiling over their dinners and wine. Not prostitutes, but a royal party from some conquered satrapy, glad enough to be on their way to wealthy and generous masters.

There was a slight scuffle of feet and the tall-headed man who had been walking toward him, was turned deftly by two men in suits who ushered him out the door. Oh, oh. Rom punched some numbers into his pocket messenger, changing his identity and starting his cargo toward a safe holding port on another planet.

One of the women was looking at him desperately, her dark eyes beseeching above the mole on her cheek. Her hand moved slightly toward him, in a gesture of appeal.

What a risk! She was a step away from death and knew it. He was still uninvolved and could stay that way. The agents had slipped up, arresting their man too soon. He could be gone in seconds.

But that look! A princess, at least.

It took Rom less than a minute to break into the guard's messenger and learn everything about him and the shipment he was safeguarding. Easy duty for a mid-level security guard, now full of wine and half asleep. In another minute, Rom had inserted himself into the guard's messenger, so that he could send directives purporting to be from the slavemasters. A crude "man in the middle" tactic, but it would hold long enough to get the girl free.

His message read: "A buyer has been found for No. 5. An agent is approaching your table. In exchange for the girl, he will give you the codes for a shipment of sapphires, as well as your transfer fee."

Before the guard had finished reading, Rom was at his table, holding out an open pouch of gemstones and a memory stick with the codes that would allow his sapphires to be transshipped from their holding dock. He had realized from the shipping manifest for the women that there had to be a real payoff this time—one big enough to persuade the slave cartel not to pursue the matter—though the hapless guard might find himself dangling in a lava vent on Morgad.

The guard checked the memory stick, swept the gemstones into his pocket, and motioned to the woman.

Outside, Rom thrust a key and some banknotes into her hand. She took them as if by right, without thanks, hauteur betrayed only by a gleam of amusement in her dark eyes. "Take an urbicruiser to Bay 37 in East Port," Rom told her. "The key will admit you, and the ship will launch automatically in two hours for Sogdan. The password on the key will open the ship's computer—search for Arvind-gi and you'll find friends in Sogdan."

He stepped quickly away into a hovercab that took him to a bare room on Regensgirt. There he painstakingly destroyed every trace of his existence, before taking another cab to an equally bare room across town. His former employers would write off as a business expense whatever accident had befallen their trusted agent and his cargo.

He would miss the human contact. He never went anywhere, and the brief handover meetings had been a diversion. But they were getting too dangerous, and his aim was to remove all risk from his operations. From now on *everything* would be done by computer.

But those eyes! That slightly marked cheek!

Into his mind came words from an old Earth poet. Hafiz, he reflected, had also laid out all his treasure for an Unattainable, in songs of such tenderness

> *that listening to them, Heaven's Lord*
> *tossed me from Heaven as reward*
> *the small change of the Pleiades.*